The New Rakes

'I'd like to know what's under that skirt,' he said, ducking his head a little as though he could peer up it from across the kitchen.

'Too bad,' Kara said, but she shifted in her heels as she spoke, remembering how exposed she was underneath the thin skirt.

'You owe me a favour, remember?'

'Not now,' Kara said.

'Show me,' he said, standing his ground and not moving a muscle. He had one hand in his pocket and something in the way he stood, that cocky, slovenly slouch, seemed like a challenge. Kara hesitated. The thought of showing him her artfully dressed crotch was appealing. She knew exactly what effect it would have on him, and her body was longing for gratification after a sleepless night and a whole morning spent thinking about fucking Mike.

Standing with her back to the kitchen counter, Kara bent and lifted the hem of her skirt. She pulled it upwards, slowly revealing her stocking-clad legs and the creamy skin that was bare at the top. Tam waited, like a cat watching its prey, his body held utterly still. When Kara's skirt was high enough for him to catch sight of her naked pussy he took a deep breath. She knew that he was taking it all in – the neatly trimmed black hair, the cleft between her legs where her thighs were pressed tightly together.

The New Rakes
Nikki Magennis

This book is a work of fiction. In real life, make sure you practise safe, sane and consensual sex.

Published by Black Lace 2008

2 4 6 8 10 9 7 5 3 1

First published in Great Britain in 2008 by
Black Lace
Virgin Books
Random House, 20 Vauxhall Bridge Road,
London SW1V 2SA

www.black-lace-books.com
www.virginbooks.com
www.rbooks.co.uk

Addresses for companies within The Random House Group Limited can be found at:
www.randomhouse.co.uk/offices.htm

The Random House Group Limited Reg. No. 954009

Distributed in the USA by Macmillan, 175 Fifth Avenue, New York, NY 10010, USA

A CIP catalogue record for this book
is available from the British Library

ISBN 9780352345035

Penguin Random House is committed to a sustainable future for our business, our readers and our planet. This book is made from Forest Stewardship Council® certified paper.

MIX
Paper from
responsible sources
FSC® C018179

Printed and bound in Great Britain by Clays Ltd, St Ives plc

Typeset by Palimpsest Book Production Limited, Grangemouth, Stirlingshire

1

This was the moment she loved most of all. When her skin was sticky with sweat and the atmosphere sparked with tension – when the whole audience was fixed on her, waiting for her next move.

Kara kicked at the speaker in front of her, scuffing the black surface with the toe of her kitten-heeled shoe. There were whoops, a couple of whistles. In the black mass of the club, eyes and teeth glinted, people watched. They wanted her to get on with it. Behind her, she knew the band was waiting too. Tam restlessly strummed the E string on his guitar, a little nervous, a little agitated.

Good, she thought. She liked to draw the moment out. Silently she paced across the front of the stage, ignoring everyone. The click of her heels sounded hard in the tight hush of the packed room, like a metronome marking out time. Kara stood still, closed her eyes and swayed her hips from side to side. She felt the roughness in her throat, the beat of blood in her veins. She felt, too, the slick of wetness in her knickers – her body oiled and aroused like it always was when she performed. The next song was the one she loved the best, the one she needed to really feel in her bones before she could sing it.

'Turn on Me'. It was a song about fucking and jealousy and getting turned on even when you were angry. About bodies thrashing against each other, locked in passionate battle.

She looked into the dark of the auditorium. Dust motes danced in the beams from the stage lights – white floods whose heat she could feel on her bare arms. Then Jon started playing a looped sample – a buzzing electric bass line. It made her teeth rattle, gave her dark shocks every time she heard it. The audience picked up on it instantly and the cries started up again, building this time, gathering speed.

Kara smiled, wrapped the mike cord around her arm and lifted the silver head to her mouth.

'This one's for Tam,' she said, her voice low and hoarse.

And then they were moving. The music swelled, the stage lights became a dazzling white halo and Kara was immersed in sound with reverb clanging in her ears.

She sang, letting her voice wash over the crowd like a velvet tide. This is where she felt most alive, up on stage exposing herself, shameless and breathtaking. Tam played a bone-shaking bass note, Ruby thrashed hell out of the drums and Kara held onto the moment. No matter that they played loud – her voice rose above it all. The critics called it her gin-and-tonic voice, sweet with a twist.

Singing made her high; she'd be out of breath and dizzy afterwards and her throat would rasp for two days. But it also made her horny. Kara sang with her whole body, closing her eyes and running a hand over herself, her fingers snagging in the slashed holes in her T-shirt and tripping over her bare midriff, digging under the waistband of her skirt and tugging it down. There were shouts from the crowd as she lost herself in the thrill of exposure, showing them the swell of her belly and the shaved, pale swell of her pubis. God knows what stopped her from stripping and playing with herself. She was close enough to it.

Just as she was squirming around and wishing for something to rub up against, Tam drifted up behind her. He leaned in to her back, pushed his shoulder against hers. His fingers strumming out chords on the fret board didn't falter, as though he'd already rehearsed this movement and knew exactly how Kara would respond.

She unrolled her spine against him, felt the neck of his guitar dig into her hip and the muscles in his wrist tensing against her side as he plucked a few fat, dark notes from the bass. Kara turned and clung to him, sticking her neck in the crook of his shoulder.

The lyrics were for him, he knew that.

> *'In the morning we're going to scream*
> *blue murder.'*

Her voice rasped as she sang, half to Tam and half to the audience. She could smell the mix of sweat and spiced after-shave at Tam's neck, feel the music vibrating through his bones as they stood crushed against each other, playing together, performing for each other as well as the crowd.

When Jon picked up the middle eight on the keyboard Kara pressed herself closer to Tam, letting the tips of her braless breasts brush against his arm. Nobody but her would have noticed the slight stumble as he played – one missed note, nothing more. It was enough for Kara. She gave him a little nip – just a small bite on the exposed skin of his neck as the piano break came to an end – and smiled as he flinched, spinning round to swear at her.

'Fuck,' he spat, murmuring low so the mike wouldn't pick it up.

Still perfectly in time, she winked at him and turned back to the crowd to belt out the chorus, feeling the tingle in her nipples as they stuck out proud and stiff under her T-shirt. Perhaps the fabric was damp from her sweat, or Tam's, and that's why the crowd surged forwards, hands reaching up towards her. Maybe they were just feeling the music. Kara didn't care. She liked the attention either way.

The rest of the band would tease her about it afterwards, but she knew their eyes were fixed on her when she danced, just as bewitched as the audience. And they certainly didn't complain about the crowds that had started to appear when The New Rakes played, ever since Kara had reinvented herself as Lady Lick and started practically frigging herself onstage.

The New Rakes had been causing a stir in the past few months. At first people had come to see if it was true that the front girl got off in front of everyone while they played. But when they came, they got into the music as much as the show, the dirty electro stuff with the sugar-sweet melodies.

Because nobody could deny it was good. Lately, they'd been selling out every gig. The bigger the audience, the wilder Kara got. She could feel them watching her, knew they appreciated a glimpse of her tits under the see-through T-shirt. And the others made a pretty sexy backdrop. Tam, with his cheekbones and his scowl, just standing there hanging onto his Rickenbacker and jutting out his hips. He was a rock-star wet dream in the making. A couple of student girls hung as close to the stage as they dared, staring at him intently through kohl-rimmed eyes.

Jon, too, had his admirers. With his doe eyes and his long delicate fingers, he attracted the sensitive types – male and female. They might have known he was Ruby's boyfriend, but it didn't put them off. Probably encouraged them – even stuck behind the drum kit, little black-haired Ruby got her share of attention. Raucous whistles when she did her solo, and a string of guys buying her drinks after each gig.

Sex fuelled their performances. While The New Rakes played,

Kara could feel the tension zinging about the stage, brimming under the surface of every song and driving it forwards.

After a show the band would be bathed in an aura of longing. Sweat soaked and exhausted, they'd still be high from adrenaline, ready for drinking and fucking their way through the night. The after-parties were almost as much fun as the gigs, nights leaching into days full of wildness and electric moments – everything loud and urgent and reckless and accompanied by a soundtrack of Kara's own devising. When she thought about it, Kara felt as though she were caught on the crest of a wave that was gathering energy and threatening to crash in glorious slow motion at any minute. She felt unstoppable. With the band behind her, anything was possible.

At the back of the club, Mike Greene sat on a barstool and watched. His shirt was undone at the neck, partly to cool himself from the fetid air of the club and partly to look less like a middle-aged guy at a gig where everyone else was under twenty-five. It didn't matter any more, though, because now he was watching Kara and the only thing he could think of was sinking his cock into her sweet, open red mouth.

He hadn't intended to stay long. Just long enough to satisfy his curiosity, to see what had become of his most difficult student since she'd dropped out of music lessons. As he watched Kara writhe and pout on stage, he couldn't help but admit she would have been wasted slogging away at the piano, learning her classical composers by painful repetition. This was her natural habitat, this dark and electric world.

He took a swig of his drink and let the glass dangle from his hand. He wondered where her wild sexual energy had come from. In lessons, she'd always been taciturn and slightly moody, a goth girl in too much eyeliner who hunched on his piano stool and stared back at him through a badly cut fringe. Up on stage she was a different story. A dazzling creature that he couldn't take his eyes off. She was, he realised, a woman that he'd give almost anything to fuck.

He looked at his watch. Lina would be waiting for him at the party, he was missing a glorious opportunity to schmooze, and his car was parked in a dodgy alleyway round the corner. There were a thousand good reasons not to stay.

And then, onstage, Kara turned to lock her eyes on his. Something flared in her expression, a shock of surprise as she recognised him. Mike held her gaze. His cock was half hard, stretching upwards and pressing against the front of his trousers as he watched the sheen of sweat on Kara's neck and imagined licking it from her skin, tasting the sweet salt of her. She was biting her lip as the guitarist on her left played a solo, marking time with a bump of her hip. And staring straight at her old teacher like she knew exactly what he was thinking.

When she came offstage, Kara's voice was hoarse, her ears were ringing and sweat stung her eyes. Adrenaline was fizzing in her veins, and the others were full of it too. Under the harsh strip lights of the backstage corridors everything seemed slightly unreal. Kara looked at Tam – his eyes wired, a tiger's grin plastered on his face and his hair drenched with sweat – and knew she had the same dazzled, half-crazed look.

The dressing room – a glorified store cupboard with smoke-stained walls and a battered old sofa along one wall – was quiet, but the music still pounded in Kara's ears, ringing and echoing and making her itch to keep moving.

Ruby and Jon had their tongues down each other's throats almost before the door had swung closed. Kara watched with a skewed smile as the two of them sank into the red cushions on the sofa, oblivious to everything but each other.

'Ain't love grand,' she said, turning just as Tam pulled his soaking T-shirt over his head. As he stretched up she admired the light gold of his skin, the gentle ripple of his muscles and the fuzz of black hair that trailed from his stomach to the top of his trousers. The glory trail. Kara bit her lip.

Tam glanced at Jon and Ruby and gave a shrug. He fetched a bottle of beer from the coffee table and cracked it open with his Clipper. He carried attitude in every movement, the way his hips rolled and his arms swung loose by his side. His muscles rippled like a panther's.

'Well, it does tend to make you horny,' he said, pushing his hair back from his forehead. 'Doesn't it?'

Kara shrugged.

'Oh come on, you coy bitch,' Tam insisted, moving closer to her. 'It's pretty obvious what's going through your head when you're up there.'

'Fuck off, Tam,' she said mildly. But her body betrayed her – she felt an inevitable, horrible, hot pink blush creeping up her cheeks. Guilty.

'Hot?' Tam asked, standing right at her shoulder. 'Allow me.' Before she could stop him, he had pressed the ice-cold bottle of beer to her neck. The shock made Kara gasp, and she felt her nipples pinch as Tam rolled the chilled glass down over her chest, his fingers brushing her skin as he did so. 'Nice?'

Kara gave him a crooked little smile. That was the trouble with Tam. He was moody, unpredictable and frequently obnoxious, but he knew how to make a girl feel good. And Kara still remembered how he tasted.

'I bet you're wet right now,' he whispered in her ear, his breath tickling her.

His mouth connected with her skin and Kara fought to keep herself steady. She should push him off, she thought, only the feel of his lips against her neck was delicious. His tongue flickered over her pulse point, sending jolts right through her bloodstream and making her knees weak. Kara closed her eyes. Tam held the bottle against her breast, rolled it over her nipple. The cold and the pressure were such exquisite torture she couldn't bring herself to move. Behind them, Kara heard a clink that was unmistakably a belt buckle being undone, and remembered Jon and Ruby on the couch.

She flinched and pulled away. 'We agreed, Tam,' she said struggling to breathe normally. 'Remember?'

'One fuck can't hurt,' he said, leaning in to kiss her.

Kara's eyes fixed on the twist of his smile and she allowed herself to imagine how it would feel to have that mouth against hers for just one moment. His lips, she remembered, were lithe and quick. His tongue was skilled. Then she shook her head. 'Bad idea.'

'Worried you might like it?' Tam said, slipping his free hand round to grip hold of her arse. He gave a squeeze, and Kara arched her spine before she could stop herself.

'More worried about the aftermath,' she murmured, but her hands were slipping around his hips and she was pulling him into her so that his belt buckle and the bulge of his cock under his jeans bumped up against her stomach. She let their bodies press against each other so that she could feel his heartbeat against her chest. 'Get out here,' she said finally, throwing open the door and pulling Tam into the corridor.

She shoved him up against the white-painted breeze blocks with a force that made him raise an eyebrow and smile at her, even as she was slipping a hand inside the waistband of his trousers and groping for his cock. The shaft sprung up to meet her fingers, plump and promising and already leaking a little drop of pre-come.

It was always a slight shock, feeling Tam's prick in her hand – like discovering an old friend in an obscene pose. Which was exactly the situation, she decided, letting him grip her wrists and pull them up, swinging her round until she was the one with the hard scrape of the wall behind her.

'My turn, I think,' he said, sinking to his knees in front of her and then burying his face in her lap. Through the thin fabric of her skirt, the heat of his breath scorched her pussy, turning her molten and making her thankful for the hard wall at her back.

Meanwhile she could feel the wiry strength of his fingers working their way up her legs, pawing at her skin like a cat working its claws. He pushed her clothes aside, shoving her skirt up and tugging her knickers down simultaneously to reveal the light fuzz of her pubic hair and the little deep-pink bud of her clit, which he kissed, softly.

Tam knew the power of contrasts. The strong burn of his hands kneading her arse versus the lightest of feather kisses on her burning clit was enough to make Kara feel she was being turned inside out. She wanted to fuck his face, right there in the basement corridor, wanted to feel his tongue plunge inside her and bring one quick, dazzling, hard orgasm before they were discovered.

'Quick, for fuck's sake, quick,' she gasped, squirming in his hands. And then wished she hadn't spoken when Tam pulled back to look at her.

'In a hurry?' he asked, and Kara saw the glint in his eye – the warning sign – as well as the shine of her wetness on his lips. But more than anything she felt her buzzing sex – the awful lack of his mouth against her and the cold air that did nothing to ease her desire.

She knotted her fingers in his hair and locked her eyes on his – something she usually tried to avoid. There was too much trouble waiting in their gaze. Like flint striking against flint, when they looked at each other sparks would fly.

'Please,' she whispered, knowing that one simple word would

work quicker than any explanation about the time that was pressing on them and the night that waited for their presence.

As Tam nodded and buried his head back between her legs, his tongue working vigorously now on her clit to wring an orgasm out of her, Kara silently let her thoughts drift. While Tam lapped at her, letting the point of his tongue dance and slip back and forth, winnowing between the folds of her lips and touching the mouth of her sex just enough to make her sigh, she thought of the guy in the audience, sitting right up at the back of the bar.

Tam's tongue was replaced by his finger. His tongue slid back up to flick at her clit and give a starburst of sensation while he wriggled one, then two fingers inside her. He brought her on like an expert, knowing exactly how much pressure she wanted and when, working his hand into the rings of her pussy while his mouth fired up the burn of her clit. Kara felt the beat quicken, like music playing louder. Her body tensed and she remembered the figure at the bar, his lean frame and the familiar angle he held his limbs in.

She was full and brimming with her orgasm now, devoured by Tam's mouth and invaded by his fingers, doubled over and rushing towards a climax with blind, wild, unstoppable need. It hit her like an avalanche and images flashed into her head unbidden as she jerked against Tam's mouth.

As she came, she thought not of the boy on his knees in front of her, but of a man in a quiet room, standing next to a piano. His hands on her shoulders and his breath on the back of her neck, both of them watching the keys, her hands moving steadily faster, both listening as the music grew louder and flowed over them, drowning them in furious sound.

2

As the aftershocks faded, Kara looked down at Tam. He was on his knees in front of her, hanging on to her hips as if they were a life raft, yet somehow it was him that seemed in control. His mouth was wet and his eyes searched her face. She wanted suddenly to shake him off, scatter him and run outside into the cold fresh air.

'We'd better move,' she said, wriggling under his grasp, looking round at the whitewashed corridor as though someone were about to crash through the double doors and find them there, leaning against the wall with their clothes undone and faces flushed.

'Always in such a hurry, aren't you?'

'Let's not get into this now,' she said, shrugging Tam's hands from her hips and pulling away. He stayed on his knees, still watching her. Kara refused to look at him. She pulled her skirt down and felt the tremor in her legs, shaky from flexing against the wall.

'So we'll move,' Tam said finally, 'but remember you owe me one, sugar.'

'I'll buy you a drink,' she muttered, 'later. Right now I'm gonna go get the stage cleared.'

Silently, she added: *Please don't follow me.* Kara was hoping there'd be somebody out there that she didn't want anyone else to meet right now. Was he at the bar, waiting for her? She briefly thought of washing her face, cleaning the scent of sex and sweat from her skin. And then changed her mind.

'I didn't know you were such a natural-born performer,' Mike said.

'There's a lot you don't know about me,' Kara said, taking a long sip of the deep-red drink in her glass, 'Professor.'

Keeping her eyes on Mike, she stretched, pulling her muscles taut and lifting her arms upwards so that her breasts swung. His eyes flickered over the points of her nipples, sticking through the thin cotton of her T-shirt.

Kara smiled. Mike may have liked to play it cool and aloof – the world-weary artist nobody could provoke – but his reactions were as predictable as a teenage boy's. And she liked having him ogle her, that pale-blue gaze stroking over her body.

They were sitting at the bar, waiting while the crew cleared up the gear from the concert. Her hair was still damp with sweat, sticking to her face in dark strands, and her T-shirt clung to her skin. Kara felt gloriously dishevelled, like a boxer fresh out of the ring, the fighter emerging victorious to meet her admirers.

'You liked the show,' she said, bold as brass. 'How did I do?'

'Mm,' Mike said, nodding. 'Less tortuous than listening to you butchering your arpeggios, I have to admit.'

'And the music?'

'Not bad. It helps that you're so delectable to watch.'

Kara hid her face in her glass, sucked up an ice cube and crunched it. Was he damning her with faint praise? she wondered.

'So, what are you doing here?' she said eventually.

'Oh, I had an hour to kill. I've got the Blue Star launch party in Queen Street and thought I'd slip in for a drink.'

'Right,' Kara said. 'Happy coincidence.'

Mike was leaning on the bar, his white shirtsleeves rolled up so Kara could see the tanned skin of his forearms and the brush of gold hair that ran to his wrists. Her eyes rested on his hands. So familiar. They were large, long fingered and thick knuckled. His fingers tapped restlessly on the black marble counter.

'I have to go,' he said, checking his watch, 'but I can put your name on the door if you want to come along.'

'For the party? Would that be cool?'

'Oh yes. Very cool.'

'What about the others?'

'What others?'

'The band: Tam, Jon, Ruby.'

Mike shrugged. 'Why not.' As he stood up to leave, he leaned closer and brushed his lips against her cheek, so that she felt the slight scrape of his stubble against her skin.

'And don't worry about changing. I like this –' he tugged on her damp T-shirt '– very much.'

He lingered at her neck for a split second too long, Kara thought, as though he were inhaling her patchouli, the fresh spice of her sweat. Could he smell the scent of sex on her too? Could he tell she'd just had her pussy licked and sucked? In the shadows of the half-empty bar, she felt her face flush deep scarlet for the second time that night.

'Tell me again where we're going,' Tam said, scowling at the bitter wind that whipped across their faces as they walked west towards Queen Street. Kara zipped her jacket up to her chin and gritted her teeth. She almost wished she hadn't asked Tam to come with her. Their little scene backstage hadn't helped clear the air; in fact, she was already starting to curse herself for giving in to the temptation of a quick orgasm. Tam was going to be as difficult as possible for the rest of the night, that was clear.

But there was no way she was walking into the Kasbah on her own and something told her she shouldn't miss the party. Jon and Ruby had gone home to finish the fuck-fest they'd started on the dressing-room couch and Kara had decided Tam was a better escort than nobody at all, even if he was in a foul mood.

'It's a launch party, Tam. A new label.'

'And who'll be there?'

'Scouts, producers, movers and shakers. Everyone we need to be meeting.'

'And your old tutor.'

Kara couldn't miss the sneer in Tam's voice. She pulled up short and wheeled round to face him. 'Yes, Tam. My old tutor. Is that a problem?'

'Not as long as you don't mind him leching all over you, no. Guess it might be worth it for a shot at the big time, eh?'

'Fucking grow up,' Kara spat, walking on again as fast as she could. The streets were dark and cold and slick with rain and she had a nervous, scratchy feeling in her stomach that she couldn't quite explain. Partly butterflies, partly the ache that she felt after a strong orgasm.

Ahead, the smooth white steps of the Kasbah led up to high double doors. The black-suited figures of two doormen stood rigid at the top, silhouetted in the gold light from the hallway behind them. Kara paused, fixing a brazen smile on her face as she approached. Just like performing on stage, she thought, you've got to be ready to dazzle them. And if you don't feel it, fake it.

Inside, the place felt like a gin palace. Polished floors, great dripping chandeliers and waiters in perfectly ironed black shirts slipping in and out of the crowd with trays of glasses.

Tea lights flickered on the tables and the air was scented with lilies. Kara thought she could even smell cigar smoke, faintly, as though it were soaked into the wallpaper. Against this opulent backdrop, the party was in full swing. Not Kara's idea of swing, though.

'Christ,' Tam said flatly as they looked at the crowd – men in silk shirts and women in tailored suits, everyone tanned and practically dripping with money. A display took up one wall, with the Blue Star logo projected across the domed ceiling and flunkies handed out CDs. Kara recognised the gravelly laugh of a fading pop star, wearing Chanel and standing surrounded by guys with greying ponytails and waistcoats, who could only be execs.

Kara was suddenly very horribly aware of her cut-off denim skirt and rain-spattered parka, her bare legs and scuffed shoes and chipped purple nail polish.

But nobody else seemed to notice them. In the dim glowing candlelight and with a soundtrack of slinky blues piano running under the noise of loud conversation, everybody was clearly too occupied with impressing each other to care if a couple of scruffs crashed the party. Tam shouldered his way into the crowd and Kara followed, glimpsing faces she vaguely recognised, looking furtively around for Mike.

She caught sight of him standing at the back of the room, deep in conversation with a red-haired woman. As Kara stared at the two of them, Mike turned and caught her eye. He fixed her with a look that made the butterflies in her stomach swirl higher than ever.

Tam pressed a glass into her hand and she clutched it, thankful for something to hang on to. He was talking to her, cracking a joke about some journalist that he'd spotted in the corner, but Kara wasn't listening.

There was the ragged roar of conversation and the flowing

melody of a piano, and there was Mike, giving that lazy smile of his while he nodded at the woman he spoke to and looked straight at Kara. One hand in his pocket, his sandy hair brushed back to show his tanned, weather-beaten face. His foot tapping, slowly, deliberately. Always marking time, thought Kara. Counting the beat.

She moved towards him, swaying through the crowd, noticing him press his lips together and frown a little like he was appraising her.

'You made it,' he said as she reached him, his words cutting through something the other woman was saying. 'I'm so glad.'

'Lina, this is Kara,' he said, motioning the two women together. 'A starlet in the making.'

Kara felt the hot glare of Lina's attention sweep over her and regarded her rival with the same curiosity. She was a striking woman – long limbed and slender with a waterfall of dark-auburn hair which cascaded over her shoulders. Kara took in the sculpted cheekbones and fine, arched eyebrows. Lina must have been about thirty-five, a bit older, but she had that well-maintained look.

'Lina's our publicist,' Mike said. 'Mistress of the well-turned phrase, aren't you, Lina?'

'You flatter me, Michael,' Lina said. She turned to Kara. 'So you're Mike's latest kick, are you? Very pretty. A musician?'

'A singer,' Kara said. 'Lead singer.'

'Wonderful,' Lina said, with a sphinx's smile.

'You should see her onstage,' said Mike. 'She's mesmer-ising.'

'Oh, I love the indie bands. It's great that everyone feels they have the chance to make their own music these days. Now, I hate to be rude, but I've just seen someone I must talk to,' Lina said. She squeezed Mike's arm before slipping into the crowd.

The bracelets on her arm jangled as she walked, leaving a trail of brittle music in her wake.

'Ouch,' Kara said. 'She's sharp.'

'Yes, it always seems like the room gets a little dimmer when Lina leaves,' Mike said. 'But I have you to add a little sparkle to the evening, don't I, Kara?'

'Hmm.' Kara gave a half-laugh and shifted awkwardly in her heels. 'Actually I'm starting to feel a little tarnished.'

'I'm not surprised,' Mike said, 'given your performance earlier. Why don't we find somewhere quiet.'

It wasn't a question. He was already steering Kara towards a booth at the edge of the room, one hand in the small of her back, a heavy warm pressure through her T-shirt. The crowd parted respectfully as they moved, people nodding and smiling as Mike passed. Kara felt suddenly at the centre of everything, like she was moving through a smooth and beautiful sea. Now that she was with Mike, people took note of her. She could be his latest protégé, or his lover. Either way, she was a curiosity.

A camera flash went off, blinding Kara temporarily. Of course, the press was here. The launch of a new record label merited a half-inch in the music columns, at least.

'This one of your artists, Mr Greene?' asked a dark-haired man in glasses.

'Could be,' Mike muttered, frowning.

'You promised an interview? *Evening Star.*'

'Ah. Yes. Do you mind, Kara?'

Kara shook her head. 'I'll go find Tam,' she said, moving away.

'Oh no, sit in with us. It won't take long,' Mike said, motioning to a booth that sat, shadowy and tucked away behind red velvet curtains. He grabbed a waiter and ordered champagne before sitting, then pulled Kara down beside him. The bench was low, the deep seat piled high with fat velvet cushions and Kara sank into them. The journalist had already flipped out a notebook and started asking questions. Kara could feel Mike's thigh against hers, the long taut muscles pressed close and tight. Was that accidental?

But Mike seemed oblivious, answering the journalist's questions with practised ease and pouring wine for them all as he did so.

'Blue Star Records are starting on the crest of a wave, of course,' he was saying. 'The music scene's never been so vibrant. New talent practically spilling from every bar in the city.'

'And you're focusing on this new talent?'

'Absolutely. It's fresh, sexy and ripe for the plucking.' Mike smiled.

Kara started as she felt something brush against her leg – a spider's touch, crawling along her thigh. Under the table, Mike was stroking her, lightly, gently. As though he weren't aware he was even doing it. She fixed her eyes on the journalist, scribbling in his notepad, oblivious to Mike's little game. They were hidden in the dim candlelight of the curtained booth and she was trapped in the corner, unable to move or make a sound.

As Mike continued, waxing lyrical about the plans for Blue Star Records, his hand continued to dance over Kara's lap, tracing an unpredictable pattern, then ran along the hem of her skirt and tugged gently. His fingers slid under the fabric, reaching to where her flesh was warm and tender and as smooth as satin. There they rested.

Kara held her breath, waiting for him to move. She could feel her pulse in her throat, feel the blood fizz in her veins as though they were running with champagne instead of blood. Dizziness washed over her so that she struggled to focus on the conversation. All she was sure of was the position of Mike's hand, definitely not accidental, now he'd crawled his fingers to the top of her thigh. Between her legs another pulse was beating, dark and desperate.

'... the idea that you're manipulating young artists?'

Kara caught the tail end of the journalist's question and felt Mike stiffen next to her.

'That's nonsense. Success doesn't fall into your lap,' he said, his voice showing a glimmer of anger. 'And we know what sells.'

He was digging his fingers into Kara's flesh now, kneading at her insistently. She couldn't help tipping her pelvis forwards, trying to inch closer to his hand. The conversation had piqued her interest now too, and she teetered on a knife-edge, wanting desperately to listen as well as feel.

'So there's no truth in the rumours about why Lina Warren left ABC?'

'John, I'm terribly sorry, but we're out of time,' Mike said. He poured another glass for himself and Kara, leaving the journalist's pointedly empty. He barely nodded goodbye as the other man rose and left.

'I don't want you to say a word,' Mike murmured, and his voice was smoky and sweet as Kara remembered it, flowing over her like notes from a cello. Under the table he was pushing her skirt up, exposing her knickers. Now he took her hand, still cold from holding the champagne flute, and rested it over the crotch of his cords.

'Isn't it a little public ... ?' Kara started to say, but Mike murmured, 'Ssssh,' as he let her feel the bulge in the front of his trousers. His cock was hard. Even through layers of fabric she could feel the long curve of it pressed along his thigh. When she stretched her fingers over the tip she heard Mike sigh with relief.

She started rubbing, slow and deliberate, moulding her hand

round the shaft and pressing down hard. Though she'd imagined touching him when she was his student and though of course they'd brushed against each other, she'd never gone this far with him. To have her hand on his cock felt beautifully dangerous, as though she might waken a sleeping monster with her touch.

The thought thrilled her rather than worried her. Suddenly Kara hardly cared if their surreptitious hand movements were noticeable – she felt invincible somehow, as though she'd entered some different universe where all the rules had changed. The glittering night seemed full of danger, full of sex, full of wanting. The bar was a fabulous depraved film set, where nothing was forbidden. Kara could get on her knees and take Mike's cock in her mouth and the party would continue around them, photographers snapping pictures and the poisonous Lina cackling with laughter as she watched.

'Jesus, that feels good,' Mike said through clenched teeth. He was bent over the table now, obscuring them from the rest of the room, and still working at Kara's knickers with clever fingers. He was an inch from feeling how wet she was, Kara knew, an inch from where she wanted him to be. They could finger-fuck each other right here. But it was too soon. She had to force herself to wait.

'Mike,' she whispered, 'what that guy was saying ...' She paused for a moment and let her hand fall limp in his lap. Waiting until he turned to her, face set hard and eyes glowing. 'Manipulating artists. How does that work exactly?'

Mike pressed his lips together. He was breathing harder, she noticed, and his expression had grown intense. Something about the way he held himself almost scared her – the control; the distant, level gaze.

'Are you just looking for a record deal?' he said eventually.

'Is that why you're sitting here like a wanton little slut with her hand on my cock?'

Kara recoiled. Before she could pull her hand away though, he had grasped her wrist and held it tight against his lap. 'Not that I'm insulted, Kara. Far from it. Some of the best creative partnerships benefit from a little sexual frisson.'

'There was always ...' Kara noticed how small her voice sounded.

'Tension?' Mike asked, still not releasing her hand. 'Of course there was. Almost enough to make me consider leaving the job. Not the done thing, to be fucking your students, is it?'

There. He'd said it. As soon as the words left his lips Kara realised the tension was there again, in spades. Kara felt it bloom against her, warp the air around them. Her heart beat and it seemed she could hear the metronome again, clicking steadily, swiftly, precisely, as it counted out the practice hour.

'But you're not my student any more,' Mike said. 'You're a chanteuse with a very fuckable body and a pretty good voice.'

'Singer-songwriter,' Kara said automatically. 'I write the songs.'

'Sure,' Mike said, shrugging. 'Not really important. Anyway, we could talk about a deal. A demo.' He relaxed, and sat back in his seat. 'It wouldn't hurt to try you out in the studio. See if that stage presence translates on tape.'

'Really?' Kara said, wanting to hear him talk at the same time as she wanted to feel his hands on her again, working at her and drawing the moisture from deep within her. The champagne fizz, his words, her shimmering pussy and the dregs of the adrenaline in her blood mixed together until she felt dizzy with possibility.

'Certainly,' Mike said, pouring the last of the wine into their glasses. 'I suspect you could be something quite special, given the right handling.' He lifted his champagne flute in a toast: 'And I do intend to give you just that.'

He drained his glass, leaving the promise hanging in the air between them. Kara looked past him to the party that still broiled in the overflowing bar, saw the men and women with sparkling smiles and flashing jewellery and eyes that flickered, every so often, to where she sat with Mike. She saw the want in them, calculating, curious and hungry. She felt their desire lapping at her.

When she caught sight of Tam, slouched against the bar and glowering at her, she felt a sudden strong tug that she couldn't explain. As though he were gripping her still, kneeling in front of her and holding on to her hips like he would never let go.

She could still feel the buzz in her pussy from when Tam had his mouth on her only two hours before, and yet the lingering sensation only seemed to make her hungrier for Mike.

It was a mix of alcohol, spite and arousal that made her lean in closer to Mike then, brushing her breast against his arm, and lay a hand over his. She smiled like a serpent, thinking of the heat of their under-the-table game and the way he handled her, covertly and blatantly all at once.

'Why don't we get out of here?' she asked. 'Come back to mine.'

Mike laughed. 'Such an impatient woman, aren't you? But much as I would like to take you home, strip you and fuck you, I really can't leave my own party.' He pulled his wallet out and gave her a card. 'Call me. Tomorrow. I'll be in the studio.'

'Alone?'

'Yes, Kara. Alone.' He looked her over again. 'Go home, go to bed. Sleep naked. I'll be thinking of you.'

3

Kara woke with her whole body aching. She rolled out of bed and winced as the sharp winter sunlight flared in her face. Her limbs hurt from dancing and from getting mauled by Tam in the corridor, and her head was full of the dull thud of a champagne hangover.

What surprised her most of all, though, was the shiver of arousal she felt still tingling in her sex. It had stayed with her all night, a restless, hungry excitement that compelled her to twist around in bed until the sheets were a tangled mess and she wanted to scream. She'd barely slept, but felt wired with a nervy energy she couldn't shake off.

As she showered and made herself breakfast, she was aware that her body was practically thrumming with desire. As though Mike had struck her with a tuning fork, got her pitch perfect, so in heat that she wouldn't be able to rest until she'd fucked him.

And it was looking likely that she'd be doing so that very afternoon. A quick phone call yielded the promise of seeing him alone in his studio, the thought of which made her palms damp and her legs shaky. Even their brief conversation turned her on – the sound of his voice tickling her ear like a promise.

She had two hours. The flat was empty – Kara shared with Ruby and Ruby was at Jon's. The two of them were barely apart these days. Which meant that Kara had free access to Ruby's wardrobe. Last night she'd been dressed in her stage clothes.

Louche, maybe sexy in a rough, punky way. But today she wanted to make damn sure she got screwed, and she was dressing specifically for Mike.

It was a ritual she enjoyed. Putting on 'glamour', artfully creating an outfit with the full intention of having it taken off again in the not-too-distant future.

To set the scene, Kara rifled through her record collection and found the perfect soundtrack: Ella Fitzgerald, a little scratched and hissy, but loaded with atmosphere. She dropped the needle on the turntable, cranked the volume up loud and opened the door so the sound would carry through the house as she dressed.

She chose a pair of lipstick-red heels, which were shockingly vivid against her pale white skin. A black corset – left over from Ruby's goth days – fixed with a row of thirty hooks and eyes that cinched in her waist and pushed her tits upwards. After some consideration, Kara fetched a pair of stockings from her room, pulled them on and fastened them to the corset's hanging clips, leaving her pubis bare but flanked by nylon, straps and lace. It reminded her of the Magritte painting: a pussy in a frame. She wrapped a pencil skirt around her hips, admired the slit at the side that showed a sliver of stocking and the curve of her thigh.

It was the kind of outfit she didn't wear very often. Retro in a noirish dame kind of a way, restrictive enough that she had to walk with small steps and swaying hips. Most of all it was the type of outfit that turned her on as she got dressed. If she leaned to the side, the lace tops of the stockings would scratch against her clit. The underwiring in the corset gripped her breasts like they were held in two claws. Nylon slid against nylon as she walked and every part of her body felt caressed, constricted, fixed and prepped for a fucking.

As she dressed Kara felt her confidence growing. She was as

sleek and bold as a Hollywood film star, and the clock was ticking towards the hour when she'd meet Mike again. She was midway through applying a mask of foundation, blusher and eyeliner when the door buzzer went, and she nearly blinded herself as the pencil jerked in her hand. Definitely on edge, she told herself. Swearing, she went to answer the door. Tam was standing there.

'What the fuck are you wearing?' he said.

'Hi, Tam. Nice to see you too.'

'So, are you going to let me in, or what?'

Kara sighed, but she stood aside and let Tam push past her into the hallway. 'Got any coffee?' he asked dryly.

'There's coffee in the cupboard, just like there always is.' Her eyes flicked to the clock on the wall. She followed Tam to the kitchen, for some reason very conscious of the clicking noise her heels made on the wood floor.

'So what's the occasion, Miss Moneypenny?' Tam asked, his head already in the fridge. Apparently too lazy to make coffee after all, he pulled the milk carton from the fridge and took a swig, licking off the white milk moustache as he waited for Kara to answer. She fiddled with her watch, pulling the strap a notch tighter.

'One of your eyes is squint,' he said eventually, breaking the silence.

'Well thanks,' Kara said, folding her arms. 'Anything else you want to tell me? I'm in a rush.'

'I'd like to know what's under that skirt,' he said, ducking his head a little as though he could peer up it from across the kitchen.

'Too bad,' Kara said, but she shifted in her heels as she spoke, remembering how exposed she was underneath the thin skirt.

'You owe me a favour, remember?'

'Not now,' Kara said.

'Show me,' he said, standing his ground and not moving a muscle. He had one hand in his pocket and something in the way he stood, that cocky, slovenly slouch, seemed like a challenge. Kara hesitated. The thought of showing him her artfully dressed crotch was appealing. She knew exactly what effect it would have on him, and her body was longing for gratification after a sleepless night and a whole morning spent thinking about fucking Mike.

Standing with her back to the kitchen counter, Kara bent and lifted the hem of her skirt. She pulled it upwards, slowly revealing her stocking-clad legs and the creamy skin that was bare at the top. Tam waited, like a cat watching its prey, his body held utterly still. When Kara's skirt was high enough for him to catch sight of her naked pussy he took a deep breath. She knew that he was taking it all in – the neatly trimmed black hair, the cleft between her legs where her thighs were pressed tightly together.

Displaying herself like this was enough to make Kara squirm, standing like a doll in front of Tam's hungry gaze and itching to have him cover the distance between them, break the tension, turn this strange exhibition into a sex scene already.

But he seemed in no hurry.

'Turn around,' he said, 'put your hands on the counter and bend forwards.'

Kara bit her lip and frowned. After a moment's hesitation she decided to play along. Swivelling round, she gripped the edge of the kitchen counter and did just as Tam said. With her head down, she could no longer see what he was doing, only hear his movements. Screwing her eyes shut, she struggled against the impulse to turn round or speak. Let him have his moment of fun, she told herself. Truth be told, she enjoyed playing these games as much as he did.

Her skirt was still rucked up around her waist, the heels tilting her on tiptoe and forcing her bare arse upwards. Ella Fitzgerald's voice drifted through from the sitting room. Over the music, Kara heard the suck of the fridge door opening. She flinched. Was Tam ignoring her? It would be just his idea of a joke to leave her hanging there half naked while he made a cup of coffee. But before she could turn, she heard him move.

The atmosphere seemed to thicken as she felt him behind her, close enough for his breath to disturb the air around her. It was almost as though she could feel him regarding her naked rear.

Without warning, he slapped her hard on the buttocks, giving her a stinging blow that was over before she could shout or move. Only the feeling lingered, her skin burning and buzzing, like a wasp sting spreading over her cheeks. Kara stiffened, but as she opened her mouth to swear at him, two more blows rained down.

She could have twisted out of the way, of course, but each smack came as an exquisite surprise, shocking her and making her body hum all over. It was electrifying. Kara arched her back, bit her lip and waited. She was ready for whatever his next move was. *Unpredictable*, she reminded herself, realising just how thrilling that could be. There was the low ripping noise of Tam's zip, and his hands on her, cupping her buttocks.

The smacking had made her instantly wet. Just as well – that was all the foreplay she got or wanted. Immediately she felt the head of Tam's cock butting up against her slit and nuzzling at her, until it found where she yielded and pushed inside. Kara's nails scratched uselessly at the counter, trying to hold the precarious position. As she swayed on the heels, unbalanced and shaking, Tam drove himself further. He went deep enough to make her gasp this time, so she could feel herself clinging and stretching around his cock.

Pinned against the counter like this, Kara was barely in control. Only Tam's hands on her hips and his cock inside her connected them. He thrust hard and fast then, screwing her decisively to his own rhythm. Kara braced her arms, held herself high on her toes to find an angle that opened her as wide as possible. She wanted this breathtaking, vigorous fuck; she wanted to be thoroughly screwed.

And Tam was obviously pleased to oblige. He was working something out from the night before, Kara could tell. This sudden, almost brutal coupling was his way of trying to impress his mark on her. He clutched her hips hard enough to leave bruises; she twisted under his grip and heard him moan.

Struck with sudden lewd inspiration, Kara arched her spine so that Tam's cock could sink in as deep as possible. His balls slammed against her arse as he screwed her to the hilt, and she felt the pang inside as he hit her centre, thumped against her cervix like the bang of a deep bass drum.

It was enough to send him over the edge; Kara heard his sharp intake of breath as he bucked once more, jerked against her and slipped out suddenly.

She heard him cry out as the warm rain of his sperm scattered over her arse, cooling almost as soon as it touched her skin. His voice sounded surprised, like she'd tricked him somehow. It was such a swift and explosive climax Kara almost laughed. But the frig had exhilarated her – barely taken the edge off her horniness and primed her nicely for her next assignation. She liked the thought of visiting Mike ready-fucked.

Kara held her skirt up gingerly, taking care not to let it brush against the wet spots on her ass. Tam's hand was shaking as he did up his zip. 'Fetch me a tissue, will you?' she asked, and felt herself slip back into control as he did her bidding, fetching a cloth from the radiator and dabbing at her. It was pleasant, the feel of him rubbing the slick of his sperm into her skin, acting almost tenderly now as he cleaned her carefully. His breath was still ragged, as though he was recovering from a shock, and Kara smiled.

'I think that makes us quits,' she said as he finished.

She expected him to laugh, and got a surprise when she looked up to find an expression on his face she'd never seen before. His jaw was tight and his brown eyes as sticky as tar, and for a moment she wondered if they were due another tantrum. The inevitable fight that seemed to happen every time they fucked. Kara stuck her chest out, ready to argue the toss. But Tam just tore his eyes away, balled up the towel and threw it at the laundry basket.

'Tam?' she said, confused.

He was leaving, already, walking slowly towards the door with his usual lazy swagger a little exaggerated. He didn't turn and Kara watched open-mouthed as he disappeared down the hall.

'Not even a goodbye?' she said. 'What the fuck was that – wham-bam-not-even-a-thank-you, ma'am?'

The front door closed quietly, leaving Kara alone with Ella still wailing 'Bewitched, bothered and bewildered,' in the next room.

Kara swore, crashed through to the sitting room and kicked the stereo with the point of her shoe, sending the needle skidding across the record and abruptly cutting the song short. 'You can shut up, too,' she muttered.

The studio was an old church that looked over the park, converted tastefully with a lot of glass and polished wood dividing the large space. Slick, Kara thought as she approached. She buzzed and waited, checking her hair with a quick glance in the reflection of the plate glass.

Mike eventually strolled to the door, smiling as he unlocked it. He was in a shirt and chinos, sleeves rolled up as though he'd been working. If he'd had a late night at the launch party it hardly showed – he was as coolly handsome as ever. Like an actor, Kara thought as he pulled the door open.

'You look amazing,' he said, waving her in.

'Thank you.'

'Come through to the office,' he said, 'I'm just finishing some paperwork.' He led Kara across the reception area and upstairs into a bright airy room. It was sparsely furnished – an upright piano stood against one wall and there was a desk by the open window. The place smelled of fresh paint, and a vase of freesias on the window sill overlaid the air with their sweet honeyed scent.

'Wow,' Kara said. 'Nice.' She walked to the window and leaned in to examine a framed record hung on the wall. The lettering was small – gold on red. 'Michael Greene – *Greeneblue*'.

'Before your time,' Michael said, moving to stand behind her. 'And probably not your cup of tea, either.'

She turned and looked coolly at him. 'How do you know?'

'I imagine your tastes run to the more ... blatant,' he said, letting his eyes run over her stockinged legs and down to the lipstick-red heels.

'Blatant, huh? Sounds nasty,' Kara said.

'Not at all. There's something to be said for shameless exhibitionism,' Mike said. 'And you carry it off very well.'

'You seemed to like it last night,' she said, pacing away from him across the room. Something about Mike made her restless, like a moth trapped in a light shade. She ran her fingertips along the lid of the piano, tapping a light tattoo on the lacquered black surface.

'Want to play?' Michael asked smoothly.

'Am I auditioning for something?'

He laughed, reaching up to rub a hand over his stubble. 'Perhaps you are.'

Instead of lifting the lid though, Kara pulled herself up to sit on the piano, sliding her bottom onto the lid and resting her feet on the stool. She let her skirt slide up to show the lacy top of her stockings and arched her back so that her breasts jutted forwards. Everything about the outfit and the situation made her feel like she was acting out a scene from a film.

She gave him her best Bette Davis look. 'So, what do you want to play?' she asked.

4

Kara perched on the lid of the piano while Mike circled her. He came so close that she could smell the coffee on his breath. When he rested his hands on her thighs and pushed them gently apart, a tremor of uncertainty flickered in her mind. She had the sudden irrational sensation that he could tell she'd just been fucked – as though Tam's touch had marked her, written her secrets across her skin in scarlet.

Mike rolled her skirt higher. Bit by bit, he revealed the lace bands at the top of her stockings and her bare flesh. His hands were quick and delicate, his long fingers skilled and precise. Of course she should have guessed he would play her as expertly as he played the piano.

He tucked the skirt back so that she was fully exposed. Barely a flicker passed over his face as he examined her pussy. Kara had a sudden urge to pull her knees together and hide herself, but when she flinched Mike gave her a slight frown. His expression was the perfect echo of the cool impatience he used to show as her tutor. His fingers dug into the soft flesh of her thigh.

'Focus,' he whispered, and Kara bit her lip. 'Good enough to eat,' he murmured softly, holding Kara's knees splayed open wide so that her hips ached.

She tensed her muscles involuntarily, as though a little twitch of her pussy could scratch the itch brought on by Mike's cool gaze. But the slight ripple and clench between her legs only made her more desperate for friction, for his hands or mouth or cock, something she could rub up against.

'Undo it,' he said, nodding at the corset.

Kara reached round eagerly to unfasten the hooks and eyes. Her lungs filled with a welcome rush of air as her breasts fell loose, freed from the stiff clutch of the black net. Spilling from the half-undone corset with her skirt crumpled round her waist, she felt more than naked. Mike was stripping her of everything, piece by piece. His fingers traced the red indentations the underwiring had left tracked across her skin, from her hip to her sensitive underarm. Her nipples had pinched into points; they blushed a deep apricot against the white of her skin. The back of his hand grazed the side of her breast and made her leap inside, as though his touch was electric.

Never mind that she'd been fucked so shortly before – she needed it again, and badly. But Mike was in no hurry. He pulled away and left Kara hanging on the edge of the piano, leaning forwards into midair. She missed his touch immediately, and the distance between them made her ache right to her fingertips.

'Stand,' he said, at last.

Kara slid down off the piano. She left smudges on the glossy black lacquer, blooms of condensation from the heat of her body.

Mike frowned. 'You've smeared it. That'll need to be polished,' he said.

He took another step back, widening the cold distance between them. 'Take off the skirt.'

Kara reached for the buttons on her hip. She forced herself to undo them slowly, trying to calm her heartbeat as she paused between each one. The skirt gradually came loose and slid to the floor. Kara instinctively wanted to kick aside the puddled fabric but she hesitated, waiting for Mike's instruction. He gave no indication of what she should do, but instead spent a good long moment looking her over as she stood with her skirt round her ankles.

'When were you last fucked?' His voice was low and quiet.

Kara half laughed, half gasped.

'You won't tell me?' Mike walked around her, circling, drawing closer but not close enough to touch. He moved behind her and Kara heard the soft click as he raised the lid of the piano.

The sound unlocked a hundred memories in a sudden vivid rush – turning up for her first lesson in a crop-top and belt-short skirt to find Mike at the piano in a shirt and polished shoes. How he'd been so calm and offhand. The way she'd withered under his gaze. The memory made her cringe again, and blush, even as another picture replaced it – Mike slapping the top of the baby grand, making her repeat a passage over and over until she'd learned it perfectly by heart. The way her fingers would ache during a session, reaching desperately to catch all the notes and tripping over themselves, making painful mistakes. With every sour note, she winced and Mike gritted his teeth.

Afterwards she would be aching too, inside, with frustrated want and horniness. She remembered how he'd grown sterner and more withdrawn over the year they'd practised together, barking out orders and barely smiling even when she played flawlessly.

Kara was wrenched back to the present and the sunlit office as Mike started to play. She didn't recognise the piece, but the deep chords touched something in her. Mike played as lightly and effortlessly as he always had. The music spilled out of him and Kara allowed it to sweep over her, the high trills sending little shocks down her spine and the low notes marking an insistent rhythm.

She stood, half naked and abandoned, lost, while Mike bent

over the keyboard. Had he forgotten her? Was he having second thoughts? Her skin tightened. Maybe she should cut her losses and leave now, before he humiliated her any more. As she bent down to pick up her skirt though, Mike's voice stopped her.

'I wouldn't do that if I were you.'

He didn't stop playing, not for a moment. The notes still tumbled from the piano, deep and light at the same time. Kara watched his hands, the tendons in his wrists long and taut as he stroked the keys. She searched his face. Expression had marked him; laughter lines curved deep at the side of his mouth and his forehead was scored with a slight frown. His face was scarred with stories, but to Kara his expression was unknowable.

At last, the piano fell silent. An echo vibrated in the air between them.

'Touch yourself,' he said, barely whispering. The tip of his tongue darted out and flickered over his lips. A tiny movement, barely a gesture. But it was enough to give Kara a glimmer of hope. Uncertain, she reached up to stroke her throat. Mike watched her with a sidelong gaze.

'Lower,' he said. 'Feel your tits.'

Kara swallowed. She cupped her right breast. Her nipple stiffened automatically and she let her thumb scuff it. The zing of sensation made her feel stronger and she arched her back, vulnerable and provocative, all at once. Under his pale-gold stubble a muscle in Mike's jaw flexed as he watched.

She imagined the prickle of his face against her, his rough cheek brushing over the soft skin of her inner thighs, and a pulse flowered in her sex.

'Show me where you want to be touched,' Mike said.

Her hand went straight between her legs, her fingers pointing out her desires more easily than she could have spoken them. Just the kiss of her own hand on her clit was at least some relief from the gnawing want that was driving her crazy, and Kara pressed down harder, hardly caring if Mike wanted her to or not.

How long would it take him to touch her? Kara rubbed herself slowly. She pressed her thighs together and trapped her hand there. With her other hand she carried on playing with her breasts, teasing each nipple in turn. She was lost in the pleasure of touching herself and it was becoming difficult to stand steady. Her knees were on the point of buckling and her cheeks were flushed. She bit her lip hard and watched as Mike shifted on his seat and reached into his back pocket.

His movements deliberate, he pulled out a tuning fork and held it in his open hand. The sight of the dark metal object laid across his palm sent a shiver through Kara.

'Stop,' he said, then rose and walked towards her. Though it wasn't easy, Kara dropped her hands. She was weak and reeling from the build-up of tension, and it was almost a relief to hear him instruct her.

Mike reached out with the fork and brushed the cold steel over her collarbone. Kara was breathing hard and the jerking movement of her chest made the edge of the metal jump against her skin. Lazily, Mike dragged the flat side of the fork around her breast, leaving a faint white line trailing in its wake. With the tuning fork against her ribs, he gently lifted her breast and bent his head. Without touching her at all, he pulled her nipple into his mouth.

His attentions were precise, catching the sensitive point between his teeth and tugging gently. Kara got an exquisite jolt of hard pleasure concentrated in that one small spot. The smell of his hair – a faint whiff of rosemary and something woody – hit her as his warm wet lips closed round her and sucked. Though they were so intimately connected, his mouth to her breast, Mike deliberately kept his distance.

At last he pulled away, leaving Kara swaying, her nipple smarting and the pulse of want still beating in her sex. Mike's expression was lit up now, a spark danced in his cool grey eyes and his mouth was wet and hungry. Kara's attention was drawn to his crotch, the forbidden territory of his naked body under those casually rumpled trousers.

Mike's body had always fascinated her, the lines and long flat curves of it. She had hunted for the subtle clues of how he would look naked – the way his muscles tensed as he moved, the way his trousers hung from his hips. His burnished skin and the wiry blond hairs of his arms hinted at a well-used body, one that was weathered by sun and exercise, and his slight stubble and loose, overlong hair broadcast the fact that he wore his good looks carelessly.

Kara stumbled forwards and pressed up against him, seeking out the hot naked skin of his throat and latching on with a half bite, half kiss. She tasted sweet salt as she licked the hard line of his collarbone. Then she bit the tender part of his neck as his bent knee slid between her legs.

He didn't push her away, but lifted her and pushed her backwards onto the piano, dropping her ass onto the keys so that they clanged a loud, broken chord. A handful of notes played as she shifted and opened her legs for him.

Mike unzipped with one hand and fiddled with a foil square with the other, while Kara rolled forwards so that her ass teetered on the lip of the piano. He had the condom on so swiftly she barely had a moment to catch her breath before he surged back against her and slid the whole length of his cock swiftly inside her.

He fought to fuck her then, while she held bunches of his shirt in her fists and dug her heels into his flanks. She balanced on the edge, using the angle to better spike herself on his cock, and pulled his shirt aside to find the burning satin smoothness of his skin. With every thrust, Mike's muscles bunched and contracted, and the hardness of his body felt like it might bruise Kara.

As they fucked, their entwined bodies released a slow-burning perfume – the smell of his body, the sharp rich smell of his sweat and that complex mixture of smoke and leather and rosemary that was Mike's own. She reached to kiss him and met the rough scratch of his stubble and the blunt, rude intrusion of his tongue forced between her lips. There was not a single suggestion of softness about the kiss, only the force and hunger of his mouth.

The tuning fork fell to the floor as he gripped her hips, adding another clang to the cacophony that they were wrenching from the piano, the dreadful chords and off-notes that resounded every time Mike plunged forwards. Kara almost laughed, hearing so many months of painstaking piano practice massacred, thinking it was ironic that the glorious mess of their fucking should produce such a jarring noise.

But she was struggling to remember to breathe as Mike hammered against her, charging onwards with unstoppable force. His hands gripped at her buttocks and ground them hard, a finger worked between her cheeks and searched out the dark hidden crevice of her asshole. Kara whined and pulled him closer. His hips crowded between her legs, pushing them so far apart that her groin ached. Kara didn't care. She needed as much of Mike as she could get, the weight and push of his body crushed against hers, and his fingers in her mouth, her pussy, her ass. Mike responded easily, swarming over her and licking, biting, nipping at her while his hips kept up their steady rhythm, pushing into her until her head swam.

'Oh, Christ.' Kara wasn't sure how much more she could take before her world exploded, and she wondered briefly if Mike fucked this relentlessly just how much thundering noise would there be when they came?

'Is this a duet?' A woman's voice cut through the messy symphony.

Mike froze, clutching Kara so tightly she couldn't move. He glanced behind him, and cold shock crashed over Kara as she realised Lina was standing by the door, watching.

'Nice to see you again.' Lina spoke calmly. She was dressed as soberly as Kara was lewd and dishevelled – black polo neck, black jeans, no make-up, her face expressing not a hint of shock but not smiling either. She looked like the harbinger of all that was sane and normal, as though reality had just gate-crashed the party. Kara felt her face burn up. Her stockings and heels and naked breasts suddenly seemed like a trashy mistake.

But inside her, Mike's cock swelled. Although Kara's body pulsed automatically in response, her sex echoing his tiny movement, her mind reeled. Was he enjoying this? He made no move to withdraw. In fact he ground himself a little tighter inside Kara as he spoke.

'We're a little busy, Lina. Can we talk later?'

'I expect you'll want me to draw up a contract, will you?' Lina asked, her face deadpan.

It only made Kara feel even more like a cheap slut and she fought the sense of rising panic in her chest. 'Can't you leave us alone?' she blurted out, forcing herself to meet Lina's eye. What she saw in the other woman's expression frightened her – a cold contempt that showed she valued Kara's input less than nothing.

'A little privacy, Lina?' Mike said, and at last Lina responded, nodding to him as she left and closed the door

'Oh, shit,' Kara said once they were alone again. 'I can't believe it.'

'Don't let it bother you,' Mike said. 'Lina isn't easily shocked.'

He reached his hand between her legs to pinch her clit. 'I don't think catching me in flagrante delicto will be much of a surprise to her.'

'What, you do this often?' Kara pushed him away, her orgasm shrivelling and dying inside her as she struggled to cover herself, the sweat already cooling on her body. Mike's unconcern confused her. Even standing there with his cock hanging out of his trousers, he was unperturbed.

'Don't bother with the coy act, Kara,' he said. 'I doubt you're as pure as the driven snow.'

'That's none of your business,' Kara said.

'No, not usually,' Mike admitted. 'Unless you're fucking Tam, of course.'

'What's Tam got to do with anything?' Kara said. She scrabbled about with the fixings of her suspender belt, trying to pull on her skirt at the same time. Most of all, she wanted to run out of there, get far away from her embarrassment and Mike's far-too-direct questioning. The recording studio suddenly seemed like a minefield.

'It's clear there's something between you,' Mike continued relentlessly. He tucked himself in and zipped his trousers. 'And if I'm going to be producing your record, I need to know that there's no chance you're going to screw things up.'

His words stung. With one sentence, they'd gone from high-octane sex straight back to business.

'I can assure you I'm capable of being totally professional,' Kara said, trying to forget the fact she was half undressed and still smelling of Mike. It didn't help when he threw back his head and laughed.

'Dear Kara,' he said. 'I'm under no illusions of what you're capable of. I don't need a prissy little businesswoman to sell records.' He reached out to run his hand over her flank and patted her ass. Like someone buying a racehorse, Kara thought bitterly.

'I just need you to be up there on stage, pouting and jiggling and oozing sex like the proper little slut you are. I don't want to *tame* you, Kara. I want to corrupt you.'

When Kara was angry her eyes turned cold and dark. She imagined right now they must be as black as obsidian. She walked towards the door with her spine very straight. She didn't bother to fix her hair or straighten her clothes – Mike could go fuck himself if he thought she was interested in making a record with him.

'Kara,' he called. There was the old warning note in his voice, the one he used to use when she talked back to him in lessons. The only answer Kara could muster was the bang of the door.

Kara's hand held on to the stair rail so tight her knuckles had turned white. She stood on the landing and did her deep-breathing exercise, waiting for her heart to slow to a trot. What a bastard of a day, she thought. It seemed she'd spent it getting wound up and missing her chances – ending up with insults and arguments instead of the orgasm she so desperately wanted. She had half a mind to put her hand in her knickers and bring herself off there and then in the elegant stairwell.

No, she thought. Later. Right now she needed to get home and get in the shower, wash off Mike's sweat and that charged masculine rosemary smell of his that was clinging to her skin. As she went down the stairs she resisted the urge to kick the freshly painted white walls.

Behind the desk at reception, though, a different problem appeared. Kara's heart sank as she saw Lina sitting in the chair, swinging back and forth thoughtfully as she looked at a computer screen. Kara stuck her chin in the air and kept her eyes on the door as she crossed the hall, but she knew the other woman was watching her. She could just imagine the look on her face.

'Leaving so soon? It didn't go well, then.' Lina had one of

those deep-honey voices that sounded like years of late nights and smoky clubs.

'What would you care,' Kara said, not breaking her stride.

'Not so much, darling. Mike's little kicks never last that long.'

Kara stopped in her tracks. She turned on her heel and noticed with some satisfaction that a flicker of doubt crossed Lina's face, the smallest tremor twitching at her eyelid.

Kara leaned over and splayed her hands across the drift of papers that covered the desk. Lina was polished, sure, and sophisticated. But Kara wasn't in the mood to be intimidated.

'Do you have a problem with me?' she asked. 'Or are you always this much of a bitch?'

Lina gave her a brittle smile. 'Of course not. Actually, I just feel a little sorry for you.'

'How's that?'

'That you have to resort to fucking your way into a record deal.' Lina spoke airily, flicking her fingers towards the door.

'Get a grip,' said Kara, spitting the words through her teeth.

'Here's a tip, dear.' Lina leaned in close. 'Next time, don't give away the goods until you've got the contract signed and sealed.'

Kara spun round and ran for the door. If she didn't leave right now, she'd be tempted to slap the woman – and any pride she might have managed to salvage would be in shreds. She could just picture herself, cat-fighting on the floor of Mike's oh-so-elegant studio. That would be a perfect way to round off her day. As she barrelled through the door and marched to the park gates across the street, Kara dug her fingernails hard into her palms and swore repeatedly under her breath.

In the office, Lina smiled as she picked up the phone. 'Mike,' she said. 'I take it I should rip this up.' She held the contract for the Rakes' first album pinched in her fingertips.

5

Kara turned on the shower and waited for the heat to run through. She wanted the water scalding. As she stepped under the stream, she closed her eyes and tried to clear her head. Her thoughts were spinning in circles and she bounced from humiliated to confused to horny. Tam, Mike, Lina. Everybody seemed to want something different from her and Kara wasn't sure who she could trust. Something Mike had said to her repeated over and over like a stuck record: *'I want to corrupt you.'*

Although his words disturbed her a little, she had to admit they also got her hot. And even if everything between them was strictly business, there was no doubt Mike could make her career skyrocket.

But she'd ruined that chance. Blown up at him and run away. She'd managed to screw up her golden opportunity so badly it made her wince. Furious, she scrubbed at her thighs with her body brush, wishing she could scour away the day, her temper, her mistakes and, most of all, the raging horniness that got her into situations like this.

Damn, she thought as the tingle spread over her body. Vigorous exfoliation wasn't helping. The more worked up she got, the more she wanted to fuck someone, and the more horny she got the more she thought of Mike. His dry smile irritated her, but it made that pulse boom between her legs. It was dangerous, what he did to her. Kara didn't want to be that hooked on anyone. She needed to stay away from him.

Luckily they were unlikely to bump into each other – though the music scene in Glasgow was small, they moved in different circles. Very different circles. Not much chance of running into Mike in the spit-and-sawdust joints that Kara was used to. He spent his time sipping overpriced drinks with the glitterati.

Kara remembered the feel of his tongue on her nipple and felt a pang of arousal, the slightest trace of regret as she poured lavender shower gel into the palm of her hand. She soaped herself slowly, noticing a couple of bruises as she did so. Noticing, too, that her nipples had puckered at the thought of Mike licking her. She thought about giving herself a quick orgasm to burn off the horniness, but her clit stung at the thought.

'You need to learn to control yourself,' she muttered, yanking the shower firmly off and stepping onto the cold tiles of the bathroom floor. She rubbed the steam off the mirror above the sink and stared at herself. Her reflection was wired; cheeks pink and eyes tired but with a curious spark to them, like she'd drunk too much coffee. She combed the tangles out of her wet hair with one hand and steered her thoughts towards work.

Kara paid her rent by doing a few shifts in a pub every week. Her shift started at seven – five hours in a West End bar serving hair of the dog to red-eyed punters, with the music on low and nobody speaking too loud. Sunday was an easy ride. At least for one night, she'd be saved from dealing with all the people she'd pissed off. She might even get time to work things out in her head, write a song – something about sex and tangled desire.

Yes, she thought, that could work. Something dark, something angry. The one thing that might keep her sane was getting down some lyrics and making music out of the whole sorry mess. As she reached for her eyeliner, Kara was already writing the first lines in her head.

Cobalt was one of the new wave of Glasgow bars, with large glass windows, black leather sofas and potted palms. So hip it hurt. Which meant Kara didn't have to be overly worried about pleasing the clientele. She could scowl, sulk and generally take the mickey, so long as she looked good and knew how to mix a Screwdriver.

As she'd expected, the place was dead when she arrived – half-a-dozen guys in crumpled shirts nursing pints of lager, and a group of dressed-down city types by the big fake marble fireplace trying their hardest to look like people out of a magazine style supplement. Besides making a few Bloody Marys, it was looking like an easy run till midnight. Kara nodded at Bernie, the carefully laid-back bar manager. He grinned at her and rolled his eyes, which were bloodshot as usual.

'Good night last night?' Kara asked, knowing that Bernie very likely hadn't been to sleep yet.

She listened to his jumbled account of an illegal party under the railway arches, nodding every so often to show she was listening. In fact, her attention was fixed on the song taking shape in her imagination.

She'd had the first line going round in her head for an hour, with the melody repeating in a loop. If she got it down on paper quick enough, she might end up with something more to show for the evening than smoky hair and sore feet. When Bernie wandered off to chat to one of his clubbing cronies at the end of the bar, Kara pulled an order book out of the drawer under the till. 'CORRUPTED', she wrote along the top of the sheet.

'*I don't want you tame.*' Kara bit her lip. '*Slide guitar?*' she added, and closed her eyes to replay the melody in her head.

*   *   *

Kara was bent over the bar working on her song an hour later, tapping out a rhythm on the wood with the end of a biro. Her hair fell over her face so that potential customers were conveniently invisible, and so she didn't see the deliveryman come in.

Although she'd been pretty oblivious, the sudden wave of scent pulled her out of her reverie. Kara looked up to see a bouquet about as big as the man carrying it advancing towards the bar; white lilies dusted with rusty pollen and those ludicrous spiky orange flowers called paradise-somethings. They were showy as hell, but pretty impressive, she had to admit. Orchids trailed from the bottom of the bouquet. Kara grinned. One of the yuppies on the sofa by the fireplace must be making some kind of grand statement.

But the guy stopped at the bar. 'Kara?'

She raised her eyebrows, the smile dropping off her face.

'I'll put them here, love, shall I?'

Before Kara could say anything, the deliveryman had dropped the flowers on the end of the bar and hurried away again. Aware that Bernie was watching her with a bloody great smirk on his face, Kara approached and sniffed gingerly at the lilies. A small white envelope was tucked into the spray, but she hardly needed to open it to guess who'd make a gesture this ostentatious.

The message was handwritten – Mike's elegant signature looping across the card under the few words he'd put: 'Let me make it up. Call me.'

'That's some posy,' Bernie said, sneaking up behind her and trying to read the card over her shoulder. 'Whoever he is, he's after something.'

'Hmm.'

'Gonna call him?'

'Not sure.' Kara chewed the end of her biro grimly.

Bernie laughed, flicked a dishtowel at Kara and shook his head. 'Don't tell me the wee diva is turning shy?'

He swaggered away before Kara could smack him. She watched his ass as he walked down the length of the bar, the way his jeans clung to it and the top of his boxers peeked out from the waistband. Under Bernie's close-shaved hair, the indigo spikes of his tattoo curled over the nape of his neck. Yes, Kara thought, he was foxy enough. Surely if she needed someone to burn off her jittery frustration with she could tumble him, instead of getting into something complicated with Mike? A nice straightforward fuck, a boy-man with smooth olive skin and a smile full of white teeth. No strings. No angst.

She watched Bernie as he flicked through the sports pages of the newspaper. He scratched his neck and whistled 'The Lady is a Tramp' – tunelessly.

No strings. But no butterflies, no tension and no chemistry, either, Kara thought wryly. She slid the envelope into her back pocket and looked at the flowers again. For a moment she thought about binning them, but then she shrugged. They weren't doing any harm sitting on the bar smelling gorgeous. And she had to admit, Mike knew how to make a statement.

By the time the clock hit twelve she was tired and jumpy. As the bar cleared out and she wiped down tables, turned chairs over and emptied ashtrays, she forced herself to stop thinking about Mike. The idea for the song had dissolved since the flowers turned up, like the scent of them had forced all her thoughts out of her head. She tried to remember how the hook had gone, sung it over quietly under her breath.

'Kara.'

At the sound of her name, she dropped the glass ashtray she was holding. It hit the floor with a loud crack and she swore as she looked up. Tam stood by the door, his clothes crumpled and his hair looking like he'd just rolled out of bed. He gave her one of his dark grins, sweeping his sleepy eyes over her black shirt and wide-legged trousers.

'Got to love a girl in uniform,' he said, leaning against the door frame. 'You finished?' He was carrying a leather holdall in one hand, the battered bag that he usually dragged his guitar round in. 'Thought you might like come back to mine for a jam.'

Kara searched his eyes, suspicious, but there was no trace of the bitterness she'd seen in them earlier that day.

'No tricks,' Tam said. 'Ruby and Jon'll be there too.'

Kara nodded. 'OK,' she said, slowly. 'Good. There's a few things we need to talk about anyway.'

'You did what?' Ruby shouted. 'Kara, that was the best fucking chance we've ever had!'

'Steady,' Tam said. 'Blue Star isn't the only record company in the world.'

'No, but it's the only one who's offered us a deal on a plate,' Jon said. He paced across Tam's living room, stepping over the tangle of cables that stretched across the carpet. 'Could you not have kept a lid on your temper for a week or two, Kara?'

Kara sat slumped in a chair, chewing her thumbnail. 'I wouldn't work with that bitch if my life depended on it,' she said. 'Besides, I'm the one who put in the effort to get us the contract in the first place. I don't see anybody else taking the initiative.'

'Must have been a lot of hard work,' Tam muttered.

Ruby sighed. 'Maybe if you could go back and apologise –'

Kara cut her dead with a look. 'I don't do apologies,' she said, flatly. 'So let's just drop it, OK? I've got a few lyrics I was working on.' She pulled the crumpled order pad out of her pocket, tore off the top sheet and passed it to Jon. 'Think you can work this into something?' she said.

He took the paper reluctantly and glared at Kara's scribbled notes. 'I'm sure I could,' he said, 'but is it worth it?'

Kara pressed her lips together. She'd had a long day, her head was fizzing, and she wanted to lose herself in the song. She knew it was the only way she'd be able to unwind. Take what was bugging her and twist it into music, make it new.

'Jon,' she said quietly, fixing her gaze on him, 'please?'

He sighed. 'You singing?'

'Yep.'

'Key?'

'B flat.'

Jon walked over to the keyboard that was set up under the window and played a few chords. Tam swung his guitar onto his lap and followed the tune, while Kara listened, waiting for the right moment. She could make this good, she knew she could.

They played into the small hours, forgetting their arguments for the time being. Kara took all her anger and horniness and poured it into the song, letting the sound carry her elsewhere. It was only after Jon and Ruby had left, when she put on her coat and got ready to leave that she noticed the rust-orange pollen spilt all over her sleeve. She caught the scent of lilies and remembered the flowers, still sitting on the end of the bar, filling the place with their sweet heavy scent.

Tam noticed her frown and took her arm.

'What's that?'

'Just a stain,' Kara said, brushing at the pollen.

'Want to stay over?' he asked, catching her hand.

Kara raised her eyes to his. 'You said no tricks.'

Tam gripped her wrist. 'No tricks.' He smiled. 'Thought you might want a little comfort, that's all.'

His thumb stroked the inside of her wrist. Kara fought the urge to pull away. She liked fucking Tam, but when he touched her like this, so gently, it made her jittery. She could feel him watching her too, with a look that was more compassion than lust. She couldn't stand his sympathy. She preferred Tam when he was dark and smouldering, gripping her because he wanted her not because he thought she needed comfort.

'It doesn't matter, you know,' Tam said.

'What doesn't matter?'

'That Mike Greene blew you off.'

'He didn't blow me off,' she snapped. 'I told him to stuff his contract.'

Tam shrugged. 'Whatever. I'm just glad you're not –' He broke off.

'Not what?'

A chasm opened up suddenly, yawning with possibilities that Kara didn't want to look at. Tam's hand circled her wrist as tightly as handcuffs and she felt as though she couldn't breathe. She pulled away, bumped her way towards the door. 'I need to get home,' she said. It was freezing outside, but she wanted to feel the cold air on her face. All the dangerous emotions were struggling inside her, making her feel like she was walking a tightrope over a deep drop, pushing forwards because she was too scared to look either side of her.

'Kara,' Tam said as she reached the door. 'Stay a while. Please.'

The fight went out of her when he used the word 'please'. It fell into her heart like cool water, and she found herself staring at him. He stood in the doorway in a T-shirt with the ragged hem, with his hair all mussed up and hanging into his eyes so that his fringe twitched when he blinked. Even with his broad shoulders and sulky mouth, his well-hidden sweet side was showing.

Kara looked at the mattress on his living-room floor. The ticking was bare, and it was covered with a zipped-out sleeping bag. Sheets of song notes and magazines were strewn over the blue nylon. Tam didn't give much thought to anything besides music and fucking – in that order.

'Perhaps I just want more, Tam,' Kara said quietly.

'More what?' He approached her, moving carefully in his bare feet. His jeans were hanging off his hip bones and she could see the pale white line of the scar on his lip, drawing her eyes to his full luscious mouth. When he reached up to tuck her hair behind her ear, Kara was startled. His hand was shaking. What could he possibly be afraid of? They'd fucked, fought, made up and forgotten about it a dozen times. Why would this time be different?

But as he stroked the nape of her neck, working at her muscles with his fingertips, Kara felt a little flip in her stomach. Tam's eyes were wide and dark and she couldn't escape their depth. This wasn't the prelude to a seduction, she realised. His jaw was working and his breath was ragged, as though he was working up the confidence to speak. When it came, his voice sounded forced and unnatural.

'He's no good for you, Kara. You can't trust a man like that.'

She pulled back and opened her mouth to answer, but Tam raised his voice and kept going: 'I know you like to think you know how to play him, but he'll chew you up and spit you out. It's not worth it, honey.'

'Honey? Since when was I your bloody *honey*?' Kara couldn't keep the anger out of her voice.

'Don't get like that. I just want to ...'

'Tam.' Kara folded her arms and nodded at him. 'I'll see who

I like, when I like, as often as I like. The last thing I need is advice from a wannabe muso whose career high is getting an email from Keith Richards.' Kara turned and made for the door, not waiting to see how Tam would react.

She gave it a good slam behind her and ran down the steps into the still winter night. There was frost in the air and it stung her lips as she breathed in but she was glad for the sudden shock, the physical sensation that seemed to help clear her thoughts. She walked fast through the dark streets, her footsteps echoing in the early-morning silence. Twice that day she'd run away from a nasty situation. Now she was going home to an empty flat – by the end of the late-night session she and Ruby still hadn't been on friendly terms. She was alone, pissed off and confused.

In fact, the only glimmer of pleasure she could think of as she tramped up the hill to her flat was that ludicrous, extravagant bunch of flowers and Mike's handwritten message – short, but full of promise.

Just how would he 'make it up' to her? she wondered. She pictured Mike's wry smile and the way his eyes flickered over her. Something about him conjured up images of grand and glittering horizons – sleek cars and endless glamorous parties. Kara let herself imagine a succession of five-star hotel rooms. Silk sheets, camera flashes, champagne and oysters and Mike's cool hands sliding over her thighs.

By the time she'd reached home, the lit up dreams in Kara's head were more vivid than the dark rooms of her flat. She dropped her coat on the sofa and saw the pollen on her sleeve again. For the first time in hours, she allowed herself a smile.

6

'So, we have a deal?' Mike held the bottle tilted over her glass.

Kara smiled. 'Sure. Just as long as it's clear.'

'Crystal clear.' Mike poured until the champagne frothed over the rim and spilled down the stem.

'The contract has nothing to do with you and me. Whatever else we choose to do –' Mike drew his finger through the condensation on the side of the glass '– is a private arrangement. And I can be as discreet as you need me to be.'

'I'll drink to that,' Kara said. She had painted her eyes smoky and now she gave Mike the full-beam effect from under sooty lashes. In the dim candlelight of the club, everything glowed with understated elegance. Kara felt as though the glamour had rubbed off on her somehow. From the moment he'd picked her up outside her flat, Mike had been treating her differently – no edge of mocking amusement in his eyes, no condescending tone in his voice. He was as sincere and humble as a Benedictine monk. Only Kara was pretty sure monks didn't take every opportunity to stroke a girl's hand or glance at her cleavage.

He'd brought her to his private club – marble floors, silent staff, mysterious doorways – and in the 'quiet lounge', presented her with a contract. Kara had barely skimmed it, but she caught sight of enough phrases like 'video production', 'marketing' and 'airplay' to make her mouth water. She tucked the envelope carefully into her leather satchel and smiled.

'And now we've dealt with business,' Mike said, giving the cuffs of his shirt a little tug, 'we're free to amuse ourselves.'

'In any private way we please,' Kara said.

'Quite.'

At that moment, a waiter arrived and refilled their drinks, tilting his head at Mike in deference. Kara smirked. She didn't doubt that if the man had had a forelock, he would have tugged it. Mike seemed to have that effect on people.

Mike rubbed his chin and gazed at Kara across the table. He'd shaved – whether for the sake of Windigo's dress code or to try to impress her, she couldn't tell. He wore a freshly pressed shirt with silver cufflinks and a silk-lined suit that fell in softly tailored lines from his shoulders. Kara felt her spine straighten as she looked at him. Mike was perfectly at ease being waited on. He wore his power lightly, as though the world naturally revolved around him. It gave him a cool magnetism that sent ripples through Kara, more used to the rough-and-ready attitudes of twenty-something boys. Mike was, without doubt, a whole hell of a lot more. And he was completely focused on her.

The silence between them stretched, even after the waiter had left – practically bowing as he backed away from their table. Kara felt the champagne haze wash over her, bubbles dancing through her bloodstream and making her pleasantly dizzy. There was a low-level buzz of anticipation in the air between them. This time though she had a better idea of what to expect. There would be no coy uncertainty; Kara knew an encounter with Mike would be highly charged and unsettling. And she knew that she liked it.

'I want to know everything,' Mike said at last. 'What turns you on, what you dream of late at night, when you're alone in your bed with your hand jammed between your legs. I want to know the pictures that you see in your head and exactly how you feel when you're horny.'

His voice was low but clear and Kara automatically huddled closer, looking about warily to see who was sitting near them. It was as though she was sitting in the waltzers and someone had just spun the seats round – she felt the delicious spark and the nervous lurch, her surroundings blurred so that she had to focus on Mike and Mike alone, as though anything else would send her spinning off into space. Her mouth opened but she didn't know what to say.

'This isn't going to be some swift and sordid affair, Kara. I'm not interested in knee-tremblers in the back of a car, even if it is hard to resist the urge. I said I wanted to fuck you thoroughly and I mean it. That means I want to know you. Your body and your fantasies through and through.' He leaned forwards. 'Am I shocking you?'

Kara bit her lip. 'A little.'

'Good. I like it that you're shockable.'

'And what about your tastes and fantasies and yada yada yada? What do you want?' she asked.

'I should have thought that was obvious.' Mike took a cigarette from his breast pocket and twisted it between his fingers. He smiled. 'I want to drive you mad with desire, of course. But first I want to find out which buttons to push.'

Kara laughed. 'So what, I should write you a laundry list?'

Mike said nothing, twirling the cigarette between his knuckles.

'Are you going to smoke that thing, or are you practising for the majorettes?'

'I gave up.'

'So why do you have one in your pocket?'

Mike gave her a thin smile. 'Like I was trying to show you, Kara, anticipation is more than half the pleasure. If you knew that I'd booked a room here, for example, with the serious intent of taking you upstairs later and fucking you, you'd start to feel a little ... heated.'

Kara swallowed. 'And have you?'

'Maybe. But tell me, if I had, what would you imagine?'

'Uh, you ripping my skirt off and fucking me senseless?'

'Bullshit.' Mike shifted in his seat and frowned. 'Would I be slow and deliberate? Would I be rough? Would I kiss you before I stripped you?'

'There are people ...' Kara looked urgently over Mike's shoulder, to where a table of businessmen sat idly chatting.

'I'm not interested in them. Start here. Start half an hour from now.'

'I'll be half cut by then.'

'You're sitting in your seat.'

Kara inhaled. 'OK. I'm sitting in my seat.'

'Your breasts feel tight. Your nipples are hard. You know what we're about to do.'

Kara swallowed. The thought of admitting her fantasies to Mike was like standing on the edge of a shark-infested sea, wondering whether they'd bite and how hard. She shut her eyes, took a deep breath and jumped. 'I'm already wet.'

'Where?'

'In between my legs.' Kara lowered her voice to a whisper. She leaned forwards now, put her arms on the table and shook her fringe over her eyes.

'Don't hide behind your hair. You're wet between your legs.'

'Yes.'

'And then what?'

'You, you take me by the hand and we go upstairs.' Kara stared at her glass, at the bubbles that clung to the side before tugging free and lifting to the surface. 'We go slowly.'

'Why?'

'It's hard to walk. I'm so turned on I'm shaky. And you're feeling me as we go up the stairs.'

'I slip my hand under your skirt, check how wet you are,' Mike added. 'And then we get to the room.'

'You push me up against the door. I'm trying to open the door, but I can't find the key because you're kissing my neck, biting me.'

'Actually, no.' Mike's voice had lowered. In the dull light of the bar his cheekbones were shadowed and his eyes glinted. Waiters and club members moved around them in a low murmur of hushed sound, but Kara felt as though she was connected to Mike with an invisible rope, a line that stretched from her groin and her belly and down through her arms to reach out to him. When he talked, she watched his mouth and felt it on her skin, when he played with the cigarette, she felt him tangle his hands in her hair, tease shivers from her body. 'I won't touch you. Not until the door's closed and you're standing in the centre of the room, with your hands hanging by your side.'

Mike sat back in his chair, legs splayed. Kara let her gaze fall to his lap, where she could see a tightening of the fabric of his suit – loose as it was, there was a definite outline where his cock pressed against his thigh.

'Because,' he said, 'we're not just fucking, are we? We're playing a game. The rules of which we're deciding now.'

'I thought you wanted to hear my fantasies?'

'Yes. And how they intersect with mine. I'm not interested in the way you are with Tam or any of your other paramours. I want to hear your deeper fantasies. The ones you wouldn't dare admit to.'

Kara pressed her lips together. The bar was growing slowly busier with professionals and the lazy rich, mostly men, a few women moving among them with poised glamour, leaving trails of Chanel in their wake.

'I'm standing in the centre of the room,' she said finally. 'You undress me, and I don't move. When I'm naked, no, wait, half naked –'

'I've taken your underwear off, but left this on –' Mike reached over, lifted the strap of Kara's white camisole '– so that I can see the line of your breasts through it, the curve of your hip, the shadow of your hair.' He trailed the back of his hand down her arm as he sat back, giving her goosebumps.

Her eyes burned. 'You feel me, just a little, enough to make me gasp. And then …' She looked at his clothes. 'Then you take off your tie. Pull my wrists behind me and knot them together.'

Mike raised an eyebrow. 'Interesting.'

'So I can't move, while you do whatever you please.'

'And you want this?'

The two of them sat now with their gazes locked on each other. Kara nodded. 'Oh yes.'

'I can lift your top and play with your tits. I can push you backwards until you fall on the bed. Will you like that?'

'Keep going.' Kara gritted her teeth.

'If I get bored, playing with your body, I can turn on the TV and find the movie channel. Watch some porn.'

Kara could feel points of heat burning on her cheeks and she was breathing with her mouth open. She wondered if it was really possible to come just from listening to someone speak.

Underneath her sequinned red skirt she was wearing a pair of string knickers, the kind that tended to curl up and cut into her skin. For a change, the irritating strip of fabric had become a blessing – it gave her something to rub up against if she rocked very slowly back and forth, letting the tight edges saw against the side of her clit.

The pictures in her head flickered faster, coming in sudden

bursts now: Mike's hand between her legs, the blue glow of the TV screen in the corner of the hotel room, Mike unzipping himself.

'Then,' she whispered fiercely, 'you take out your cock. You push me onto my front and open my legs. You drive yourself into me, until I can feel your balls against me and your cock fills me completely. I'm so fucking horny, but you won't touch my clit, won't untie my hands so I can make myself come.'

'Even if you beg me. I just keep fucking you. And then I start feeling your arsehole.'

Behind them, Kara saw a waiter turn round and give them a curious look, before turning away quickly. She wondered if this kind of conversation happened a lot at Windigo's. Did men bring their mistresses here? Hookers? Was that why the blinds were pulled down and the lights were so low?

'And then I sink my cock into your arse,' Mike said, laying his hand on her knee and squeezing.

'Uh, no, hold up,' Kara said. 'Don't go there.'

'No? OK. Maybe later. I'll break you in slowly.' Mike smiled. 'So then, I fuck you harder. Pull out and come over your back. Let it cool.'

'But don't let me shower. Leave me there, tied up, sweating, begging.'

Mike narrowed his eyes. 'I'll bury my face between your legs and lick you. Just lightly. Slowly, like I'm eating a particularly delicious bowl of ice cream.'

'Sounds good,' Kara said, digging her nails into her palms. She glanced quickly at the champagne, noted how much was left in the bottle.

Mike continued talking. 'I'll draw it out until you can't stand it. Until you can't think and can't speak and can't breathe. And then I'll tweak your nipples and suck on your clit and make you come so that you scream into the feather pillows.'

'OK,' Kara said. 'We need to go upstairs. Now.'

'I don't know,' said Mike. 'Perhaps we need to work out the finer –'

Kara stood up abruptly and dragged him to his feet. 'Where are these rooms?' She jiggled her foot.

'Are you sure you –'

Kara hissed in his face. 'I don't care where we're going, Mike, or what the "agreement" is – we need to fuck, right *now*.'

He mock-bowed to her, like the waiter acceding to his patron's demands. 'Madam. I'll be happy to take you up to my room and play dirty games with you. Just let me pay the bar tab first, OK?'

As they stood at the desk waiting, Kara gripped her hands behind her back. The warmth of Mike's body was just a few inches away and the knowledge of what his hands and his mouth would soon be doing to her made her feel as jittery as a schoolgirl. She wandered over to the window and looked out onto the square, tried to distract herself by watching the crowds of black-clad teenagers congregating like flocks of crows under the art gallery's pillars. Finally, a man in a pinstriped suit appeared behind the desk. Kara turned and watched as his impassive face creased into a smile.

'Mr Greene,' he said smoothly. 'I've reserved room five for you. I hope that's to your satisfaction.'

'Wonderful, thank you Robert.'

'I know Ms Warren –' The man's eyes flicked towards Kara and widened abruptly. 'I beg your pardon,' the man murmured, lowering his gaze and sliding a set of keys over the desk to Mike. 'Enjoy your stay,' he said, his face darkening under his white stubble as he turned and hurried away.

'Shall we?' Mike said, gesturing to the stairs.

Kara stood in silence. Her heart lurched and then froze, as

though a sliver of ice from the champagne had lodged in her chest. She felt as though she was rooted to the spot.

'Something the matter?' Mike asked, a note of irritation creeping into his voice. 'You're not going to run off again, I hope.' He rattled the keys and shoved a hand in his pocket. When Kara didn't respond, he walked to her and took her arm. 'If you want to walk away now, that's all right. But this will be the last chance I'll give you, Kara.'

She looked at the stairs. Small white lights dotted each tread, like the lowlights in a theatre that showed you where to walk when the power went off. In the hallway the scent of lilies was overpowering, as sweet and heavy as a drug. Mike was next to her, stroking the underside of her arm where the skin was soft, and breathing evenly. It didn't matter that her heart was squeezing in her chest. Kara's body was still oiled, weak and ready with want for Mike. She let him lead her, across the hall and up the staircase, towards room number five and whatever awaited her.

7

He closed the door behind her. 'Christ, you're quite pale,' he said.

She looked around. A lot of polished wood and white linen. More flowers on the table, black tulips this time, the stems bowing under the weight of the full, sleek blossoms.

'Nice,' she said faintly.

'Well, it's a hotel room. What were you expecting – chains and a rack?' Kara pressed her lips together. Mike laughed. 'I don't need any fancy props right now. Just you.'

His voice had changed, subtly. There was a dark quality in his words that she could hear very faintly, like the flow of an underground river. Kara wanted something to hold on to but there was nothing near her, and so she stood in the centre of the room just as he'd told her she would, waiting.

He was unknotting his tie, pulling it through his hand to loosen the creases, and she listened to the faint hiss of silk as it slid over his palm. She was shaking a little, the ghosts of uncertainty and anticipation whirling around her. As Mike came close to her and took her hands, Kara concentrated on the feel of him, on how he held her so gently as he looped the tie round her wrists.

It was all new and she let the movements unfold in a series of strangely delicious sensations – the feel of her arms pulled back behind her so that her breasts thrust forwards, the tight binding of the fabric against her wrists that felt surprisingly like a very warm, very safe embrace. Most of all, she felt a rushing, a widening expanse that flowed from her joined wrists and her rigidly bound arms. She recognised it, suddenly, as the sensation of power finally slipping away from her, and wondered how it could make her feel quite so free, almost as though she were flying.

He tugged on the knot to test it and stood behind her, running a finger down the curve of her spine.

'Remember, any time you want to stop, say "Stop",' Mike murmured, his mouth next to her ear, his lips brushing her lobe. And then his hands were slipping under her arms, sliding over her belly and digging under her waistband. She leaned back against him, trying to push her buttocks against his groin, but he held himself at a distance.

With Mike behind her, and her wrists tied, she could do nothing to stop him and nothing to help him. He continued at his own pace, pushing her skirt down to her knees and leaving her like that, naked but not graceful, twisting her hips in midair.

Just as he'd told her he would, he reached up to undo her bra, pulling it up so that her breasts hung loose inside her shirt, tender but tight, her nipples burning against the slight rub of the ribbed cotton. Kara was undone, her front bared and Mike's hot hard presence behind her unbearably impossible to reach.

She let a sound escape her mouth, half sigh, half moan, and it was as near as she had come to saying 'Please.' Words built up inside her, meaningless fragments, dirty words; she almost wanted to start chanting a litany of obscenities, a list of pleas and incitements that might prompt Mike to do what she asked.

But she bit her lip. Something told her that the more she begged for, the less Mike would give her. His hands were hovering over her naked skin now, brushing feather light under her ribs and over her hip bones. His palms were dry and warm and wide, his fingers rhythmic and deft, working steadily closer to the points where she burned and buzzed and needed to be touched.

'Is this what you wanted?' he asked, letting her lean into his shoulder.

'Mm,' she answered, not trusting herself to say more.

'I think it's more than that,' he continued, sliding one hand into the brush of hair between her legs and curling his fingers there. He tugged, gently, pulling enough to make the blood rush right to her clit. Kara's centre of gravity shifted. 'It's what you needed,' Mike whispered, tracing the slit of her lips with the very tip of his forefinger.

Her body needed so badly to move that she bucked against his hand.

'God,' Mike said as his thumb pressed against her clit. 'You're so responsive. Just the right type to tie up and tease.'

Although his honeyed words made Kara's knees sag with desire, unease started to prick at her. What other type was he thinking of? Who else had he tied up in this room? The answer came back to her immediately.

Lina. Kara saw the other woman's face vividly, the curled lip of her bitter smile, her copper hair. She almost thought she could catch the scent of her hidden somewhere in the hotel room. And though she was lost in Mike's game, almost drunk with horniness, the image sobered her like cold water splashed on her face. She struggled, considered shouting 'Stop,' had the word on her lips but held back. Was she being compared? How would Lina react to being tied up and teased?

Mike sensed the change. He dropped his arms and stood back. Kara was left swaying, angry at the loss of his touch and confused by the mixture of want and fury that fought within her.

'Hm,' Mike said. 'I think that's all you need for the moment.'

This time he walked in front of her and started to undress. Through narrowed eyes, Kara watched as he tugged his shirt buttons undone and pulled himself free. His skin was the colour of pale sand, as smooth and sharp as a desert landscape, and when he moved his muscles rippled like shifting dunes. There were faint freckles on his shoulders, and his nipples were as pale as shells, tight knots on his long, elegant torso. His was a body she wanted to explore slowly, the lines and angles and curves of it.

Mike was unzipping his trousers. Kara found her eyes drawn to the springing hair that crept down his belly and trailed lower, to the shadowy groin where he was reaching to free himself. He pulled out his cock and held it slung in his hand. Thick and straight, it was a darker gold than the rest of his body and nicely stiff.

Mike wasn't watching her and seemed to have almost forgotten she was there. He leaned forwards and spat in his hand, curling his wet fingers over the head of his cock. He started to rub. His eyes closed and he sighed, tipping his head back so Kara could see his Adam's apple rise and fall in his throat. It was sheer, private pleasure, just Mike and his cock, but she knew he was doing it for her benefit. It worked. He stood with his legs wide apart and his arm, strong and tense, worked slowly at the fat hard-on held just out of her reach.

When he gritted his teeth and pushed air through them in a rough hissing sigh, she was ready to weep with desire for that body and that cock.

Had he done this with Lina? Made her beg? Kara was starting to care less. She licked her lips and strained at the silky bonds that kept her powerless and frustrated. If she wanted this man, it was clear she was going to have to find a way to take him.

And if she had to get round his tangled past to do it, she'd find a way.

With her arms tied and her pulled-down skirt hobbling her, she sank to the floor. The carpet was soft and her knees sank into it as she shuffled over to him, feeling ridiculous but ready to crawl if she had to. When she reached Mike, she butted her cheek against his cock, nuzzled against his thigh and tried to bury her face in his coarse bush of hair. She struggled against him blindly, darting her tongue out to lick the hot salt of his skin.

'Bobbing for apples, are you?' he asked, laughing softly at her while he continued to jack away at himself. But when Kara keened with frustration, he relented and slowed his movements, cupped the back of her head and moved his cock into her mouth. She sucked on it gratefully, feeling the full roundness of his head and the tight hard length curling into her cheek. 'That's it,' he said softly, angling his hips to move deeper.

Kara jammed as much of him as she could into her mouth, pulling back slowly and then surging forwards to hear him sigh as he pressed hard against the roof of her mouth. She worked at his root hard, dragging her teeth over the lip of his foreskin and closing her lips tightly around his girth, holding him hard and sucking relentlessly. Spit welled in her mouth and ran down her chin, but she kept going, listening with pleasure as she heard Mike's gasps come faster.

When he clutched at her, she knew he was losing control. With every grunt he made, every moan she drew from his lips, she felt stronger. At last, when his hips locked rigid and his skin swarmed against her lips, she pulled away.

'Fuck me,' she said, breathing hard.

Mike didn't answer, but took hold of her shoulders. He lowered her slowly, folding her over so that she rocked back on her heels, supporting herself with her bound fists. Automatically, her legs spread wider, and she gasped. She felt like she was falling backwards. Her hips curved so that her pubis stuck forwards. Her head was tilted back and she couldn't move, and for a moment she struggled.

Then Mike's mouth was on her, licking full lazy strokes across her clit and lips, his tongue running nimbly into the fold of her thigh. She didn't need much stimulation. One more hard fabulous suck of her clit and he was going to make her come.

When he drew away, she was left hanging in awful space for a long moment, bereft. She heard the crinkle of foil as he tore the wrapper from a condom and she balanced dizzily on the edge, waiting.

Two heartbeats and his cock was at her slit, surging inside her at last and rising deep, right up to the hilt. Jesus, she thought. She was angled so that his cock pressed hard against her sweet spot and, as they rocked in and out of each other, even with the ache in her wrists and the pain in her thigh muscles, she felt the orgasm start to blossom between them.

'Say my name,' she said.

When he didn't answer, she curled her head up to look at him. Their eyes locked. 'Say my name,' she repeated, insistent, holding herself still, trapping his hips between her thighs so that he couldn't move.

'Kara,' he said at last, pushing into her with a deep driving stroke. 'Kara.'

At the same moment, they tipped over the brink.

Her orgasm nearly broke her. It crackled and hummed up her thighs and wrapped itself round her arse, broke deep in her pussy where his cock was squeezing, shot out through her arms and rose up, until she was blind and deaf and dumb, rigid with the force of it.

Mike clutched at her waist as he fell forwards, coming soundlessly, mouth open, eyes screwed shut. Shocks rippled across Kara's body and she rocked against him, bumping like a boat hitting the harbour wall, waves rising and falling and pulling the ropes tight until they sighed, finally, and fell back, looping slowly into the water.

Then she spread out like an oil slick, the feeling rushing back into her limbs and her kneecaps stinging from carpet burns. She twisted onto her side and they came loose, doubled over and panting. The room was full of stars for a moment and Kara's head swam; she'd been dropped, suddenly, back into the world of the living and it was a shock. There was sweat trickling down her back and drying already, and Mike in front of her pushing his hands into his hair, composing himself, steadying his breathing.

Though she was trembling and as weak as a newborn puppy, Kara managed a smile. Whatever strange game they had started, full of undercurrents and secrets, she looked at his face, slack after the orgasm, and felt like she'd just won a round.

Afterwards, she sprawled on the king-size bed and stretched out.

'I could get used to this,' she said. 'Come here.'

Mike glanced at his watch. 'Much as I'd love to, I have things to do.' He bent down and gave her a brisk kiss on the cheek. He was already tucking his shirt in and looking for his jacket.

Kara bristled. She rolled out of bed and snatched her clothes from the floor, avoiding Mike's eyes.

She dressed quickly, feeling the ache in her arms and legs. Mike watched as she fumbled the buttons on her skirt and hunted for a lost shoe.

'There's no need to rush,' he said. 'They don't rent these rooms by the hour, you know.'

'Oh, I wouldn't want to keep you,' Kara said. If her voice was bitter, she couldn't help it.

He caught her arm as she headed for the door. 'Call me,' he said.

Kara nodded. 'When I have the time,' she said, giving him an icy smile.

Outside, the streets were full of rain and rushing crowds. The late-shift workers and the early drinkers mingled on the wide streets of the city centre, dodging salesmen in neon jackets and charity workers, sweeping past the buskers with their guitars echoing under archways and in doorways.

Kara walked fast under the violet streetlights, her raincoat pulled tight and her collar lifted to cover her face. The burn from Mike's stubble was hot on her cheeks as she went westwards, passing gusts of heated air from the shops with their open doors and smelling the first early-evening kitchen smells of garlic and grease and beer. Her legs, bare and tight in the cold winter air, were still aching, but her pussy had that tingling, well-fucked feel that put a spring in her step.

She pulled out her phone and wrote a text with one hand as she walked, closing the other around the folded contract in her jacket pocket.

'Meet me in Sleazy's,' she punched in. 'I've got good news.' She scrolled through the names in her phone, past Jon and Mike and Ruby, reached Tam, and hesitated. As she waited at a junction, she bit her lip and let her thumb hover over the send button.

Around her, people surged forwards as the lights changed, bumping her shoulders. Kara snapped at someone, swore and marched onwards, skirting the traffic as it drove forwards and picked up speed.

When she walked past a pub with the doors propped wide open and heard a blast of music thumping into the street, she smiled. The city was full of music, spilling out of every corner, and she was just about to turn the volume up even louder. Even as the rainstorm grew heavier around her, Kara felt her heart lifting and surging as she reached the motorway junction.

Traffic swarmed under the flyover, flowing south over the river and east towards Edinburgh, streaming out in every direction from the heart of the city. Kara looked down at the cars and felt again the faint ache in her wrists, a reminder of her and Mike's game. She remembered the noise he'd made as he'd come inside her and the rush and roar of the road beneath her sounded as charged and exciting as sex.

Everything's coming together, she told herself. Don't lose your nerve. Taking a deep breath of the smoke and rain-sodden air, she lifted her phone and pressed the button. Just as long as you don't screw this up, Tam, she added.

Slipping her phone back in her pocket, she turned and hurried onwards, walking faster straight into the rain.

8

Sub City Radio was blasting through the house when she got home. Kara followed the noise to the kitchen, where her flatmate clattered around making coffee. The sink was piled with dirty plates and a load of laundry was scattered on the floor: fishnets and ballet skirts and red flannel sheets. It was just the way Ruby lived – 'creative chaos', as she called it. Kara was too psyched to notice. She was wet from the rain, her cheeks burned with wind chill and stubble rash, and her body ached with exhaustion, but inside everything was sparking like fireworks. She leaned against the kitchen counter and said hi. Ruby barely looked up.

'We're out of milk,' Ruby snapped, slamming the door of the fridge. 'If you want coffee you'll have to have it black.'

'I've got news,' Kara said. 'Good news.'

Ruby turned. Her make-up was blurred on her face and her hair fell around her face in a mass of black curls. 'Oh yeah?' She peered closer at Kara. 'What happened to you? You're soaked and you look kind of ... wired.'

Kara looked at her flatmate's rosebud lips, her open freckled face, and savoured the surprise she knew was going to make her freak. 'We've got a deal.'

'A deal. A deal. A record deal? Blue Star?' Ruby froze. 'Oh my *God*. This is major. This is ... Oh God.' She looked down at the kettle in her hand. 'Screw the coffee. We need alcohol.'

Kara laughed. 'I'm going to meet Tam in Sleazy's. But I don't know if he's going to be exactly over the moon.'

Ruby winced. 'Ah. Tam trouble.'

'Mm. He's got some chip on his shoulder.'

'That boy's always been a headcase,' Ruby said. 'But yes, it's been worse than usual lately.' She laid the coffee jug on the counter and looked at Kara. 'You do know why though? I mean, it's fairly obvious.'

Kara sniffed. She pushed Ruby out of the way and started spooning grains into the pot. A cup of scalding-hot strong coffee suddenly seemed like a good idea. She was running on fumes after hours of fizz and fucking with Mike, and she had a feeling she'd need her wits about her to deal with Tam. Everything seemed to have speeded up in the past few days, as though she was falling head first into the future. It made her exhilarated and nervy all at once.

'I mean, you can't have failed to notice –'

Kara cut Ruby short. 'I need to get going. Are you coming or not?'

Ruby lifted her eyebrows. 'Whatever.' She picked up her phone from the table. 'I'll call Jon. He's going to bite himself.' She spun round as she reached the doorway. 'Uh – you might want to put on a bit of slap before we go and meet Tam.'

'Huh?' Kara said. 'Tam's seen me without make-up plenty of times. I don't think it'll help.'

'No.' Ruby nodded, a smile twitching at the corner of her mouth. 'But that stubble rash is *nasty*.'

'Where the hell is he?' Kara said, rattling the ice in her glass. Three-quarters of her band sat in the half-empty bar, under kitsch blue-tinted paintings and a disco ball. They'd taken over a bench by the window and sat looking out into the rain. Celebratory drinks were half-drunk in front of them. The contract lay spread out on the table, with three signatures on it and the ink smudged where Ruby had carelessly set down a beer bottle. The space next to Tam's name was blank, the street outside was empty and Kara's mood was turning dark.

'God knows,' Jon said. 'Tam moves in mysterious ways.' He shrugged.

'I could kill him,' Kara said. 'We're recording in two days. Two days.'

Jon looked up. 'Give him some time to cool off,' he said. 'You know he can pick up a tune as easy as blinking.'

'He'd better,' Kara said, 'I won't let him ruin this.'

Ruby sat with her arm looped over Jon's shoulder. 'Maybe you should call him, Kara,' she said quietly.

'Oh screw that. I've got enough to do without running round after Tam.'

'Give him a break,' Ruby said. 'His feelings are hurt.'

'Poor thing.' Kara rolled her eyes. 'I think Tam needs to realise the world does not revolve around him and his fucking feelings.'

'I'm aware of that.'

Kara's head snapped round. Tam stood behind them, wearing his leather jacket and four-day-old stubble.

'So, what is it we're playing?'

Tam directed his question at Kara and Kara alone. She looked at him, shocked. When did he get so pale? she thought. His cheekbones stood out razor sharp and his eyes were bruised with dark shadows. He looked as though he hadn't slept for a week. 'Playing?' she echoed.

'New songs.' Tam dropped onto a chair, ignoring the seat next to Kara. He was ragged, but she couldn't help noticing how it gave him an extra layer of sexiness. A dissolute, surly rock-star look just dripped from him. Kara looked him over.

Anger suited him. It made him sharper and ever so slightly dangerous. His eyes were dark, but they burned when she caught

73

his gaze, burned cold. He looked at the uncertain expressions on the faces around him and sighed.

'We're recording a demo, I take it. From the looks of this –' he picked up the contract and skimmed over it '– Mike's picking you up after all.' He looked at Kara again and she felt like his gaze was flaying her. They'd always been sparring partners, but this time she saw something new in his expression. It looked uncomfortably like hate.

'Picking *us* up, Tam,' she said, shifting in her seat. 'So you need to be ready for it. No fucking around. Show up on time, etcete-*rah*.'

'You want this?' He was asking Kara again, waving the contract in her face. She locked eyes with him. Nearby, someone dropped coins into the jukebox and an old Pixies tune started playing.

Kara's hand rose to her collarbone, rubbed at the hollow of her throat. 'Yes, I want it.'

Tam nodded slowly. 'OK. Then I'll be there.'

He pulled a pen from his jacket pocket and added his signature to the page. Nobody spoke and Tam's face was grim. It wasn't quite the celebration Kara had been expecting and she found herself digging her nails into her palm to match the tension that was stewing the air over the table.

'Rehearsals?' Tam said, throwing the pen on the table. He kept his head bent and when Jon answered him with arrangements for their next meeting merely nodded. 'See you then,' he said. He got up and left without a backwards glance. The door swung closed behind him.

As he walked past the window Kara watched through the glass. For a moment, she saw him as though she would a stranger – a young guy with troubled eyes, locked in his own private world. His shoulders were set very square and choppy strands of hair whipped around his face as he strode into the wind. Even in scuffed baseball boots and faded jeans he moved like he was in possession of some secret strong enough to carry him. Maybe it was the clean lines of his bones or the clarity of his brown eyes, but Kara sensed a quality about him that she'd never recognised before – something quiet and strong that didn't break.

'Too much testosterone,' she murmured, turning away from the window. 'The boy drives me up the wall.'

Jon and Ruby said nothing, sitting twined around each other on the bench. Their hands were out of sight under the table and Kara wondered if they were playing with each other or just holding hands in that way they did, lightly and constantly, as though they were magnetically drawn to each other. She frowned and looked away, watched the lights of the fruit machine on the other side of the bar chasing round in circles and flashing insistently.

'Well,' she said, 'screw him anyway. He's signed. And that means we're in business.' Raising her glass, she swilled the watery vodka in the general direction of the bar. 'Here's to The New Rakes. Let's rock the fuck out of everyone.'

Lina bumped the door open with her hip and carried the hot paper cups over to Mike's desk. She had a few files tucked under her arm and her top two buttons were carefully undone. She wore patent-leather heels, in a deep blood red, and walked as smoothly as a dancer.

'Well,' she said, dropping into a seat and blowing on her coffee. 'You got her to sign. That's great.'

'Yes,' said Mike, smiling at her. 'Isn't it?' His eyes were dazzlingly blue, as though they'd been charged with cold, hard spring light. Lina noticed his shirt wasn't ironed. Instead of cufflinks, he'd rolled his sleeves up in messy bunches, showing the tanned muscles of his forearms. A CD was playing on the

B. & O. stereo in the corner – she recognised the flowing piano tune from long ago.

Mike was leaning back in his chair, with thin rays of sun bursting through the window and slicing the desk between them into bright lines. Something had shifted, Lina sensed. That gaze was shockingly familiar to her, that heady, intense, powerful way he had when he was fired up with something, someone. It hit her right in the solar plexus. She inhaled and shifted her hips so that she was sitting with her spine straight.

'I've been thinking about how to do this,' Lina said.

'I've booked an engineer,' Mike said. 'We're recording next week.'

'Fine. But there are a few other things.'

'Meaning?'

Lina pursed her lips. 'Are we happy with how everything looks?' She opened a file and placed a photograph on Mike's desk. 'This is what we have,' she said. 'Two girls. Attractive, good bodies, one particularly ... ambitious.' She paused to watch the smirk that rippled over Mike's face. His hand moved to his chin in that gesture she knew so well. 'Two boys, a little rough around the edges.' She studied the picture of the band. 'How will this work,' she murmured. At last, she looked up at Mike, focused. 'Who's the most fuckable?' she asked, bluntly.

'Kara, of course.' Mike gave her a full hard smile this time, his eyes flashing like he was daring her to disagree.

'Of course. So we sell everything on her. More tit, more ass, more gloss.' Lina tapped the table in time with her words. 'How far will she let us push her, d'you think?'

Mike raised his eyebrows. 'You're taking quite an interest. I thought you couldn't stand her.'

Lina shrugged. She let one long fingernail trace the outline of Kara's figure in the photograph. 'You want to fuck her, that's your business. I'm interested in what we can get out of her.'

'Intending to go to work on her, aren't you?'

'She needs polishing. We have to push that sex appeal that seems to have knocked you for six, turn her into a drop-dead irresistible product.' Lina sat back in her chair. 'Fuckable singers are two a penny,' she said. 'We need shock and awe tactics, here.' She smiled, lifted her hair and stroked her neck. 'I'll turn your rough little slut into a gold-plated diva. Just give me some time.'

Mike nodded. He lifted his feet onto the edge of the desk and stretched out, swinging back and forth in his chair. 'And the rest of the band?'

'I'll deal with them. Should be interesting to see how it all shakes down once I've licked Kara into shape.'

'Now there's a picture.'

Lina gave Mike a long smile, ran the tip of her tongue over her lips. 'Isn't it just?' She leaned forwards and let her shirt fall open a little further. She placed one hand on Mike's leg and stroked gently along his calf bone. 'I do think we can have a little fun with this, don't you?'

'Sure.'

'It could be just like old times.'

At this, Mike swung round to face her. His expression was blank and Lina's hand curled automatically away from him. 'Don't,' he said, curtly, and the smile dropped from her face.

'Oversensitive.' Her lip curled as she said it. 'You do bury your grudges deep, don't you, Michael?'

'I don't want to have this conversation, Lina.'

He was rifling through a drawer, head bent in concentration, and an onlooker would almost have believed he was ignoring her, so calm was his expression.

'Oh, come on,' she said, 'I'm only playing. Don't tell me you'd turn down a little ménage with your latest toy. And the lover that knows you best.' She reached for the amber pendant that hung round her neck and toyed with it, listening to the faint sawing noise as it slid along the chain necklace.

Mike was turning out to be trickier than she'd anticipated. Still, there was colour rising in his cheeks. It could have been anger, but Lina guessed he wasn't completely immune to her overtures. She'd seen his face when she'd walked in on him and Kara after all. It had that dark spark of desire flickering on it, even as he was inside Kara.

He tossed a piece of paper onto the table. 'Kara's number,' he said. 'Try not to frighten her off, will you?' Their conversation was clearly over.

Lina nodded as she rose from her seat. 'That's sweet, darling. You care about her. Well, don't worry.' Lina lifted the pictures from Mike's desk and slid them into a folder. 'She won't know what hit her.'

With that, Lina left, leaving a trail of Obsession in her wake and Mike with a strange twisted feeling in his stomach.

9

'Is this a bad time?' Lina stood on the doorstep, shaking her car keys in one hand.

Kara, having just dragged herself out of bed, squinted at the other woman in the morning sunshine. Lina was dressed with a sharp, calculated sexiness that looked straight out of the pages of a Sunday style supplement. Designer trousers, designer shirt, designer fucking lipgloss, no doubt. Kara was damn sure that she spent more money on her appearance than Kara paid in rent.

'I thought we'd best get moving early,' Lina continued. 'We've got so much to do.' With this, she gave Kara's faded-to-grey Goldfrapp T-shirt and bare legs a sly once-over, as though she couldn't quite believe the new face of pop slept in such shabby gear.

'Uh,' Kara said, combing her hair with her fingers. 'Shit, we're not recording today, are we?' She fought the urge to tug her T-shirt down further over the threadbare pink knickers she was wearing.

'No,' said Lina, flexing back and forth on her knee. 'Today we're branding.'

'Which means?'

Lina gave her a smile as hard and fake as her impossibly pert breasts. 'Shopping. Aren't we a lucky girl?'

'For what?'

Lina pursed her lips. 'For the next big thing,' she said. 'For sex, in loud, bright, shiny, glittery packaging.'

'I don't quite –'

'We need to brand you, Kara, before we can sell you. Add a bit of spin. So we're visiting a good friend of mine, dressing you up and taking you out to play. Think of it as a crash course in pornification,' she added, in a stage whisper.

'But I'm not –' Kara waved her hand in the air, at a loss for words. She had no idea what the crazy bitch was talking about, but it sounded like the wrong kind of wild.

Behind them in the hall, Ruby emerged from the bathroom and moved tentatively towards the daylight. 'Morning?' she said, blinking at Lina in confusion.

'You must be the drummer.' Lina nodded curtly. 'Hi. Kara and I are just about to leave.'

'But Ruby,' Kara said, latching on to an idea suddenly. 'Rube needs to come too, yeah?'

'Not necessary,' Lina called, already turning to descend the steps, waving one gloved hand in the air. 'You're the sex kitten, Kara. The others are just background.'

Kara cringed. She spun round to see Ruby drawing back into the hallway. Ruby was silent; the hurt showing in her hunched shoulders and a sudden coldness in her face, the way her rosebud mouth tightened.

'I'll be in the car,' Lina was shouting as she pointed to a black Mazda double-parked outside the terrace. 'See you in ten.'

Lina drove fast, but without ostentation. It took them ten minutes to slip through the early-morning traffic; they reached the Merchant City before Kara had time to rub the sleep out of her eyes. They pulled to a stop in front of a redbrick warehouse with a heavy steel door set between frosted-glass panels – unmarked and unremarkable. Lina was out of the car and already on the phone getting them buzzed in by the time Kara got a chance to register that this was not a shop, nor anything like one. She felt a mix of resentment and curiosity as she waited for a shadowy figure behind the glass to get to the door – she still had very little idea of what Lina was setting up, and Ruby's displeasure had left a bitter taste in her mouth that wouldn't leave.

'Jerome!' said Lina, pronouncing the name with a soft 'J'.

'Hi, hi, come in.' A shaven-headed man with a wide mouth and a hurried, fretful air waved them in, kissing Lina lightly on the cheek and zipping his eyes up and down Kara's figure. They walked swiftly across the marble hallway and into the lift, where Kara was free to look closer at their host in the mirrored wall. He was a strange-looking type – ugly in the conventional sense, with heavy-lidded, small green eyes and deep lines bracketing his mouth. Only there was something in his manner, in the tense, brusque way he ignored both women and held himself braced against the wall that intrigued Kara. Though his head was bald and smooth, dark wiry hair sprouted from his roll-neck T-shirt and his skin looked tough and leathery.

'So,' he said as the lift doors opened and they spilled out into a large airy studio flat overlooking the City Chambers, 'what is your pleasure today, Lina darling?'

Lina launched into the same speech she'd given Kara earlier about branding and sex appeal, while the man, Jerome, nodded and hummed, with his glittering green eyes fixed squarely on Kara. Feeling uncomfortable under his critical gaze, she looked around. The space was a workplace as well as a home, a large table dominating the centre of the room, covered with sheets of tracing paper and sketches. Scraps of fabric were scattered on the floor and a rack of clothes was pulled close to the table. Jerome's furniture was bright and modern and looked hellishly uncomfortable – turquoise plastic chairs and a clear Plexiglas coffee table sat on a zebra-striped rug that was placed, artfully squint, across the slate flagstones of the floor. Kara's attention was immediately drawn though to the poster-sized photographs that hung on the bare brick walls. Mostly monochrome, at first they appeared abstract, but among the curves and shadows Kara picked out a few recognisable elements – the pointed tip of a tongue, curling upwards, the bony ridges of knuckles and scribbled shadows that on second glance revealed themselves as being body hair trailing across skin.

'Help yourself, take a look,' Jerome called to her, gesturing with a big pawlike hand towards the sitting area. Kara walked closer, leaving the others to talk in a low intense murmur while she examined the pictures.

There were women and men, hidden in shadows as black as pitch. Kara's eyes followed the lines of their limbs: intertwined, wrapped in thin rope, crushed against other bodies. When she noticed a thick erect cock gripped in a fist and pushed against a mouth, Kara smirked, but she also felt the rush of wetness flowering between her legs. The photographs were beautiful and the more she looked at them, the more she saw: the silver stud in a tongue, glowing dully under a curved buttock; fingers sinking into mouths, crevices, hollows; the sheen of wet skin – fresh sperm or women's secretions brushed against a thigh. And a recurring image, one that pricked her attention most, was the glossy wet-black fabric that clung to hips, breasts and stomachs.

'Latex,' Lina said in Kara's ear. She seemed to have come out of nowhere. 'It's Jerome's special talent. Come,' she added, taking Kara by the elbow and leading her to the table where Jerome had looped a measuring tape over his shoulders and stood watching her with his hands on his hips.

'We want something to shock, yes?' he asked, directing the question at Lina rather than Kara.

Lina smiled in assent. 'Absolutely.'

'Full length? Sleeves? Hood?'

'Hood?' Kara said, too loudly. She looked at Lina, but the other woman's face was perfectly bland.

Jerome approached and reached out to grip her waist.

'Hey!' Kara pulled back, only to hear Jerome make a guttural laugh in the back of his throat and see Lina roll her eyes.

'Please, Kara, calm yourself. We need to take your measurements.'

Jerome's froggish face became serious. 'Don't worry. You'll find this an enjoyable experience if you just relax, I promise.'

Kara inhaled and let Jerome's fingers scuttle over her body, pinching and testing. He whipped the tape from round his neck and looped it under her breasts; she tried not to flinch when his knuckles bumped against her nipples.

'I think something slashed, yeah?' he asked Lina, drawing a line from Kara's throat to her navel with his fingernail. 'Expose the breasts, maybe even a little snatch.'

Kara stood silently while Jerome drew imaginary lines on her body like she was a mannequin, putting a hand on her hip to turn her round and tracing across the very top of her buttocks. He made noises as he worked, little sucks and clicks of his teeth like he was beatboxing. Even through her clothes, it felt as though he were cutting her up into slices, portioning her like a butcher's diagram. 'Legs are good too, Lina,' he said. 'Hobble skirt maybe, something that clings to her arse and makes her wiggle. You like the sound of that?' he said loudly, slapping Kara on the bottom and laughing like a drain.

Kara's lips curled back to snarl at him, but she caught a warning look from Lina and managed to perk her mouth into a fierce smile instead. She focused on a fleck of spittle in the corner of Jerome's mouth and watched his pointed tongue curl to lick it away.

'I think I've got something that could work,' he said, turning to the dress rail and flicking through the hangers. Each garment was shrouded in cellophane and labelled with a paper tag and, as he rustled through them, he called over his shoulder, 'At the risk of sounding forward, darling, drop your clothes on the chair for me, would you?'

Kara cocked an eyebrow at Lina. The older woman had settled herself into one of Jerome's bucket chairs and looked as though she was thoroughly enjoying herself. She nodded at Kara.

'Jerome has worked with the best,' she said pointedly, as though that absolved him from perversion. 'Do as he says now.'

'Quick, quick,' Jerome added, snapping his fingers at Kara. 'No point in being coy.'

Kara undressed as quickly as she could, pulling her top over her head and shuffling out of her denim skirt. She dropped them, as Jerome had directed, on the chair, and stood awkwardly holding her elbow, as though one arm over her belly could cover her nakedness.

'Everything, Kara,' Lina said, 'latex is very unforgiving.'

And so, while Jerome chose a hanger and turned to lay the bundled plastic in his arms reverently on the table, Kara unhooked her bra and draped it over the rest of her clothes, pulled off her knickers and bunched them in her hand. For some reason, she didn't want to let go of them, no matter that she was standing gloriously naked under the studio's strip lights with two strangers. Her skin was prickling with goose-bumps and her nipples pinched tight in the suddenly cold daylight.

'Not shaved,' Jerome said, frowning at Kara's pubis. 'Shame.'

Silently, Kara gave thanks for the triangle of dark hair that curled over her pussy and covered her most intimate parts. Without it, she would be one degree more naked, one particularly obscene degree. It might be obvious how her clit had darkened and swelled, how she was bizarrely excited by the situation she found herself in – ashamed, but unable to stop her body from reacting. She kept her thighs pressed together and hoped the wetness between her legs was not visible. When Jerome approached, she held herself rigid, arms clutched at her sides.

Apart from her shame at being so publicly exposed, she hadn't showered that morning, had changed at breakneck speed to accompany Lina on this twisted 'shopping' expedition. There was a lingering smell on her, the rosemary scent of Mike's aftershave and pungent traces of the night before. She was nervous now, starting to sweat, and the sweat was enlivening every sweet and earthy fragrance that clung to her. Kara was keenly aware of the rich scent of body odour trapped in all of her hidden crevices.

But Jerome wanted her to lift her arms. He held a bottle in his hand with his finger on the spray nozzle and he aimed it at her while he motioned for her to put her hands up. Kara put her hands on her head, like a criminal surrendering. She closed her eyes and pressed her lips together. The spray hit her body with a cold tingle that spread and lay on her skin, cloying and slick. Jerome worked steadily over her, coating her from her neck to her ankles.

'Lube,' Jerome said, turning her and spraying her back, bottom and legs. 'You can use powder, but this –' he smiled, spritzed the crevice of her buttocks and let the liquid dribble slowly into the crack of her arse '– I think this gives more pleasure.'

Then his hands were on her, surprisingly rough and warm. He brushed lightly over her skin, as though trying to warm her, slapping at her hips and sides, gliding gently over her breasts, moving so fast that Kara didn't have time to protest or even register how his rough massage made her skin thrill all over.

'OK. Let's try this baby out.'

Jerome unwrapped the hanger and pulled aside the plastic to reveal his creation. It was purple – vivid blackcurrant purple – and shone like polished fruit. The dress held its shape even without a body to fill it, curving round at the hips and bust, tapering at the edges where it would fit tightly to her.

Kara nearly burst out laughing. 'It's a cartoon dress,' she said, suddenly feeling ridiculous. 'It doesn't look real.' Nervously, her eyes darted to Lina, but she was smiling and Kara relaxed. The dress was jiggling as Jerome removed the cocoon from its wrapping, the gleaming surface quivering like jelly, and although it was bizarre and surreal, she really had to touch it suddenly, like a kid reaching out for sweets.

Kara felt her legs gliding together as though they were oiled when she moved across the floor. When she pressed the rubbery sheeting of the dress between her fingers she felt it bounce a little, slippery and cold, almost like wet flesh. A faint plasticky smell rose from it, tangy and artificial. Despite her bemusement, Kara wanted this against her skin, wanted to feel herself encased in it.

Jerome helped her ease into the dress. She stepped into it, holding on to his shoulders for balance, and let him slide it inch by inch up over her hips, felt the tight, slick rubber pull at her skin and suck at her. Somehow she felt quite comfortable, even when he pushed the flat of his hand in between the dress and her body to drag it up, even though she could feel his breath hot on her side, panting as they worked together to shoehorn her into the crazy outfit.

It hugged every part of her body, stretching tight over her curves and following every dip and crevice as though it were painted directly onto her skin. Her breasts and belly and ass were cupped and moulded, squeezed into the hourglass form, constricting her breath and pulling at her in an all-enveloping embrace. Jerome led her to a mirror, Kara shuffling in tiny steps because the skirt restricted her movement, and when she looked up, her eyes widened.

'I look like a computer graphic,' she said, 'not real.'

'Perfect,' Lina said, approaching from behind and placing her hands, with their long painted nails, on Kara's hips.

Where the dress stretched tight, it reflected a distorted image of the studio around them, and when Jerome spritzed more, it gleamed. Kara watched in the mirror as he worked more lubricant onto the dress and was so mesmerised she hardly noticed he was rubbing her breasts, her nipples, her hips through the rubber. The wetness between her legs had smeared on her thigh, merged with her sweat and the spray Jerome had applied and she was all liquid, pliable and taut and rippling, trapped in the dress and glistening with ripe sexiness.

'But where the hell would I wear this?' Kara asked, turning to check the eye-popping curves the dress gave her, lifting herself up on bare feet to curl into a Jessica Rabbit 'S' shape. The slit from neck to crotch showed a long pale wedge of flesh, her breasts straining at the latex and threatening to spill out of the dress altogether.

'We'll take some pictures here,' Lina murmured, dragging her palms across Kara's flanks, all the while holding eye contact in the mirror. 'Jerome's studio's set up next door.'

Just then, a tinny blast of music sounded from her pocket and Lina pulled her phone out and flipped it open.

'Good,' she said, a smile dancing over her lips, 'I'll send Jerome down.'

Lina was holding Kara's chin and smudging dark-crimson lipstick over her lower lip when the door opened. Jerome approached them, rubbing his hands, nodding at the sight of Kara sprawled across his white leather sofa in the ludicrous dress. And although Lina held her chin with a firm grip, Kara twisted round, curious to see who was behind him.

'Jon?' she asked, bewildered.

'Wow,' he said, shoving his hands in his back pockets and bowing his head. He was wearing a red T-shirt and blushing to match it. His eyes didn't leave Kara, not for a moment. 'You look ...'

'Why's Jon here?' Kara demanded, looking straight at Lina.

The other woman slipped the lid back on her lipstick and shrugged. 'Symmetry,' she said simply. 'The two of you look good together.'

In the background, Jerome was setting up a tripod, screwing a camera onto the base and sweeping the lens over Kara where she lay on the sofa. He fired off a few quick shots, the bursts of the flash half-blinding Kara so that she froze, uncertain, with the feeling she was trapped somehow and not in control of what was happening.

'Just try to relax,' Jerome said, 'and let Lina direct you.' He stood and folded his arms across his chest. Beside him, Kara noticed that Jon was looking at her curiously, almost as though they didn't know each other. 'You should be pleased to be working with her,' Jerome continued. 'Very clever woman, Lina, very clever.' He smiled again, and walked over to the high windows to draw the blinds.

10

'That's it, lean over towards her. Turn your chin a little. More.'

Jerome had put a CD in the stereo and a lush string symphony spilled from the speakers. The music bounced around the high echoing space of his living room, softened the edges of Kara's nerves and lulled her into silence.

Of course they'd need promo shots. And she might feel slightly ridiculous in her porn-star get-up, but she had to admit at the same time she also felt curiously sexy. Confused, a little dazed and yet weak-at-the-knees sensual.

She lay back on the giant velveteen cushions and allowed Lina to direct her, meanwhile listening to the strings and the tight clicks of the camera shutter. Jon hovered behind the sofa, holding himself stiff and awkward as Jerome took the shots.

'You really need to loosen up,' Lina said. 'Come down on the floor here, Jon, in front of Kara.' He did her bidding silently, sinking onto his knees on the zebra-print carpet and flicking his hair out of his eyes. His usual light-heartedness had evaporated, and Kara almost reached out to touch his shoulder, give him a little shake. Something held her back. Jon had avoided her eyes since he'd arrived, his gaze darting over her rubber-clad body but quickly sliding away, and where his delicate lips would normally twist into a smile so easily, today his expression remained dark and unreadable.

'Oh, they'll love it, Jon,' Lina said. 'Just curl in a little closer. Your hand on her hip, maybe? Yes. Now look at her.

'Delicious naif, isn't he?' she asked Jerome, who was pushing the tripod closer and refocusing.

'Hm,' he agreed, straightening and running a hand over his shaved head. 'We should maybe work with that.'

'Props?'

'Good idea.' Jerome nodded and disappeared into the other room, leaving the others hanging in uncomfortable tension. Jon's hand was as heavy as lead on Kara's thigh and under the dress she was growing hot and sticky.

'You're doing wonderfully,' Lina said, dropping into the armchair facing them. 'This is just what we need to sell The New Rakes – tension, a little shock value, lashings of sex.'

'And here I was thinking we should be working on the new songs,' Jon muttered, pulling at a loose thread in the rug under him.

Lina ignored him. 'Of course, it'll all feel a little strange at first, but trust me, you're in professional hands. If you want to win, you need to play the game.' She gave them a twenty-four-carat smile. 'And I know the rules.'

Kara flinched. The mention of rules tended to bring her out in a rash. Part of her wished she was back in Tam's bedsit with the band, cranking out rough and ready songs, listening for the hook and arguing with Tam about guitar riffs. She was ready to tell Lina where she could stick her rules, but at that moment, Lina's phone rang. She stood up to take the call, talking fast and loud, as though there was no one else in the room.

'This is kind of weird, isn't it?' Kara said to Jon.

He still hadn't looked at her and although he was sitting only inches away he kept his back turned when he spoke. 'I don't trust her,' he said, watching Lina as she gestured wildly with her free hand and jabbered into her phone.

'Fair enough, Batman. But I guess it's part of the deal. You know, get on the merry-go-round, sell your soul, become a superstar. The end.' Kara shrugged, trying to keep the mood light.

'I just don't like the way she's ordering us around.'

'Yeah, well you're not the one in rubber,' Kara said, and watched as a faint crimson blush swarmed over the back of Jon's neck, ruddying his china-white skin. Was he actually that innocent? She smirked before she could help herself. 'D'you like it?' she asked, wriggling further down the seat until she was close enough to smell his shampoo. Pursing her lips, she blew into the nape of his neck, where the hairline trailed to a point. He shuddered and Kara laughed quietly, just as Jerome walked in with a cardboard box.

'Should be something we can use in here,' he said, laying the box at Lina's feet.

She glanced inside it, snapping her phone shut at the same time. 'Oh, Jerome,' she said, 'this is wonderful. Give me a hand?' She pointed at Jon, who got slowly to his feet. Lina lifted out a coil of black rope, knotted into a neat bundle. Kara felt a little thrill rush up her spine as she watched. This was a woman who knew exactly what she was doing. Lina was smiling at Jon as she unwound the rope, her movements slow and deliberate.

Kara could tell she was enjoying herself from the way she pulled the rope through her hand and from the way she looked at Jon with lowered eyelids. The rope fell silently to the floor and Lina doubled it over, held on to one end, tensing it between her hands. Finally, she reached out and pinched the hem of Jon's T-shirt between her finger and thumb, lifting it so that Kara caught a glimpse of his belly, pale as paper, flat and perfectly hairless.

'Uh,' Jon started to protest, shrinking away from Lina's curling fingers.

'Come on now. Kara's not been shy, has she? Let me tie you.'

Lina motioned with her hand, a little beckoning gesture, asking Jon to take off his T-shirt. When he did, sullen and kind of helpless, pulling it over his head in one movement, Kara swallowed. A half-naked man in the room made her feel somehow that she was also a layer more exposed. Jon's body was slim and long and pale, with baby-pink nipples and muscles drawn in delicate pencil line across his abdomen and along his arms. He shrank away as Lina moved closer, squeezing and releasing his fist so that the tendons in his arm flexed.

'OK?' Lina asked. 'Remember, we're just play-acting. You can stop anytime you want to.' She smiled. 'But I don't expect you will.'

For a moment nobody moved. Kara realised she was chanting to herself, in her head: Do it, do it, do it. At last Jon nodded and held his wrists up readily, the gesture making it look for a moment as if he was begging to be tied.

Kara had always seen Jon as an appendage to Ruby, one skinny half of a couple, never looked at him directly. Now he stood in front of her, vulnerable and exposed, and she let herself consider him as a man. He had a body full of nerves and muscle and sensation, and for sure his sex drive didn't begin and end with Ruby.

Lina looped rope around his wrists and his body became something other than Jon – a man's torso, a man's flesh, bound and restrained. With his hands crossed over each other, Lina wound the rope back and forth, pulling it slowly under itself and tying it finally to leave one long trailing end.

Jon tugged, but his wrists were pinned fast. With that one knot, Kara was disarmed. She imagined herself pressing against Jon's soft, glowing white skin. Now he was tied, it seemed he could finally look at her and when their eyes met it shocked her. His expression held nothing of the soft affection or the playful sexiness when he looked at Ruby, but instead was full of the dangerous, predatory look of raw desire. His doe's eyes were wet and his long lashes drifted down as Lina pulled on the rope to lead him back to the sofa.

'Now, get on your knees,' Lina was instructing again, and Kara was already rising to stand in front of him. They didn't need to be choreographed any more; it seemed entirely natural for her to reach down and bury her hand in Jon's short, choppy brown hair. She rubbed his head, as if stroking a pet, and could almost convince herself it was just a friendly gesture. Even when Jon sagged against her and Kara felt the heat of his body through the rubber dress, his cheek pressed into her stomach and his chin digging into her hip, she didn't let go.

Meanwhile Lina murmured encouragement, Jerome took picture after picture and the music continued to pour into the room. Kara moved as her body dictated, arching her back and pulling Jon closer to her crotch, letting him squirm against her and struggle to stay upright. Lina still held the end of the rope and she circled the two of them, winding the length around Kara's waist so that Jon's hands were pulled upwards and held tight against her, his knuckles pushing on her pubic bone. He wriggled a little and his fists locked in place, a hard welcome press that Kara wanted to lean into.

She was sticky now, the dress rubbing against her where she'd sweated and pinching under the arms. Lina was pulling the rope around, trailing it over Kara's shoulder and binding the two of them together. She handed the end to Kara.

'Up to you how hard you pull,' she said, letting her hand trail up Kara's arm and squeezing her shoulder. 'But if you keep the rope tight, it'll look better in the pictures.'

'Move slowly,' Jerome called from behind the camera. 'I want these crystal sharp.'

Kara held onto the rope, contemplating what would happen if she gave it one hard tug. Jon was slipping, the shiny and oiled surface of her dress not giving him enough purchase. If she didn't help him, he'd be on the floor any minute. Thoughtfully, she pulled on the rope, dragged him up and felt the smooth rub of the rope as it slipped over her shoulder.

'Careful,' Jerome said. 'You don't want rope burns.'

Jon's face was against her crotch now, breathing heavily, his shoulders heaving. They moved together, bound by the rope but separated by the dress, able to feel only the heat and undefined pressure of each other. Kara was grateful for the barrier between them. Without that dress, Jon's skin would be against hers and they would cross a line that she knew wasn't right.

'Safe sex,' she whispered to Jon, trying to keep the tremor out of her voice, 'always wear rubber, right?' He didn't laugh, and Kara felt his bound fingers scrabble against her, searching for the outline of her pussy under the slippery surface. They could play-act, she thought, of course. This was just some dumb photo shoot. Just so long as nobody admitted her good friend was feeling her up. And nobody mentioned Ruby.

'Wait,' Jerome called, and ran to her with a large pair of shears. 'Just an idea,' he said, leaning down and cutting from the hem of the dress up towards Kara's stomach. Jon watched, the blades dangerously close to his face. The rubber stretched under Jerome's large hands and cut easily, the edges pulling back as the point of the scissors moved upwards, the blunt side of them cold against Kara's skin. 'There,' Jerome said, peeling one half of the dress away.

Kara's thigh was bared, the slit stopping just short of her pussy. She now felt keenly naked next to Jon's face. This is when everything falls apart, she thought, even as exhilaration buzzed through her.

Her skin was still smeared with lubricant. Moisture matted the dark curls of her pubic hair and the cold air of the studio was fresh against her clit. Jon's hot breath passed back and forth over her most tender spot. Her face burned and she held on to the rope so tight her hand hurt.

'Damn,' Jerome said, fiddling with his camera. 'Run out of space. I never blow a memory card. You two are good.' He started dismantling the camera, unscrewing it from the tripod and flipping open the side, while Kara and Jon tried desperately to hold the pose. 'Give me a minute,' Jerome told them, backing away towards the other room.

'I'll download the other pictures while we're waiting' Lina said, following him. She shook her head as though any hitch in her day was unforgivable.

And then Kara was alone with Jon and there was nothing to stop him from sighing and rolling an inch closer to her. It could have been an accident.

Neither of them spoke and Kara didn't crack any jokes. She just tugged at the edge of her dress slightly so that she was exposed. So that Jon could dip his head down and press his mouth against her clit. One soft warm kiss. So slight she might have imagined it, just a brushing of his mouth against her. No tongue, no sucking, no licking or biting. Just a chaste and heated kiss. Jon groaned and Kara felt her heart swing in her chest, knowing it was wrong but tipping forwards all the same, winding her fingers into his hair and rocking against Jon's face.

She was half praying for his tongue to dart out and curl into her. Fuck, fuck, fuck, she swore to herself. His cheek was smooth and cool against her thigh and her legs were so weak they were trembling. Kara gritted her teeth and let go of the rope. Jon slumped onto his knees, letting out a long shaky breath.

'OK, all fixed,' Jerome said, walking briskly back into the room. 'We can start again.' He looked back at Jon and Kara, now inches apart, the rope lying limp on the floor between them.

Kara clenched her teeth together and held herself very straight. She nodded at Jerome and moved back onto the couch, waiting for Lina to start shouting out directions again.

For the rest of the morning, as they moved through a variety of different poses, with rope wound around them and Jerome's music playing faintly in the background, Kara remained silent. She and Jon touched and brushed against each other sometimes, but she held it back, refused to let the elecricity flow, closed her eyes and bit her lip. Play-acting, she repeated to herself, just play-acting.

When she and Jon left Jerome's studio in the late afternoon and stood outside in the street, Kara felt a rush of relief and regret. Something clutched in her stomach and her skin was clammy from lubricant and sweat. Though she was back in her denim skirt, she could still feel where the dress had clung to her body.

'Well, that was crazy, huh?' she said to Jon, who was swinging around, looking for a bus stop.

He nodded. 'The others'll be glad they missed that session,' he said, a note of forced humour in his voice.

Kara's shoulders sagged. 'They don't ... They don't need to hear about it, Jon,' she said. 'Not all of it.'

Jon looked at her with his limpid eyes and now there was a touch of blue sadness in them. 'No, you're right. They don't.'

'Where are you heading?' she asked.

'Uh, back to your, to Ruby's flat.'

'Right.'

'Are you going that way too?'

Kara shook her head and gave him a tight smile. 'No. I think I need to cut loose. Besides, we're recording tomorrow. I'm going to go and blow off some steam.'

With that, they parted. Kara watched Jon's back as he disappeared down St Vincent Street, his hands jammed in his pockets as though he was carrying their secret buried deep within them.

Kara set off across the red tarmac of George Square. Tired, dazed and horny, she didn't have a destination in mind, but her feet seemed to know exactly where she was going. Dusk had already fallen and the sky was dark turquoise over in the west, the traffic inching in that direction almost slower than she was walking. As she fished in her bag for her phone, Kara saw the red marks on her wrist, indentations where the rope had been coiled. The lines were perfectly even, the pattern as neat and delicate as a bracelet. As she called Mike's number, she walked faster, cutting across the street by the station and dodging cars.

'Mike,' she said, raising her voice over the growling engines, 'I want to see you.'

Up ahead, Kara recognised a guy she knew from basement gigs. She swerved up a side street before he saw her, slipped down the alley where the sound was muted and the lights murky.

'Now,' she said into her phone, 'I need to see you right now.'

She sawed back and forth on her heel as she listened to Mike's reply.

'I'm at the studio. Come round.'

'No, not there.' Kara threw herself against the brick of the alley wall and sighed out loud. 'Come and pick me up.'

'Where are you?'

Kara looked around and found a street sign. 'Heckler's Wynd.'

'Bad timing, Kara. The traffic's awful.'

'I'll owe you.'

With her free hand, Kara rubbed her belly. She pressed her shoulder into the wall, in need of something soothing, or something to rub up against, she hardly knew any more. The whole afternoon had been sticky and difficult and maddeningly, strangely sexy and the rough dirty bricks at her back were at least solid and reassuring.

'Something wrong?'

'I don't want to talk about it.' Kara leaned her cheek against the stone.

'Lina sorted out the promo stuff?'

'Yes. Some twisted kind of publicity that is.' Her eyes darted up and down the street. She held the phone close to her ear, like it was a lifeline. Only Mike was playing out the line, not reeling her in. She took one deep breath and asked him straight out. 'Mike, please come get me.'

Kara hung up and closed her eyes. The poky little alley was a dodgy hiding place, but out in the street she had felt the city closing in around her. She kept imagining the hurt expression on Ruby's face that morning, and then Jon, nuzzling at her, kissing her, crossing that line from friend to potential lover. It gave her a pang in her heart and a tingle in her clit at the same time. And Mike's voice was like honey poured in her ear, soothing her but also leading her into dark and tangled fantasies. Woven through all the fantasies she had of what he would do to her and what she would do to him was the spectre of Lina, smiling that poisonous smile and running a black silky rope through her hands.

'I'm stuck in a sex farce,' she said out loud, shaking her head. She would almost have managed a laugh, if her next thought hadn't instantly been the one she'd been trying not to have for the past twenty-four hours.

Among all the bit players crowding out the feverish theatre of Kara's imagination, there was one that hovered on the edge of her mind, in the background but never far away. One sullen and petulant guitarist with his hair in his eyes. She could never quite manage to forget Tam, the weird mix of irritation and glee and desire she felt every time they were together.

This time, though, she wasn't just thinking of his nice fat dick and his Michelangelo mouth. She could see him with his three-day-old stubble and those hard angry brown eyes, walking off into the sunset like he never cared if he saw her again. It wrenched something inside her, felt so wrong that she pushed the memory aside into some shadowy place where she didn't have to think about it.

Mike was on his way with his big swish car and a whole evening of dirty lavish sex already planned out. She wouldn't have to think at all once she saw him, just let her worked-up, sticky, tired and rope-marked body take over. Kara knew what she needed – huge, mind-blowing, breathtaking, bone-crunching orgasms. Mike couldn't get there fast enough.

11

'Do you often call people and demand they drop everything to come and fuck you?'

'Only when I'm horny,' Kara said, leaning back into the warm air-conditioned bliss of Mike's car.

'You're recording tomorrow.'

'I know.'

'You need to be on form.'

'I need to be fucked.'

Mike shook his head and pulled away from the kerb, sliding the long car smoothly into the stream of traffic.

'What, I'm too crude all of a sudden?' Kara said, noticing the way Mike's jaw flexed as though he were chewing a piece of gristle.

'I might have had other plans,' he said, slamming the gearstick into third. 'I do have things to do that don't include doing you.'

'Such as?'

Mike's mouth was set in a thin line. He concentrated on the road and, for a moment, Kara had the urge to fling open the door and jump right back out again. She sighed and rolled her head against the seat.

'I've had a long weird afternoon and I just want to get ... oblivious, you know?'

The boiling mess of worry and excitement that had been rolling around inside Kara all day wasn't calming. She was wired and jittery, and she knew that a stiff cock hammering into her would help, at least for a couple of hours. She reached out to feel for Mike's zipper, tugged it open and slipped a hand inside his trousers. His prick was curled in there, warm and half hard. He might be pissed off, but he wasn't pushing her away. The heavy handful of his flesh in her palm was already reassuring and she worked at him steadily, bringing him to life.

'So I'm your therapy, am I?' Mike asked, even as he shifted his legs further apart to give her more space. They were merging onto the expressway now, turning under the massive concrete columns of the Kingston Bridge onto the road that snaked along the riverside.

Kara didn't answer. Instead, she lowered her head to his lap and tucked the head of his cock in her mouth. As she sucked, she could feel the humming of the car's engine, the way Mike tensed his thighs, his hand falling on the back of her neck, rubbing, massaging, circling. His cock grew larger, filling her mouth and butting against the inside of her cheek. She closed her eyes and rocked back and forth in his lap, tasting the salt and the slight earthiness of his skin.

The car curved round a corner and centrifugal force pushed Kara aside. She fell back, breathing hard, leaned against the door and looked at Mike. At least now he was smiling. He sat with his flies undone and his semi-stiff cock sticking upright, her saliva still gleaming on his dark satin flesh.

'Patience, Kara,' he said, flicking on the indicator and bringing them down a ramp into the sandstone terraces of the West End. 'I know right now you want to fuck yourself to a standstill. But if you can keep your hands out of your pants for an hour or so, maybe we can share something more substantial.'

As he talked, he tucked himself back in and zipped up his fly, leaving a little hump in the fabric of his trousers that Kara eyed wistfully. She'd spent the whole day holding herself back and now the man she'd thought would put her out of her misery was making things even worse. Obviously, he was going to tease her. That was his bag, wasn't it? Never ceding an inch of control, never giving her what she wanted until she was ready to beg for it. She tucked her hands under her legs and dug her nails into the soft flesh of her thigh. How long could she hold off, she wondered, getting wound up and let down and played with, before she snapped?

They were slowing now, driving the wide quiet streets where the houses sat behind large gardens and tall gateposts. Kara was curious. She'd never seen where Mike lived. Had imagined him, perhaps, in some sleek new-build penthouse, or in a warehouse like the one where she'd spent the afternoon. She looked at the square villa in front of them as they drew to a halt. Her gaze fell almost instantly though from the tall windows and the carved stone lintel.

A girl sat on the steps. She rested her chin on her hand and looked altogether neat and tidy, from her glossy black plaits down to the pretty red court shoes that peeked from a mid-length skirt. She looked like a filing clerk and if it hadn't been for the girl's large dark eyes and well-toned legs Kara wouldn't have been jealous at all.

'Who is that?' she asked.

'A student,' Mike said, turning the ignition off and letting the silence swell between them.

'You still teach?'

'Only if the student is exceptionally promising.'

'And you have a lesson booked.'

'No, not booked. Judy drops by occasionally. It's not exactly a formal relationship.'

Instantly, every fibre of Kara's body stiffened. *Other things to do?* Was this what Mike had planned for his evening? Kara screwed her head round to check his face, but she couldn't read his expression. Winter's early night had nearly fallen and in the murky shadows he could have been looking at the woman on his doorstep with hunger or irritation – there was no way of telling.

Mike got out of the car and walked swiftly towards the house. Kara wondered for a moment if she could stay where she was; sit rigid in the cosy warmth with her eyes shut and just wait for this girl, Judy, to disappear. But Mike was talking to Judy as he put his key in the door and pushed it open. The two of them disappeared into Mike's house and Kara found herself alone outside in the gathering dark.

What the hell was going on? Kara ground her teeth. There was only one way to find out. She counted to five and followed them inside.

She pushed open the door, walked down a narrow hallway hung with large abstract prints and into a sitting room where she could hear voices.

'. . . to see you, tonight.' Judy broke off when she caught sight of Kara. 'Hi.'

In the softly lit room, Kara got a better look at Mike's 'exceptionally promising' student. She was around thirty, at a guess, and pretty in a tanned, bland, clerkish kind of way. Without her coat, she was dressed in a white shirt that cinched at the waist. Not seduction gear, Kara thought, although she noticed the faint outline of a red bra through the cotton. She watched as Judy dropped her handbag on the floor casually, and leaned against the wall. A slit in the back of her mid-length clerk's skirt showed a sliver of those well-toned thighs Kara had noticed earlier.

'Is this a bad time?' Judy asked, giving Mike a lipgloss-and-twinkle smile.

Kara's gaze switched back and forth – she wanted to watch this exchange, but she pretended to be absorbed in looking around Mike's house.

The room around her wasn't what she was expecting – it was smaller and a little shabby round the edges. A window was crammed hard up against the back wall and a collection of mismatched furniture huddled in the centre of a worn charcoal carpet. An upright piano stood against one wall. Mike stood by the window looking into the black square of glass and the reflection of the room within it.

'How about we have a glass of wine, anyway,' Judy said, moving smoothly out of the room and leaving a prickly silence behind her. Kara watched Mike's back, trying to gauge by the set of his shoulders what mood he was wrapped up in.

'I wish I'd been allowed to drink wine at my lessons,' Kara said, her voice tinged with acid. 'Seems your standards are relaxing.'

'Apparently you put on quite a show this afternoon,' Mike said. 'I'm sorry I missed it.'

He was avoiding the subject. Kara played along.

'How do you know?' Kara asked.

'Lina called.'

Of course she did.

'I was just playing to the camera,' Kara said, flicking her gaze over the cluttered surfaces strewn with newspapers, scrawled notes and empty wine glasses. Mike seemed to have the whole bachelor's functional-monochrome thing going on, with unfinished patches of bare plaster on the walls and nothing to indicate anyone ever took any pleasure in spending time here. The only things that stood out were a space-age box mounted on one wall, glass and chrome and polished wood concealing what Kara guessed was a state-of-the-art stereo, and an ornate brass clock fixed opposite it, rasping as it ticked off the seconds.

The overall effect gave her a strange falling-away feeling. His home was so different from the bold, elegantly designed spaces of the studio that her ideas of Mike were shifting in front of her.

'Send her away,' Kara said.

He turned and Kara thought she saw some remnant of his old self glowing in his eyes – some glimmer of challenge.

Had she wandered into dangerous territory? When Mike licked his lips, jutted his chin at her and eyed her boldly, was he contemplating fucking her or throwing her out? Was he intending to fuck his prize student tonight, before she'd called him? Kara felt the ground see-saw beneath her as Mike gave her that look that could have been lust or hate.

Whatever his gaze meant, it had an instant effect on Kara. That electric field that sprung up between them was pulsing again, compelling her to tug at her clothes as though they itched, fiddle with her hair, chew at her bottom lip.

If Judy wasn't in the next room playing hostess, she thought, they might have already been naked or screwing on the low coffee table among a mess of papers and the agitating tick of the clock, which seemed to be running faster somehow. A surge of anger pulsed through Kara's veins and she dropped herself onto the couch, kicked her feet up onto the table and stretched her legs out fully, crossing one over the other so that Mike's view up her skirt was unobstructed.

If he wanted to play games, Kara would just have to up the ante. She could manipulate a situation just as surely as Lina, especially when that situation included fuckable men.

'Send her away,' she whispered loudly to Mike, sliding down further in the seat so that her skirt rode up even higher. As Judy returned, carrying a bottle and three glasses, Kara stared fixedly at Mike, trying to will him to do her bidding.

'Lovely,' he said to Judy, accepting a glass and holding it out to be filled. 'Kara and I were just saying how we should all spend the evening together. Couple of music lovers like you two; you're bound to get on. Care to join us for dinner?' he asked Judy, ignoring Kara's scowl and the fact that she pointedly refused to take the glass that was offered to her.

'Sounds peachy,' Judy said, sinking into the couch opposite Kara and smiling over the rim of her glass. 'As long as that's OK with you?'

'I didn't come here for a dinner party,' Kara said.

Judy narrowed her eyes. 'Neither did I, sweetie. But let's make the most of it, shall we? Besides –' she reached out to squeeze Mike's kneecap '– Mike's an excellent cook.'

At that moment, all the fight went out of Kara. She laid her head back against the couch and closed her eyes. Still sticky from the afternoon, still smelling faintly from the plastic of the dress, still so horny it was almost painful, she felt like she didn't even know any more what or who it was she needed.

'Could I have a shower?' she asked Mike. 'Please?'

She tripped down the stairs, wrapped in a scratchy white towel, swearing through her chattering teeth. Voices spilled out from the kitchen, mixed with the hissing of steam and the sizzle of oil in a hot pan. Kara barged straight in, dripping onto the tiled floor.

'The water's gone cold,' she said.

'It does that,' Mike answered. 'Good for the circulation. Makes you tingle all over, doesn't it?' He was bent over the hob, with Judy leaning close into him.

'You're giving cooking lessons now?' Kara said, moving from foot to foot and trying to keep herself from shivering.

'Judy,' Mike said, 'would you light the fire next door. See if you can get Kara warmed up. The risotto'll be done in five minutes.'

Judy dipped her head in acquiescence and brushed past Kara on her way to the living room. Kara opened her mouth to argue with Mike, inhaled the smells of garlic and herbs and realised that she was, in fact, starving. Her mouth watered and she felt the hunger tighten in her stomach.

'There's a robe on the back of the bathroom door,' Mike said, without turning round. 'Go and put it on, sit by the fire and wait.'

Kara gritted her teeth. 'You're not ordering me around.'

'No. I'm not. I'd only do that with your explicit permission.'

'Like your suck-up little Judy in there?'

Very precisely, Mike laid his spatula on the counter. He faced Kara, wiping his hands on a cloth. When he spoke, his words were carefully measured, each one bitten off sharply. 'You come to my house, Kara, demanding I satisfy every immediate whim that flits across your mind. That's fine. I enjoy your company and I like the challenge.' He leaned on the counter and splayed his hands flat on the surface between them. 'But you will either be warm, polite and friendly to my other guests or you will leave. Half naked and freezing none the less. Is that clear?'

Kara felt a lump rise in her throat. She blinked hard, several times. His territory, his rules. 'I'm sorry,' she said hoarsely. 'I'll stay.'

'Good. Now go and make yourself comfortable, and we'll enjoy the rest of the evening, OK?'

Kara nodded. When she turned to leave, Mike grabbed her wrist.

'I know a lot's happening for you right now. I know it's all new and strange and you think that you have to fight to keep yourself on solid ground. But you don't need to fight me, Kara. I'm on your side.'

Kara clutched at the towel where it was knotted over her breasts. Mike had her other hand and his grip was firm. Curious, she thought. Usually when someone held on to her she wanted to twist free. But when Mike took hold of her, all she could think of was how sure he was, how solid and certain. Like an anchor that would hold her in harbour no matter how stormy the sea. When he let go, she missed his touch immediately.

She fetched the wrap and padded through to the sitting room, where Judy had lit a fire and was warming herself in front of it.

'Better?' the other girl asked, and Kara allowed herself to relax a little.

'Yes.' She sat down and pulled the robe tighter around herself. 'I was a bit worked up,' she said. 'It's been a long day.'

Judy lifted a poker and nudged a log deeper into the grate. The bark caught quickly and flames licked over the dry wood, curling over the surface and burning into the soft, pale heartwood.

'That's what the nights are for,' she said softly, laying the poker down. 'Unravelling all the kinks of a long day.' She looked straight at Kara then and her eyes were a clear soft grey. 'That's why I'm here.'

They ate at the low coffee table, hardly talking, listening to the fire spit and crackle and the wind blustering in the chimney. Kara relaxed, notch by notch, as she emptied two glasses of wine and the plate of creamy risotto. Mike's living room was shabby, it was true, but with a cold tangled night outside and rain flecking the window, it was also a welcome escape from the uneasiness Kara imagined when she thought of the band, the flat, her life.

She felt part of a very small tight circle, lit by the glow of the fire and lulled into silence by the ticking brass clock. Judy had slid out of her court shoes and with her inky-black hair falling over her shoulders and her stocking feet hooked over the arm of a chair, she had lost that uptight clerkish look. In fact, she had a wry, easy humour that Kara warmed to and when she laughed her face took on a wicked impish look.

There was something else in the room Kara couldn't quite put her finger on, a tension dancing just under the surface. She noticed slight signals – the way Judy's eyes widened when she listened to Mike, Mike rubbing at his stubble, letting his gaze drop and roam over Judy's body. Kara recognised that move. His hand covered the smile, the one that hooked up the corner of his mouth when he was thinking something dirty. When Judy took the empty plates through to the kitchen and Mike came to sit next to her on the sofa, pulling her bare feet into his lap, Kara sensed what was coming next.

'How do you like the sound of a duet?' he asked, his voice low.

Kara cocked an eyebrow. Mike was stroking her legs, his hands running up the curves of her calf and dipping behind her knee, trailing back down to her ankle. Repetitive, soothing, promising.

She didn't answer. Instead, she tugged at the knot of her belt, loosened it and let the robe fall open. Just a sliver of skin was exposed, from her throat to her crotch, and Kara smiled as she realised how similar this was to the design of the damn rubber dress she'd worn – oh, it seemed like weeks ago. Mike put his hand over her pubic hair and held it there, applying just the slightest pressure while he watched Kara. Her heart boomed in her chest and she closed her eyes and concentrated on the tick of the clock, the warm drowsiness she felt as the wine and desire flowed in her veins.

12

Judy kissed her. Even with her eyes closed, Kara could tell it was Judy from the softness, the bloom of the girl's full lips against her own and the sweet lemony scent of her. Kara let their tongues dance against each other and concentrated all her attention on the giving heat of Judy's mouth.

Mike still held his hand over Kara's pussy. He cupped it in his palm so that Kara couldn't tell if the pulse she felt was his or her own. She sank deeper into the couch, into the kiss.

'Just a moment,' Mike said.

Judy broke away and Kara opened her eyes. The other girl was flushed and Mike looked like he was struggling to control his breath. He stood and went to rummage in a chest of drawers, while Judy sought Kara's hand and pressed her thumb into her palm, rubbing small circles. Like Kara, she seemed to need something to hold on to.

Mike came back with a length of black fabric – something dense and felty, with ribbons attached to either end. Kara's heart skipped a little when she realised what it was.

'I think this might put a nice twist on things,' he said, already reaching to cover Kara's eyes.

The blindfold wrapped tightly round her head, blanketed out the room and left her swimming in space. If Judy hadn't been holding her hand, she would have been entirely lost. Nobody spoke. Kara strained to hear anything that would give her clues, help her to guess who was close to her. After a minute, she noticed the difference in the sound of their breathing: Mike's was deep and slow, Judy's a quicker, lighter pattern.

Her robe was pulled open and cool hands ran over her body. Every touch made her move towards the person that had given it, until she was rolling around wildly, chasing caresses from her invisible lovers.

With no warning, a finger slid between her legs and tested her wetness, at the same time as a mouth latched on to her nipple and sucked. Kara moaned and rolled towards the hands, the mouth, only to have them pull away and reappear somewhere else. Someone – the size and rasp of the hands made her think it was Mike – tugged her arms gently out of the sleeves of the robe and laid her down again.

She couldn't tell who lifted her arms over her head, placed her wrists together and wrapped what felt like a thin silk rope around them. Was it another of Mike's hidden skills? Kara thought, as someone bound her and tied the knot carefully so that it didn't cut off her circulation, but held her fast. Another hand played with her clit, rolling it between thumb and forefinger, and the distraction made it harder to keep track of who was where. Bound and blindfolded, teased and caressed, she was frantic with the confusion of touches.

Robbed of her sight, Kara was disorientated. She was all nerves, all flesh that needed to be touched. When someone stroked her legs, all her attention focused on the sensation. When the hands moved higher up to squeeze her buttocks, cup and massage them, she was only aware of that part of herself, the rest of her rolling frantically in midair, hoping to collide with someone or something.

'More,' she blurted out, knowing her voice was verging on desperate. 'Please, more.'

'More of this?' Mike's voice sounded in her ear as the pressure of the hands rubbing her bottom grew harder.

'Everything,' Kara said, 'everywhere.'

'Turn her over,' Mike said, pulling away and directing his voice elsewhere. Hands, small hands, slid under Kara's hips and rolled her gently onto her front. The cuffs of Judy's shirt caught on her skin and Kara pressed down to trap her. She wanted those fingers on her, and that soft mouth. In the hot tight space between her body and the rough fabric of the couch, delicate fingertips slid across her belly and roved up to feel her breasts. Kara whimpered as Judy worked at her, pinching her nipples gently so that the tips hardened and scuffed against the upholstery.

Kara was aware that her arse was bare and exposed, and she knew Mike was standing over her. There was the sound of a zip tearing open, a belt clinking.

For a moment, she squirmed against Judy, greedy for more sensation, and then Mike's hands were burrowing between her legs, pulling her open. Quickly, he parted her lips and fed the head of his cock into her. Just the head.

She wanted to rock back against it, but one hand held her firm and steady. Mike knew how to torment her. When she thought she was going to sob with the wanting, he moved at last, running his cock into her hard and fast so that his hips banged against hers. The sudden force of his stroke took Kara's breath away.

With him in her full and hard, Judy's hands squirmed down to nestle between her legs, and Kara thought she might scream.

She was on the point of losing it, Kara knew, struggling to scrape herself against the scratchy canvas of the couch, longing for buttons and seams to roll over and sink onto. As Mike started to fuck her methodically and steadily, she opened her mouth wide, without making any sound.

In fact, she was hardly breathing. This was what she'd been

craving all day, an overload of sensation that built up until she wasn't aware of herself, only the places where her body rubbed up against other flesh.

She'd been longing for Mike, but having two people wrapped around her was almost unbearably intense.

Next to her, Judy made short, hard panting noises and rested her cheek on Kara's back while she fingered her. With her hands tied above her head and Mike holding her hips down, Kara was helpless. She couldn't do anything to speed up her orgasm, or hold it back when it came.

With a long groan, she gave up chasing it and let herself sag into Judy's hands, yielding to Mike's thrusts as they got shorter and blunter.

Mike paused, held himself motionless and taut. He was close to coming, Kara guessed. Inside her, his cock grew as solid and hard as an iron bar and Kara felt the pulse, the first twitches rising up the length of him.

She ground against Judy's fluttering fingers and butted against Mike, knowing it would send him over the edge. Sure enough, he groaned and his hips started jerking. Kara bit down on the cushions as the first rush of her own climax spread upwards. Heat swirled around Judy's busy hands, building in her clit.

When Kara came, her spine arched and she thrashed back and forth, tugging at the bonds that held her wrists. Restrained like this, there was nowhere for her orgasm to disperse. It ricocheted inside her, overtook her with a blackness even deeper and richer than the one she saw behind the blindfold and sent her spinning into a place where her body had no limits. Every atom of her body strummed with bliss. A pulse rippled along her spine and Kara cried out, singing one long sustained note.

The next thing she was aware of was Mike stroking her

hair, slowly and rhythmically. Judy's touches had fallen away and she was only aware of him, covering her with his long sweat-slicked body.

As her breath slowly calmed, Mike untied her and slipped off the blindfold, leaving her dazed and blinking in the firelight. Judy sat cross-legged on the floor next to them. Her lips were reddened and her eyes were glittering – Kara had the sense that wringing an orgasm out of her had been some kind of small victory.

'God,' Kara said, her words thick as though she'd been drugged. 'That was amazing.'

'You did well,' Mike said, nodding his approval at Judy.

'Do you want to come?' Kara asked, even though the question felt awkward in her mouth. Judy glanced at Mike. Reading something in his face, she shook her head and looked at the floor.

'Judy's very self-controlled,' Mike said, stretching out and tipping his head back. 'Something you've yet to learn, Kara. Holding back can be just as mind-blowing as getting off.' He smiled at Judy and Kara had the feeling it was part of her lesson.

Judy left soon after, sweeping her jacket round her shoulders and nodding goodbye at Kara. Her look was hard to fathom – Kara sensed complicity in her eyes, as well as a spark of something else. Jealousy? Amusement? Her hands must still smell of me, Kara thought as she watched Judy disappear down the hallway after Mike.

But although they'd shared an intense physical connection, Kara guessed there were layers to Judy and her relationship with Mike that she would never understand. Although Kara's body was sated, at least for the moment, her head seethed with questions. When Mike returned, she was ready to throw a dozen accusations at him, but something in the way he moved around and avoided her eyes made her hesitate.

'How often do you give lessons?' she asked at last, feeling herself blush even as the words escaped her mouth.

'That's none of your business,' Mike answered smoothly. He glanced at the silver watch on his wrist.

'It's late. You need a good eight hours if we're recording tomorrow.' He opened a cupboard and pulled out a duvet, blankets and pillows. Kara frowned as he spread them over the couch.

'You want me to stay on the couch?' she asked. 'God, you know how to make a girl feel welcome.'

'Your choice, Kara. Sleep on the couch or go home.'

'That ticking clock will keep me up all night.'

'And if we share a bed we'll get no sleep at all.' He approached her and pushed a strand of hair out of her eyes. 'I gave you the orgasm you wanted so badly, Kara. Now, do as I say, please.'

Kara was silent as he walked away, disappearing without even a kiss goodnight. He'd had his kicks for the evening, she thought bitterly.

Huddled on the couch watching the dying embers of the fire, Kara listened to the night noises of a strange house. Instead of traffic and shouts on the street, she heard faint creaks and the rustling of water in old pipes. The fractious ticking of the brass clock became louder and more insistent in the thick silence. She wanted to stay awake and unravel all her tangled thought-clutter, but there were too many loose ends, too many events and worries. She fell asleep with a frown on her face and her hands jammed tightly between her legs.

'See you soon,' Mike said as he dropped her off by the park's iron gates.

They'd agreed she'd go and get a coffee before following

Mike to the studio. Not that their affair was a secret. Just – private, Mike said. Not something he wanted broadcast to the world.

Kara inhaled a deep lungful of the freezing-cold air. Frost edged the grass playing fields in the park and everything sparkled. She plunged her hands into her pockets and shivered. She was nervous about the session, nervous about seeing Jon. God knows what mood Tam would show up in. In fact, when she thought about walking into the studio to face the undercurrents and secrets and ripples of jealousy, Kara almost wanted to turn and run for it.

'All right.' Tam's voice hit her like a jolt of caffeine. He stood behind her, dressed in a fur-lined parka with his guitar slung over his shoulder. Kara covered her awkwardness by laughing out loud and breathed a puff of steam into the frozen air.

'God, I'm glad to see you,' she said, reaching for his arm. She'd almost forgotten their last intense encounter when he'd scrawled his signature on the contract and left immediately. He didn't recoil, but he didn't respond to her touch either, turning to look up the street as though he were waiting for someone.

'Seen Jon recently?' he asked.

'Have you?'

'No. But I hear things are fucked up with him and Ruby.'

Kara's heart squeezed. 'Shit. How come?'

Tam turned back to look at her. There was nothing there in his eyes, no anger or desire. His pupils were just flat dark discs. It sent Kara's heart into a lurching freefall again. Raging hatred or sneering contempt would be easier to take than indifference.

'What happened, Tam?' Alarms were ringing in her head. *Don't go there*, they warned, but Kara pushed on anyway, desperate to get some kind of response out of Tam, some flicker of feeling. She was still holding on to him and now she twisted a handful of his coat in her fist.

Tam shrugged. 'I don't know. Jon said you knew all about it.'

Kara felt sick. So Jon hadn't kept their pact after all and now everything was shot to hell. Stupid, stupid mistake, she chanted in her head. How had she let herself get into that situation?

'Gonna give me my jacket back?' Tam said, giving her a curious look.

Kara dropped her hands and took a stumbling step backwards.

'Everything OK?' Tam asked. But he didn't honestly look like he wanted to hear it. And anyway, where would she start? How could she explain what was going on, when she didn't understand it herself? She buried her face in her hands and pressed her cold fingertips against her eyelids. This record deal should have been a dream come true, but ever since she'd bumped into Mike Greene, life had suddenly become a twisted game of screwing and screw-ups. Her libido was thrilled, sure, but Kara's head was spinning and she was strung out so far she didn't know which way was up. Don't look down, she told herself. Keep aiming for the prize.

Kara pursed her lips and blew a thin stream of air. 'Let's get in there,' she said. She started walking towards the studio without checking to see if Tam was following.

The door was propped open when they arrived. Kara pulled up short when she saw who was sitting behind the reception desk. Glossy and groomed and smiling brightly, Judy nodded a welcome to her.

Kara would have laughed if her stomach wasn't doing somersaults. Did Mike only work with women he'd been involved with? Or was it the other way round? Was the company just a hunting ground for new playmates?

'You work here?' Kara asked, trying to keep her composure.

Judy smiled. 'Part-time,' she said. 'When I'm not studying.'

At the mention of studying, Kara instantly thought of Mike and his 'lessons'. A prickle of embarrassment and confusion washed over her and she took a step backwards, only to cannon straight into someone. She spun on her heel.

'Hey, Jon,' she said, automatically checking over his shoulder to see if Ruby was behind him. Half of her hoped to see her drummer turn up and half of her was awash with guilt. 'Is Ruby here?'

Wordlessly, Jon handed her a brown envelope, ripped open at one end. Frowning, Kara took it and felt inside. She drew out a few sheets of thick glossy paper. They were contact sheets, dozens of thumbnails of the photos Jerome had taken. High colour, pin sharp.

Kara scanned them quickly. There she was, in violet rubber, pouting and posing. Jon was a shadowy figure lurking in the background, looking startled and uncomfortable. Laid in sequence across the page, the images reminded Kara of one of those flick-through books, each picture advancing forwards, with Jon shifting round her, reaching for her, bound to her with ropes. Just looking at the pictures made her skin prickle. They were good shots – horny, stylish, bold. And they reminded Kara immediately of what they'd led to – her with her skirt split open and Jon pressing his mouth against her. *Stupid, stupid*, delicious *mistake*.

Keeping her face blank, Kara ran her eyes over the sheets, feeling progressively more uncomfortable as the rope appeared round Jon's wrists and the shots got wilder. It didn't help that Tam was breathing down her neck, checking out the sordid poses his best friend had got tangled up in, with the girl he had a history of fucking.

'Where did these come from?' Kara said sharply.

'Someone put them through the door last night,' Jon said.

His voice was hollow and dry, as though he'd been smoking all night.

'Someone? As in Lina?'

Jon shrugged. His eyes were fixed on the sheet in Kara's hands. She followed his gaze and her breath caught in her throat as she saw what he was looking at. Half-a-dozen pictures of Jon with his face in Kara's crotch. Intimate, candid and quite clearly not publishable.

'How –' Kara's question died in her throat. How had Jerome even taken those shots when his camera had 'run out of memory'?

'Ruby saw these?' she asked Jon, with a feeling like the ground was shifting under her feet.

Jon nodded.

'But they weren't there –' Kara broke off. 'We weren't posing,' she finished weakly.

'That's probably what bothered Ruby,' Judy murmured, studying her screen.

Kara looked up with her mouth open. 'Has everybody seen these?' she demanded.

Judy ducked her head to the keyboard and pursed her lips, refusing to answer.

Kara's shoulders sagged. Behind her, Tam reached out and clapped his hand on her shoulder.

'It's OK, Kara,' he said. 'They're just a few photos. Can't be that bad.' He rubbed her shoulder gently. 'Give Rubes a bit of time to cool off. She knows you're a wild flirt. She'll come round.'

Please don't be nice to me, Kara thought. When Tam was kind to her, she knew things were really screwed up. His hand circled the tight knot of muscles at the base of her neck, and part of her wanted to sink into his hands and let him work out all her problems for her. But not here. Not now. His sympathy threatened to make her dissolve.

Silently, she handed him the contact sheet. The pictures looked more incriminating than the act itself had been. In real life it had been a hazy shimmering moment that slipped an inch too far. Captured on film, the photographs showed Jon with his face in her crotch. Her hand on the back of his head was pulling him closer. There was no ambiguity, no room for explanation or denial.

Tam's face hardened. A muscle in his jaw twitched. The hand that had been massaging Kara's shoulder slowed to a halt and dropped away. Silence fell in the bright reception hall, with nobody meeting each other's eyes.

'Is Ruby at home?' Kara asked Jon.

'Yeah. She doesn't want to see anyone.'

'And the session?'

Jon shrugged. 'There's three of us here.'

Three of us barely talking to each other, Kara added mentally.

'We'll just need to lay down what we can and fill in the rest later.'

'Tam?' Kara asked, curling her hands into fists. 'Are you ready to do this?'

'I said I'd be here,' he answered. 'And I keep my promises.' He paused, waited for the room to start clearing before he whispered to Kara in a low voice, 'One of us has to.'

13

She wasn't feeling it. They'd messed up half-a-dozen takes already – Kara kept missing her cues and forgetting the words.

'This isn't even new material,' Tam said through gritted teeth. He was downing his third coffee, leaning on a high stool and glowering at her. 'You wrote this stuff, Kara. You should know how to sing it.'

On the other side of the soundproof glass, Mike crouched over the board next to the engineer and watched everything. Kara hadn't spoken to him since he dropped her off – she didn't know where to start or if she'd be able to stop once she did. Now, she ripped off her headphones and slammed her way out of the studio. She rapped on the door to the control room. It swung open and Mike frowned at her.

'What is it?' he said. 'The clock's running, Kara. This is all costing me and we're behind schedule already.'

'I need to talk to you,' she hissed.

Mike waited, swinging in his seat. 'So talk,' he said.

Kara hung on the door, chewing her bottom lip. She glared at the engineer, who finally muttered an excuse and scuttled out of the room. Alone with Mike, Kara took a deep breath and spat our her question. 'What's with all the ex-fucks?'

'I beg your pardon?'

'Judy, Lina. All the exes you have stashed away in here. Is it some kind of sex cult?'

Mike blew out a breath. 'Get a hold on yourself, Kara.'

'I didn't know Judy worked here,' Kara hissed, crowding close in to Mike. She was close enough to reach out and rake her nails across his arm.

'Is that a problem?'

'It's incestuous,' she said. 'It's seedy.'

'What, that I've been involved with someone I work with? Why should it matter to you?'

'We're surrounded by them! All the knowing looks and secret little smiles. The place is lousy with sex. It'll drive me crazy.'

'It's never been a problem up until now,' Mike said, leaning on the door frame and drumming on the wood with his fingers. 'We're all adults here, Kara. I've always managed to keep work separate from my private life.'

'Doesn't look like that from where I'm standing.'

'And you think letting Ruby's boyfriend bury his face between your legs is less seedy? Less likely to screw up the chances of your band succeeding?' Mike leaned in close now and spoke directly into Kara's ear. 'At least be a bit discreet next time.'

'That's bullshit!' She pulled away. 'Lina engineered that whole ridiculous mess. She's poisonous.'

'I think you're jealous.'

'I think you're fucking me around.'

Mike smiled. He swung round and pushed the door open, gestured for Kara to leave. 'Play the game, Kara. Get back in there.'

She retreated into the studio, aggravated rather than relieved. She should know better than to have expected Mike to placate her. He was all about winding her up – pushing her buttons and watching her spin. Kara slid the headphones on, keeping her eyes fixed on Mike. Behind her, Tam ran through chords, repeating the same riff over and over. Though the headphones dampened the sound, she recognised the refrain instantly.

'Hold that song for a minute,' she said, into the standing mike.

There was a hiss of static as Mike opened the channel that connected directly to her. 'We're not finished,' he said.

'Later. We'll do it later.' Kara shook her head dismissively. 'I've got a new track for you right now.'

'Kara –'

The line clicked as he flicked the switch back to silent. Through the soundproof glass, Kara could see him swearing. The sound engineer was cracking his knuckles and frowning.

Kara smiled. 'This is brand new,' she said, jutting her chin towards Tam. 'Tam, pick it up as we go, OK?' She closed her eyes for a moment, nodded her head to a silent beat.

'You want a click track on this?' the engineer asked.

'Shh. No,' Kara said. She took a deep breath. 'OK. Roll.'

Everyone waited. Kara listened to the thick silence in her headphones. She let the tension in the room swell until it started to warp. Then she snapped her eyes open and looked straight at Mike.

At last, she sang in a low, sugared voice:

> 'Think you've got it?
> Think you're it.
> But since I saw you last week I'm spitting out grit.'

She glanced behind her and nodded at Tam. Lifting his chin, he chimed in with an E chord. Kara's voice swelled to match it, rising and growing stronger.

> 'I can tell you, Mister slick,
> This is not the bitch to spurn.
> She'll fight you right back, and give you one hell of a burn.
> And like the rest . . .'

Kara threw her head back and closed her eyes, just as Jon picked up a melody on the keyboard. The song was taking over.

> *'She'll bend over,*
> *she'll spread her thighs,*
> *but like the rest,*
> *Mister slick,*
> *she'll be counting the ties …'*

Kara broke off and leaned in close so the microphone was tight against her lips. Mike watched with his arms folded. His skin was dust coloured and his mouth a thin pinched line as Kara sang on.

> *'… to the men*
> *who would hold her*
> *and the boys who would try.'*

Her hips swayed and Kara felt the relief surge through her at last as she curled over the microphone and purred the last line:

> *'It's not so much the secrets as the lies that hurt.'*

She fell back, breathing fast, and watched the booth with a mix of attitude and uncertainty.

Mike said nothing. He stood with his shoulders rigid, staring at Kara as though he were thinking hard. Eventually the sound engineer broke in and defused the stalemate.

'Sweet,' he said, shrugging. 'We could use it as filler. Little end track.' While he fiddled with the mixer and asked Jon to replay the keyboard riff, Kara watched Mike out of the corner of her eye.

He leaned forwards to open the channel. Again she heard the static in her headphones and Mike's voice coming through as smooth and calm as ever. 'Clever trick, Kara. You've got a shining talent.'

There was another subtle shift in the sound as he hit more switches and then his voice came through as dark and sweet as chocolate. 'And I do enjoy watching you lead Tam around by his prick.'

Kara started, widening her eyes and spinning round to see Tam's reaction. There was none. Then she heard the low chuckle in her ear.

'I've isolated the channel, Kara. You're the only one that can hear me.' Through the glass, Mike was leaning back in his seat. The engineer had his head bowed over his mixing desk. 'But, of course, it would take just the flick of a switch to open Tam's headphones. You wouldn't want him to hear our private conversation, would you?'

You bastard, Kara thought. She flailed and reached out to grab hold of the microphone stand, needed to hold on to something cold and solid. Hearing Mike's voice when no one else could disorientated her and the thought of the things he could tell Tam made her feel sick. Pressing her lips tightly together, Kara shook her head.

'Good. So you'll do as I tell you.' Mike smiled. He had her caught like a fish on the end of a line. Worst of all, Kara couldn't speak back, only stand there and mime her responses without letting Jon or Tam know what was going on. She was boiling inside, but Mike's voice continued in her ear. 'We'll go back to "Turn on Me",' he said, 'but this time I want you to do it *with feeling*.' His smile twisted unpleasantly and he bent in low to whisper in the microphone. 'Turn him on, Kara. Make his prick hard and I'll keep all the seedy details between us.'

Kara frowned and shook her head violently. She must look

like she had a flea in her ear, she thought, but there was no way she was going to make a fool of herself in front of everyone. Tam was still in cool-and-aloof mode, his blank indifference hiding God knows how many shades of contempt.

'I know you can do it,' Mike coaxed. 'Get Tam's dick hard and you win my silence.'

He flicked the channels open, called out for the band to start the song and watched from his chair like a film director. Screw you, Kara thought, but she also felt the familiar lightness in her arms and legs, the horny adrenaline rush Mike's games always gave her.

The opening chords reverberated through her ribs and Kara closed her eyes, trying to calm her breath. She needed to tap into the rage and the arousal both at once, the memory of how Tam and she would spar and scowl at each other; the way it felt to have him slam her up against a wall and slide down her body, tugging at her clothes as he went.

She turned to him as she started singing the verse, watched his blunt fingers trip over the fret board and his face set in concentration. He wasn't even looking in her direction. The distance between them made her hurt and she felt her knees get weak, prayed that Mike would drop his new game and let her just get on with the song. If she worked hard enough maybe she could forget about Tam for the next few hours.

'Get closer to him,' Mike whispered, and she knew he was speaking to her alone.

She circled closer, stood in front of Tam and looked down at his guitar. It was slung on his lap, held close to his body. Like a shield, she thought. He wouldn't face her, kept his head bowed over the instrument and his eyes turned down. Did he know what was going on? Could she touch him?

'Let's try that again,' called the engineer, and the song broke apart, sputtered to a pause and started again.

The intro played out, but Kara held off. She was waiting. At last, when they'd repeated the refrain twice already, Tam looked up.

'Lick your lips,' Mike said in a low voice.

Kara hesitated, then did as he said, flicking her tongue over her top lip and biting down on her lower. Tam continued to play the melody, watching her now from under his dark brows.

'Don't forget to sing, Kara,' Mike reminded her.

Although her voice caught in her throat, she obeyed him, forcing the words out with a voice much huskier than usual. It was about Tam, for Tam, and she'd always sung it with him in mind. Only this time it was different. When she sung about being as wet as silk, she felt it. Between her legs and in her very centre, just below her heart.

'Touch yourself,' Mike said.

His words blazed in her mind and her hand flew automatically to her neck. She stroked her pulse point, felt the tremor of her voice as it rose in her throat.

'Lower,' he insisted.

Kara let her hand slide down over the swell of her breast.

'That's good,' Mike said. 'You're listening well.'

Kara could hear the sweet irritant of certainty in his voice, like an over-sugared drink she couldn't stop sipping at. She stroked light circles over her breasts, cursing Mike even though it felt good.

'Do it harder. Rub your nipples.'

Closing her eyes, Kara scuffed the point of her tit with her palm and gave herself little zings of sensation.

'Make them stiff,' Mike said, his voice gaining an edge. 'Let Tam get a good look at you. Let him see how horny you are.'

Kara's voice nearly broke as she played with herself, knowing that Tam was watching her, sure that he was just as keenly aware of her body as Mike. Desperate, she pinched herself hard, twisted a nipple between her thumb and forefinger. Somehow, she thought, a little jolt of pain might fix the rising agitation she felt, or soothe the hunger of her sex, or satisfy Mike. Her nipples burned, the pain white hot and achingly good.

'Now drop your hands. By your sides. Let him see you.'

As the song finished, Kara opened her eyes and dared to look at Tam.

At least she'd caught his attention. His gaze was stuck on her breasts and his mouth hung slightly open, those delicate lips parted just enough that she could see the edge of his teeth. This was a Tam she recognised and the realisation sent hope shooting in sparks straight from her heart. Was he as turned on as he looked? She imagined his cock straining against the backboard of his guitar, his balls tightening like a fist. She wanted to lean into him right there and then, let him take her nipple in his mouth and trap it between those sharp white teeth.

'OK, guys, let's move it on. "Sweet Street", from the top.' Mike's voice broke rudely into the moment.

Bastard! Kara thought. Tam swallowed and averted his face, frowned as he fiddled with the tuners on his guitar.

'Tam,' Mike said, and Kara's heart tripped a beat. 'We're not picking you up so well. Could you stand up and move closer to the mike?'

As he moved, Kara caught a slight scent of Tam – his own mix of hot skin, coffee and Dax-wax coconut. She wanted so badly to walk up and bury her face in his chest, feel the springy muscle under her cheek and inhale that smell deeply. But Mike wasn't finished yet.

'Bring it up a little higher – I want the fret board right up tight for a moment, just to check the levels.'

Tam shouldered his guitar and lifted it towards the microphone that hung from the ceiling. Instantly Kara's eyes dropped to his crotch. Under the seam of his jeans, his cock curved hard against his thigh, sticking out bluntly and stretching the denim. As he strummed a few notes, Kara resisted the urge to reach out and touch him. Not here, not now, she said to herself. Not when it's part of one of Mike's twisted games.

At least she knew she still had the power to get him hard. That must mean he still wanted her, on some level. For the moment, that was enough.

'That did the trick,' Mike said, apparently as aware of Tam's hard-on as Kara was. She felt ashamed, suddenly, to be sharing his voyeurism. What she and Tam had was complicated, but it wasn't something she wanted to share with anyone else.

'Don't like me looking at your fuck-buddy?' Mike said. 'Wouldn't you even like to see me bend him over and take him?'

Kara's heart caught in her chest. The room seemed airless suddenly, as close and hot as a sauna. She could picture it so clearly. Mike had a way of turning his words into pictures in her head and at that moment she could see Tam gritting his teeth, picture the way his face would screw up as Mike's cock nudged at his asshole.

'I need a break,' she said heavily, tearing the headphones off and leaving them swinging from their tether. She crashed across the hall and into the bathroom, running to the sink. For a few moments she breathed out through her mouth, trying to calm her breathing.

Behind her, the door swung slowly open.

'Cooling off?' Mike asked. 'Or were you just about to jam your hand down your knickers?'

Kara whirled around and would have run straight back out if Mike hadn't been blocking her path. He shifted so that his wide shoulders filled the door frame and crossed his arms.

'I'm impressed.' Mike said.

'I'm delighted,' Kara replied, making an ineffectual effort to push him out of the way. But he wasn't letting her go. He stood immovable in front of the door.

'You're insatiable, aren't you? Such a horny little slut.'

His words stung, but something in Kara responded to the harshness of the phrase. She blushed, and it wasn't lost on Mike.

'Oh, you like that too, don't you?' Mike's face grew sober. 'Undo your zip. Take your skirt down.'

Kara looked at him coolly. She could refuse. Of course she could. But for some reason she found she was pinned to the spot, unwilling to give in and unable to tear herself away.

'What, you're scared someone might see us? There are not many people in the building that haven't had the pleasure already, Kara. Or are you just shy?' His voice was as mocking as a playground bully.

Of course that was the quickest way to make her react. As soon as he taunted her, the rebellion flared in Kara's chest and she got reckless.

She popped the button on her skirt and tugged it open. She was naked underneath – yesterday's knickers were stuffed into the bottom of her handbag.

Swiftly, Mike moved to her and stuck his hand down the front of her skirt. His middle finger slid expertly between her lips and dabbled in the wetness that had gathered there. He hooked his finger inside her. Made a beckoning motion that pressed against her pubic bone, and reached for her clit with his other hand.

'This is what you need, isn't it? Good girl,' he said, as Kara sagged against him, clinging to his arm. He tugged firmly at a tuft of her hair and pulled her closer in to him until she moaned out loud.

'You just want to be fucked, don't you?' he murmured,

pinching her clit and rubbing it. 'You wouldn't care who it was, just as long as they were inside you.'

His fingers had found a rhythm now and played it, dipping in and out of her, flicking her clit back and forth.

'Cock, tongue, fingers,' he chanted in her ear. 'Tam, Jon, Judy.'

Kara clutched at his shoulder, nearly doubled over with want and arousal. Mike's words made her head spin, but the combination of his filthy whispered speech and the insistent way his hand worked at her kept her nailed in place. If he'd let go of her, she would have fallen.

'Whose cock are you going to chase tonight, Kara?' He doubled his fingers inside her, filled her with searching flesh. 'Tam's? Are you in love with him?'

As he questioned her, Mike pushed his thumb hard against her clit. It was like he'd flicked a switch – the orgasm sprang up out of nowhere and shook upwards through her body. It felt like she was breaking apart as she came into his hand, there in the dimly lit bathroom on the tiled floor. Her mouth stretched open against his shirt and she sucked at it, knew she was leaving a damp stain but couldn't stop herself.

Afterwards, Mike withdrew his hand from her and washed in the basin.

'You'd better get back in there,' he said. 'We've got a lot still to do.'

Her legs were weak and she was flushed and sweaty, but Kara knew Mike had won this battle. She nodded mutely and retreated to the studio, put on her headphones and faced the booth so that she wouldn't have to look at Tam.

The blush on her cheeks faded, but when she looked up through the glass she saw Mike and the damp spot blooming on his shirt like a badge. A victory medal, she thought. Reminding her he'd won.

For the rest of the session, Tam played his parts note perfect and tight, never missing a beat and never saying a word in between tracks. Kara listened for something in her headphones, some clue as to how he was feeling, but heard only static. She sang with her eyes shut, concentrating on the tunes and not thinking about the meaning behind the words at all.

14

It was after midnight when they wrapped up. Kara's throat was hoarse and she felt ready to drop. She crammed a chocolate bar in her mouth to perk up her blood sugar and collapsed onto a chair in reception, staring out through the glass wall. Outside the park across the street was dark, only the lit-up towers of the old churches on top of the hill showing up beyond the trees. Mike, Jon, Tam – everyone else was still in the studio, listening to the playback of the songs they'd worked on.

Part of Kara knew she should go back to the flat and try to talk to Ruby, explain how the photos had been a set-up. But she was dog-tired and so wrung out she couldn't face the thought of an angry flatmate and an empty bed. At least there was no sign of Lina in the office. She's done what she needed to do, Kara thought bitterly.

Tam walked out of the live room and across reception, wearing his parka buttoned right up to the neck.

'You're heading home,' Kara said. For a moment, she imagined walking back along the night streets with him, dropping onto his bare mattress and the two of them curling up together to sleep. Maybe she could, she thought. Maybe one night didn't have to mean anything.

'Yes,' Tam said, pulling earphones out of his pocket and slipping them on.

'Maybe I could come . . .' Kara's voice trailed away. She hated how she sounded – small and uncertain. Needy. This was not the way she and Tam worked. They snapped at each other, cracked stupid jokes. They were never this polite. Kara pressed her lips together. She'd crossed a line, played the game wrong and she knew it. Tam had a hard look on his face.

'I've got company,' he said shortly.

Kara felt as though he'd slammed a door in her face. The chocolate in her mouth tasted far too sweet, sickly and cloying. Tam was turning his phone on and checking for messages. Kara saw a flicker of pleasure pass over his face as he read the display, noticed his mouth curl, just for a moment.

'Sure,' she said. 'Well, I'll see you tomorrow.'

Who is it? she wanted to scream. Tam slipped his phone back in his pocket and pulled his hood on as he turned for the door. Kara wanted to leap up and grab him, stop him from going back to his flat to meet whoever was waiting for him. For a moment, she imagined herself throwing a full-blown hysterical tantrum there in the cool, well-designed lobby. She curled her toes inside her shoes instead, forced herself to sit rigid and still on the chair as he left.

Behind them, she heard voices as the others left the studio and pulled the doors shut. Mike was talking to Jon, loudly, something about chords and keyboard technique.

Kara watched silently as Tam pulled the door open and let in a blast of cold air. He slipped out into the night, not looking back, and the voices behind her moved closer in a wave of distracting noise. Kara turned to meet them.

'Want a lift?' Mike said coolly, and she found herself nodding before she'd even thought about what that might mean. Jon disappeared without saying goodbye, and Kara followed Mike to his car in silence.

She buckled herself into the passenger seat and felt the soft leather chill her back.

'Where am I taking you?' Kara could hear the smile in Mike's voice. She hesitated. Where was she going? To face Ruby? To run after Tam?

'My place, then,' Mike said, slipping the car into first and pulling away. He drove fast over the icy roads and Kara felt the wheels slide uncertainly every time they turned a corner.

'Are we going to be alone tonight?' she asked eventually. In the glow from the dashboard lights, she saw Mike smile.

'Yes. Judy has other plans.'

Kara nodded. She focused on the lit-up road in front of them, the brake lights of the car in front, and tried to keep her voice neutral.

'Are you two in some kind of relationship?' she asked.

'Some kind,' said Mike, 'but probably not the kind you mean.'

Mike's house was cold, the fireplace a mess of ash and cinders and the air still tinged with the smell of wood smoke. Kara shivered as she looked at the sofa.

'I'm sleeping here?' she asked, dropping her handbag on the floor. She was so tired she'd have slept in the car. Mike came up behind her and placed his hands on her shoulders. He kissed her neck, laying his dry lips on the tender skin at the base of her scalp.

'You're cold,' she said, as he pushed her hair aside and trailed the tip of his tongue across her throat.

'You did well today,' he said, dragging her arms out of her coat. Kara shrugged to help him. 'It can't have been easy. I know you and Tam have a history.' Mike thrust his ice-cold hands under her top and felt her breasts, making her nipples shrink instantly into hard points.

Kara sighed. '"History" being the operative word,' she murmured, standing quite still as Mike worked at her, his touch gentle and persistent. This was how he got her, she realised. He always gave her the unexpected. What she wanted, before she even knew she wanted it.

'Don't worry,' he said, moving round to kiss her mouth. It was a long kiss, soft and deep, and Kara felt her limbs turn to water. 'I've made sure he won't be a problem any more.'

Mike's touch was drugging her, making her slip into a warm haze of pleasure, but his words triggered a flicker of anxiety.

Kara frowned and pulled away. 'What do you mean?'

Mike tapped on her collarbone with his fingers. For the first time ever, she noticed he was having trouble choosing his words. Brushing his hair back from his face, he sighed and moved towards the stereo.

'Mike?'

He took his time choosing a track, waited for the chime of a solo piano to flow into the room before he turned to answer her. His arms were rigid, his hands stuffed into his pockets and Kara looked at him warily. It was the way people stood when they were delivering bad news.

'When I said Judy had other plans tonight ...' he started, letting his words trail away. It took a moment to sink in. And then Kara remembered Tam's face as he looked at his phone. A strange feeling buzzed over her, something like the lurch of seasickness.

'Judy,' she said. It almost hurt to say the name.

'I thought it would be fitting,' Mike said, nodding. 'Sort of poetic.'

'What are you talking about?' Kara asked, crossing her arms over her body and squeezing. 'What's this got to do with you?'

'When I said Judy and I had a relationship – it's complicated.'

'Try me,' Kara said.

Mike threw his keys on the coffee table and leaned on the

back of the couch. 'We met a couple of years ago. I didn't want to take on a student.' He looked straight at Kara. She was fixed where she stood, still hugging herself as though the room were freezing. 'I didn't want a repeat of what had happened between you and me,' he said softly. His eyes glittered. 'But Judy insisted. You wouldn't think she could be so persuasive to look at her. Such a sweet-looking girl.'

He shook his head, and Kara waited, digging her fingernails into the soft skin above her elbows.

'So I took her on, and we started lessons. Part of me thought I could make up for what had happened – what didn't happen – when I was teaching you.'

'But you just couldn't help yourself,' Kara said.

Mike smiled. 'The situation was entirely different. Judy was a private student. And besides, she made it clear she was more than willing. The whole thing was almost too easy.'

'You got bored,' Kara said flatly.

'Nearly,' Mike agreed. 'Until I saw Judy flirting with a barman one night. I suggested she fuck him and the idea went down well.' He looked into the ashes of the fireplace, lost in thought. 'I find Judy is like salt.'

'Like salt?'

'You can't eat it on its own, but added to other ingredients, it livens up a meal.'

'So now you loan her out.'

'God, no! You make me sound like her pimp. I enjoy instructing her and she enjoys receiving my instructions.'

'And Tam is one of those ... instructions.' Kara realised she suddenly couldn't feel the temperature any more. She could see every detail of the room very clearly; hear the recorded piano notes falling into the air one by one, faster and faster, and behind that the ticking clock shaving seconds off the hour. But she couldn't feel her heart.

'Just as you were the night before,' Mike was saying. 'Judy's very generous. Very giving. She likes to bring pleasure and she likes to be instructed.' He stretched out on the couch, inviting Kara to sit beside him with a wave of his hand. 'She'll be taking good care of Tam. And that leaves us free, my dear, to enjoy each other without distractions.'

Kara had to admit it was tidy. Flawless. She could sink onto the couch next to Mike and lose herself in his games, forget about Tam and the band and the heaving, tangled complications of the day. Nothing could be simpler.

But instead of sitting, she was pacing, rubbing her arms and walking from one side of the room to the other. The plan would be perfect, she admitted, if it wasn't for the fact that she felt like crying.

'Could I have a drink?' she asked, suddenly feeling the need for a mouthful of whisky, something that would burn her throat and warm her inside.

'It's not a drink that you need,' Mike said quietly.

Kara turned to him and saw how at ease he was, how certain he looked. Not a fibre of his gold, tanned body twitched, and his grey-blue eyes held hers as steady as granite. She knew how his body felt against her, how solid and unyielding he was, how firmly his arms held her as he wanted her. To be trapped underneath him, letting him manipulate her and fuck her to his own distinct rhythm seemed just the solace she needed.

At that moment, when everything around her was dark and uncertain and the night was full of lies and betrayal, Mike was a constant.

Right now, he was her only constant.

The next day, when Tam turned up at the studio with his arm round Judy, Kara managed not to scream. She went straight to the sanctuary of the live room, took her place at the micro-phone and held on tightly. All morning she kept her eyes focused on the wall in front of her and tried not to think. Mike watched everything from his position in the control booth, saying very little and only occasionally breaking in to ask them to repeat part of a song, adjust the levels or do another take.

They'd run through the eight tracks they were recording half-a-dozen times or more when Mike called a halt.

'We need a change of scene,' his voice instructed through the headphones. 'Something's not working. Everybody, break for an hour.'

Over a lunch that she didn't eat and a bottle of wine that she downed too fast, Kara listened to Mike as he tore apart the band's performance.

'I'm not hearing anything good,' he said grimly, staring down at his half-eaten plate of salad.

'We're missing Ruby,' she reminded him, trying not to let the guilt surface in her mind as she thought of her flatmate. 'Things'll pick up when she's here.'

'Will they?' Mike said. 'I sincerely hope so.'

That afternoon, to Kara's disgust, Lina appeared in the control room and sat with Mike. She watched the band, sometimes leaning in to Mike to murmur in his ear. Kara didn't like her expression – serious and shrewd – and she didn't like the way Mike seemed to be listening to her almost as much as he was listening to the music.

It bothered the others too – Jon kept messing up his part and Tam seemed to be lagging behind, tripping over himself and missing all his cues.

After they'd butchered 'Plastic Hallway' for the fourth time, Kara tore off the headphones. 'What the hell is going on?' she asked Tam and Jon, who were grimly bent over their instruments.

Jon looked haggard, she thought. 'And where is Ruby?' she asked.

Jon closed his eyes as if saying a silent prayer.

'It doesn't matter how upset she is, she needs to be here,' Kara went on. 'We only get one shot at this.'

'Wait, don't tell me – we need to be professional about it?' Tam asked, looking at her through narrowed eyes. 'That's what you were going to say, is it?'

'You're not helping,' she said, a shard of bitterness breaking into her voice.

'Neither is having your sugar daddy breathing down my neck,' muttered Tam, shoving his hand in his hair and clutching a handful of messy brown curls.

Kara's gaze flew nervously to the control room, but Mike was lost in a conversation with Lina, nodding as she talked.

Jon hit a low C, playing one long forlorn note. 'It's not working, is it?' he said, expressing in his awkward, gentle manner exactly what Kara was too scared to think.

'So we make it work,' she said, gritting her teeth. 'These are our songs. We made them. We can fucking play them, whether we're in the mood or not.'

'Speak for yourself,' Jon said.

Kara glared at him. She rattled the beaded bracelet on her wrist. 'If you don't want to be here, Jon, you'd better let me know. Just in case, you know, we find ourselves *in the middle of recording our debut album* when you decide to duck out. Christ.'

'What's the problem?' Mike's voice cut across their argument. He was broadcasting on the loudspeakers and he didn't sound happy. 'Kara?'

Kara tilted her chin up and shook her head. *No problem*, she mouthed, ignoring the guys sitting next to her with their faces tripping them. Mike nodded slowly, as though he was considering something. His eyes were cold and, although Kara had grown almost used to the way he observed her, this time she felt the chill.

They played for another hour, with an atmosphere of stewing resentment thick in the air. Kara sang as hard as she could, but her voice wasn't mixing with Tam's guitar and the lyrics fell into the mix like lead weights. No matter how much she tried to give it zest and spark, the words were coming out false. When Lina left the suite and Mike called an early finish, Kara felt her shoulders slump with relief.

Mike drew her aside as the others left, pulling her into one of the tiny isolation booths at the side of the live room. 'This is not going well,' he said, leaning back against the wall.

Kara nodded. 'Bad day,' she said, cursing the band and herself in her head.

'It's more than that,' Mike said, pulling a sheet of paper out of his pocket. 'Lina took some notes.'

'Well, great. Can't wait to hear what spiteful crap she's come up with.'

'Kara, whatever your personal feelings towards Lina, she is one of the best producers I've worked with. She knows a good thing when she sees it.'

'Really.'

'Yes. Really. And she is not seeing it here today.'

Kara felt her blood shrivel in her veins. Throughout it all, all the mayhem and fuck-ups and fights and confusion, she'd been clinging to the music as the one thing she knew how to do.

'What ... What did she say?' she asked, dreading Mike's reply.

He read over the notes, frowning. 'She said it's critical that the band can perform under pressure. What makes an act sink or swim is not just the music. It's how strong they are.'

'And?'

'And she says The New Rakes are falling apart at the first hurdle,' Mike said quietly. 'You're all over the place. Losing it.'

Kara blew out a long breath. It hurt because it was true. Lina might be a bitch, she thought, but she's right on the money this time.

'So what do we do?' she asked. 'Do we get another day to fix this?' The band was booked for three days of studio time. Maybe with one more day, they could pull something off. If Ruby would come round. If Tam would forgive her. If miracles happened.

'I'll be blunt. Lina's for cutting our losses and stopping right now,' Mike said. He put out a hand to touch Kara's shoulder, stroked her as if to soothe her. It didn't help much – she felt like the ground had been pulled out from under her. The shiny, glossy, beautiful dreams that had been blossoming in her head for the past year were crumbling. Her hands were shaking.

'But,' Mike said, kneading Kara's arm insistently. 'But I might be willing to back you.'

It was a small spark of hope, enough to make Kara inhale sharply and straighten her spine. 'Another day?' she asked, her mind already racing through all the ass-kissing and apologising and persuading she'd have to do to make it right. There wasn't much of a chance, but there was a glimmer and that was all that she needed. 'Let me talk to the guys,' she was saying already, reaching up to take Mike's hand. It felt almost like she was begging him, but for once she really didn't care. 'By tomorrow morning I'll have it fixed, Mike. We'll be golden.' She flashed a smile at him, willing him to soften and agree.

Only Mike wasn't smiling back. Instead he shook his head.

'That's not what I meant, Kara.' He turned her around to face him and placed both hands on her hips.

'I meant I'd give you another chance. Only you.'

'I don't understand,' Kara said, feeling her head spin.

Mike's hands slipped round her waist and pulled her closer.

'Your band is falling apart,' he said. 'If we can't trust these guys to show up and play well in a studio, what'll happen when we start pulling big gigs? There's no space for hangers-on.'

'But – it's our band,' Kara said. 'It's ours.'

Mike trapped her hands in his. 'It's your band, Kara. No one doubts that you're the engine running the machine. You're the one everybody wants, you write the songs and you do the legwork. It's you that keeps everything up and running.'

'But I can't do it on my own.'

'I wasn't suggesting it,' Mike said. 'But there are other options.' He was rubbing each of her hands in turn, holding them tightly as though Kara might try to run if he let go.

'I don't want to hear them,' Kara said, pressing her lips together tightly. She shook her head, struggled to pull away from Mike's steady touch.

'Calm down. Listen to what I have to say.'

'You want to split us up.'

'No. I want to make sure you get the chance you deserve, Kara. This band, these people. They're not going to give you that.'

'So I just ditch them.'

Mike shrugged. 'You change the line-up. No big deal. Happens every fifteen minutes in this business.'

'And fill in with what, session musicians?' Kara's tone was scathing.

'Maybe,' Mike agreed. 'although if you want instant chemistry ...'

He stroked her face with the back of his hand. His touch was so gentle, it surprised Kara. A lover's touch, one that could turn any moment into something more intense. He fixed his eyes on hers, gazed at her with cool intent. Mike could turn her on with a glance, and he knew it.

'... I'll step in.'

15

Kara walked along the gravel path through the park. In the moonless dark it was just a paler smudge among the pools of tree shadows. During the day, the green space that bordered the river was a wide-open sanctuary. At night, the place became something different – a place of malevolent lurkers and opportunist lovers. She walked fast, trying to make her shoulders look broader and her footsteps sound surer.

It was a stupid idea to take this short cut, but nerves had made Kara reckless and she wanted – needed – to get to Tam as soon as she could. Mike had given her a couple of hours to consider his offer. His final offer.

Trash the band, save herself. Lose the rest or sink entirely. Mike knew she couldn't make that choice, any more than she could choose which limb she'd rather lose. And so he'd made it for her – either she let the band know their dream was over or he would. He'd stood with his phone in his hand, ready to dial their numbers and deal the final blow. Part of Kara had wanted to let him do it, just to close her eyes and leave the chaos behind her, let Mike drive her back to his place and take her to bed.

The next day they'd start all over, with him on piano and session musicians pulled at random from Lina's little black book. Mike would produce something slick, a debut that could catapult her straight into the eye of the storm. Her music would reach out everywhere. All her dreams might come true.

Three old friends would hate her for ever, but that was the

price she'd have to pay. Kara heard the river rushing along beside her, the water swollen and urgent as it ran towards the Clyde. The bridge was up ahead and Tam's flat was ten minutes away. Her stride faltered suddenly. How was she going to break this to him? Kara pictured him opening the door, rumpled and sexy. Would Judy be in the room behind him, naked in his bed? As the path tilted uphill, she slowed her pace.

After that, there was Ruby. And Jon. *Sorry for screwing up your lives, guys.* She could turn round, Kara thought. Turn round right now and let Mike do the dirty work. After tonight it would be a whole new world – she'd be lifted into a different circle, taken out to meet other musicians, movers and shakers, media people, stars. She could throw herself into Mike's world, get on the merry-go-round and forget all this.

They could play dirty games, pick up other lovers anytime they wanted some added 'salt'. Fuck their way into the future.

Kara reached the gates on the other side of the park and stepped into the street to join the sparse flow of people on the pavement. Above her the university's gothic towers jutted into the sky. The little bars and restaurants on Gibson Street had knots of people hanging outside them. Further up the hill, she guessed Tam would be in his flat with his 'visitor'. And a couple of streets away, Ruby was no doubt nursing a broken heart. What a mess. A few days ago they'd had the world at their feet. Now all they had was bitterness and confusion.

As she neared the street where Tam lived, Kara found herself walking slower and slower. She came to a stop outside his door, her finger hovering over the buzzer. Would he hate her any less if she delivered the news in person? What did she owe him anyway?

Shaking her head, she pressed the button hard and stood back to wait. The intercom crackled.

'Hello?' He didn't sound angry. There was that cocky swoop

in his voice, the rough warmth that had first attracted her to him. 'Who is it?'

Kara remembered how she'd rung this bell a hundred times before, horny or hopeful or pissed off, and how she'd run up the stairs to meet him and make music or screw or just play records and drink beer until the small hours.

'Anyone there?' His voice was growing irritable.

She couldn't do it. She bit her lip as she turned away and walked slowly down the steps. Tam would be OK. He'd march off into the distance with a chip on his shoulder and fuck a hundred other beautiful women and forget about Kara soon enough.

She set her shoulders and walked away, not in the direction of her flat or Ruby, not towards home. She didn't really know where she was going, or why there were tears running down her face in unstoppable rivers.

She'd got halfway down the street before she heard the footsteps behind her. She turned to see Tam walking fast towards her, hunched and shivering in a thin white T-shirt.

'What's the deal?' he asked. 'Ringing the doorbell and running away? I thought you'd grown out of that.'

Kara tore herself away and kept on walking. She tried to wipe her eyes on her sleeve, choking back a sob.

'Kara,' Tam called, chasing after her. 'Will you stop a minute? What's going on?' He grabbed her by the elbow and spun her round, breathing hard. 'Kara, oh God, you're not ...'

It seemed Tam could handle just about anything apart from seeing Kara cry. He looked even more stricken than she felt, reaching up to touch her and then changing his mind, letting his hands flail uselessly at his sides.

'Ah, come on ... Shh, it can't be that bad.' He raised his eyebrows. 'Is this because we screwed up today? We'll just fix it. Re-record tomorrow.'

Kara shook her head. 'There is no "tomorrow", Tam,' she said, clearing her throat. Under the dim glow of a street light and with tears in her eyes, he was a white blur, shifting from one foot to the other.

'What do you mean?' He was hugging himself against the cold and Kara looked down and realised his feet were bare. He hadn't stopped to put his shoes on before running after her. Who else would chase her barefoot through the city? Was she just about to make the worst mistake of her life?

'Mike doesn't want you there any more,' she almost whispered. As she told him, tonelessly, what Mike had told her, she kept her eyes fixed on the pavement. There was no way she could watch his face as the news sunk in.

'He wants me to record with session musicians,' she said flatly. She waited for Tam's response, but there was nothing. At last, she looked up. He stood very still in front of her. If he was cold he wasn't showing it any more, and maybe the light was playing tricks with her eyes, but she could have sworn there was the ghost of a smile on his face. Though she'd been playing it out in her head for the past hour, nothing could have prepared her for how he reacted.

'You've done it. You're going to be a star,' he said quietly.

There was a moment in which the night seemed to expand around them and then Kara thought she heard a very high thin sound, like glass shattering in the distance. It could have been her heart starting to break.

This was all wrong. How could she go places without him? She started to apologise, to take everything back, but before she could get the words out of her mouth, he kissed her.

His mouth was soft and warm, and his touch was decisive. It took her off guard, and before she knew what was happening he was pushing her back against the iron railings. His arms locked around her waist and he kept on kissing her, tilting her head back and thrusting his tongue inside her mouth, biting at her lips and attacking her again, almost angrily.

Under the thin cotton of his T-shirt, the familiar feel of his taut body moved under her hands. She clutched at him and tried to pull away for a moment to explain, but he wasn't about to let go. He held her hips, rigid, bending her back until her shoulder blades dug into the fence. As his tongue plunged inside her mouth, hard and searching, running along her teeth, she realised what he was doing.

The kiss was a way to silence her. It was also his way of saying goodbye.

The tears started again, flowed silently down her face and ran into the kiss. She tasted the salt of them, mixed in with the sweet hot taste of Tam.

When he pulled away and started walking back along the street without her, Kara gave up trying to hold back and let the sobs shake right through her.

The bar was crowded with people, drunk or on their way there. Thrawn's was a magnet for all the West-End media crowd, who shoe-horned themselves into the nooks and crannys and talked loudly around their glasses of Pinot Grigio. Kara knew Mike would be there, talking over his new ideas with Lina.

She pushed through to the staircase and up to the balcony, where Mike and Lina sat deep in conversation, a bottle of wine on the table between them. Over the noise and clatter of the bar, Kara heard Lina raising her voice in anger.

'. . . chasing some wannabe diva. It's crazy.'

'Oh, I'm interrupting,' Kara broke in, pulling a chair from another table and sitting down. 'So sorry.' She gave Lina a hard smile and brushed the back of Mike's hand. 'I take it you've told her,' she said. 'So, are we celebrating?'

Lina said nothing, just shook her head and drained her glass.

Mike gave a twisted kind of smile and Kara saw a new gleam of excitement hidden in his expression. She wondered what it meant. Was it the wine, or his argument with Lina – or was it the fact he was thinking of stepping in to play keyboards with Kara?

'Lina doesn't think it's such a good idea.'

'That's the understatement of the year,' Lina said.

'Are you jealous,' Kara said, tilting her head to one side and turning to face the other woman, 'of my talent, or the fact I'm fucking Mike?'

Kara had just given up everything she cared about. For some reason, it made her feel bitchy and invincible.

Lina let out a short, astonished laugh. 'Oh, you are learning fast, aren't you, precious?' She leaned in close to Kara and laid a hand on her arm. 'I just wouldn't want you to get hurt.'

'That's sweet,' Kara said. 'But I'll be fine.'

'Even without your buddies?' Lina said. 'Must be heart-breaking leaving them behind.' She gave Kara's forearm a tight squeeze.

Kara jerked back, shaking herself free and knocking Lina's wine into her lap.

'Jesus Christ!'

'Oops,' Kara said, pulling a face.

'Fuck. These are Alexander McQueen,' Lina hissed, pushing her chair back and clutching at her trousers. She swore again as she stood up and stormed towards the Ladies'.

'That was childish,' Mike said, but Kara saw a smile twitch at the corner of his mouth. 'So,' he continued, turning to Kara. 'You're on board? We start recording again tomorrow?'

'If Lina doesn't kill me, yes.' Kara nodded. 'I'll be there.'

'Wonderful. And you told Tam?'

Kara's eyes dropped to her lap. Her lips were still buzzing, slightly bruised from Tam's kiss. Worse, the look on his face as he'd said goodbye was horribly vivid in her mind's eye. She felt like a traitor. A heartbroken traitor. 'Yes.'

'So that only leaves one thing for you to fix,' Mike said, pulling out his phone and dialling a number.

'One thing?' Kara asked.

'Lina. You just soaked the lap of the best producer in the country. And not in a good way either.'

'I'm not apologising.'

'You're not going to get very far without her help.'

Even with the phone clamped to his ear, he kept his gaze fixed on Kara. Under the table, his hand slid over her knee. As the call was connected and he started speaking, his fingers crept up her thigh and tickled the soft skin hidden under the hem of her skirt.

He liked to do this – get her turned on in public, tease her with the promise of how he'd touch her, how he'd torment her later. It was disturbing and reassuring at the same time, Kara thought. She listened, resentful but curious, as he spoke on the phone.

'I think you'd enjoy working with her. Yes.' He smiled as his hand brushed the crease of her thigh, the hot fold of her pussy. 'Mm, you won't regret it. Sure.'

He snapped the phone shut and pulled his hand from Kara, leaving her off balance on the edge of her chair, craving more of his touch.

'We're all set,' he said. 'The Polar, next week.'

'Really?'

'Radio presence, journalists, DJs. The whole sweaty media corps in fact. And you on stage, in front of them all.'

He reached up to tuck a strand of Kara's hair behind her ear. Her heart was beating a hard erratic rhythm and she was reaching for words. The Polar was a premier venue, not some dingy basement filled with penniless students. In fact,

Kara couldn't afford the place. She only went when she really had to see a band – could stand drinking tap water all night and blowing a week's wages on a ticket if the music was guaranteed to blow her away.

And the bands that played there were big. The new hip acts, the hot tickets, the must-see media darlings that nobody wanted to miss.

'That's ... incredible,' she said finally, picturing the place. A wide stage, a state-of-the-art sound system, shit-hot lighting rigs. Most of all, a thousand-capacity venue. Kara was used to playing gigs that were the size of a large house party. Halfway through a set, she could reach out and shake hands with the audience if she wanted to, recognise familiar faces among the crowd.

The Polar was a whole different ball game.

'Now, this date could knock you into the stratosphere,' Mike said, seeming to echo her thoughts. 'Launch your album, blow everyone away. But ...'

'How do we fill the place?' Kara said, her voice rising with panic. 'I don't –'

'You,' Mike said. 'don't have to do anything. This is where Lina comes into her own. If, and I do mean if, you get her onside.'

'I have to win her over,' Kara said weakly. 'Even though she hates me.'

Mike seemed unconcerned. He sipped his drink, looked around the bar and waited.

'What is her problem? I mean, what have I ever done to her?' Kara knew there was a whine creeping into her voice.

Mike shrugged. 'It's not so much what you've done to her, Kara, as what you've done to me.'

'She's jealous?'

It sounded ridiculous as she said it, but the instant she did,

Kara felt things start to fall into place. The way Lina was so tactile with Mike, taking every chance to stroke his arm or lean in close. The day she'd walked in on them, and her spiteful warnings.

'She's in love with you,' she said quietly.

'It's a little more complicated than that,' Mike said, turning the stem of his glass between his fingers. 'But yes, we have a history. A very long history.'

Kara realised she was digging her nails into the arms of her chair. She hated apologies more than just about anything on earth. But without Lina, her music-world debut would fall nastily flat. The woman might be twisted, but she had the connections, the golden tongue and the chutzpah that would make a success of the launch.

'What do I do?' Kara asked, gritting her teeth. 'Grovel?'

Mike laughed. 'That won't work with Lina,' he said. 'She can't stand emotional displays. You'll have to be a bit more sophisticated than that to bring her round.'

'OK,' Kara said. 'Seeing as you know her so intimately, what's going to sway her?'

Mike paused. 'I think you'll have to ask her that yourself,' he said.

The Ladies' was at the back of the bar, a dim-lit room with orchids on the window sill. Lina was standing at the mirrors, leaning in close to apply her mascara.

'Hi,' said Kara, leaning against a basin and looking down at her feet.

'Mike sent you in here,' Lina stated, matter-of-factly. She screwed the lid back on her mascara and looked at Kara's reflection. 'You may be able to wrap him round your little finger, but the prick-tease act won't work with me.'

Lina turned on a tap and washed her hands. Over the roar

of the water, Kara tried to think of a strategy. Someone opened the door and entered one of the cubicles and Kara squirmed as she struggled to find the right words. As Lina dried her hands briskly and moved to leave, Kara felt the panic start to spiral again, prickling through her stomach and pressing down on her chest. It didn't matter, she thought, if she made a fool of herself. She'd already sacrificed her band mates and her principles. Her pride was going to have to be next.

'I'm sorry about the, uh, the wine,' Kara said, staring fixedly at an orchid.

Lina gave a short harsh laugh. 'Of course you are,' she said. She pushed past Kara and headed towards the door. Kara saw all her hopes shrinking as Lina made to leave.

'What will it take?' she asked, shortly. 'I need you to help with this gig. Just tell me what I have to do.'

At this, Lina hesitated. Slowly, she swung back to where Kara stood biting her lip. She circled her like she was sizing up a horse, glancing over Kara's face, body, legs. Under her curious, judging gaze, Kara wanted to cover herself, but she set her jaw and stood straight, waiting. When Lina crossed her arms in front of her, Kara sensed her humiliation wasn't over yet.

'Please?' she asked, the word bitter in her mouth.

'Ah, the little bird sings,' Lina mocked, moving in so close that her sweet heavy perfume made Kara's eyes water. 'And what do you think you could possibly do for me?'

Kara swallowed.

'What the fuck do you think a wet-behind-the-ears chanteuse could do to please *me*?'

Lina turned, shaking her head, and paced across the tiled floor. 'I've seen a thousand of you already, you know. Nice voice, nice tits, bit of sparkly attitude. You won't last ten minutes out there. Once the gossip rags and the bitter old divas and the jealous young hopefuls get started on you. They'll trample all over you,' she said with relish, as though she were telling Kara her horoscope.

'And which are you?' Kara blurted out, unable to stop herself. 'Bitter? Jealous? Or both?'

Lina shook her hair. She pressed her perfectly painted, glossy lips tight together. Had Kara gone too far? She cast around for a new way to apologise.

'I didn't know,' Kara said, 'about you and Mike. I didn't realise.'

'You wouldn't have acted any differently if you had,' Lina murmured, rocking back and forth on her heels. She still had her hands planted on her hips, but her jaw was working and Kara noticed something in the other woman's expression that surprised her. Under the thick eyeliner and the gleam of superiority, Lina's eyes were glittering. She looked, for once, not fearsome or glamorous or awe-inspiring. She looked hurt.

16

'So, you want to make some kind of deal,' Lina said.

'I want us to work together,' Kara said, 'without all this shit getting in the way.'

Lina gave her a thin smile. Now that Kara was looking closely at her, talking to her instead of trading insults, she kept catching glimpses of a different woman. Underneath the quick, fierce intelligence and the glamorous sheen, Kara thought she could sense something deep and dark.

'This goes no further,' Lina said, pressing her lips together into a thin crimson line.

'You mean – I mustn't tell Mike?'

At the sound of his name, a frown passed over Lina's face and her pupils swelled large and black. She turned her head away quickly. 'Exactly,' she said. 'If you can keep yourself under control –' she threw a scathing glance at Kara '– maybe we can come to some kind of arrangement.'

Outside, the noise of the bar swelled against the door, brash laughter and clattering glasses.

'There's no point telling you to stop screwing him,' Lina said, inhaling sharply. 'He'd only get himself even more snarled up, wanting to win you back.'

Kara closed her eyes. As much as part of her hated Lina, at that moment she couldn't watch her. It was like watching someone trying to make a bargain to win back their broken heart. Lina discussed the 'arrangement' calmly, but Kara knew that the thought of it was making her skin crawl.

'Keep on playing your games. He'll be enjoying trying to break you down, I bet?' Lina asked, a sharp note in her voice. Kara's eyes snapped open. A smile twisted across Lina's mouth, but her eyes were bitter. 'It's just what he loves,' she murmured. 'Finding the weakness in a woman. Finding the place where he can snake his way in and bend her the way he likes.' Lina's shoulders sagged a little, and she leaned forwards to grip the edge of the washbasin. 'What have you been doing?' she asked, abruptly. 'Rope? Other girls? Blindfolds?'

Her questions jolted into Kara like bullets.

'And you like it, don't you?' Lina gazed into the mirror. Her eyes flicked from her own face to Kara's, as though she recognised something in the reflections. She nodded slowly. 'You spend every day fighting. For the music, the money, for all the things you think you want. And against all the things you can't stand. Everything that frightens you.' Lina played with the tap, turned it on so a trickle of water streamed over the china. 'Mostly fighting yourself. And then he takes hold of your wrists and for one hour, one evening, one moment, the fight is over.' She smiled.

It was as though Lina could see right inside her. As though she could see Kara's whole inner landscape just by looking at her through the mirror. A blush crept up Kara's cheeks and she swallowed, hoping Lina couldn't guess just how accurate her insights were. And hoping too that Lina couldn't really guess every twist and turn of Kara's sex life.

'Don't worry, you can't shock me,' Lina said. 'I told you, I've seen it all before.'

'What do you want?' Kara asked, her voice barely a whisper.

Lina's lips tightened. She folded her arms. 'Don't let him fall in love with you.'

The word 'love' deepened the blush on Kara's throat and

cheeks, and the thud of her heartbeat banged in her ears. 'That might not be up to me,' Kara said.

'You'll find a way,' Lina said, reaching for her handbag and then pulling out her phone. 'You'll work out how to break the spell. But just in case –' she waved her phone at Kara '– I'll take an insurance policy.' Lina's eyes narrowed and flashed. 'Tam's number.'

His name hit her like a punch in the solar plexus. Kara looked at Lina, at her polished skin and carefully maintained figure. There was a lot of power tucked into the designer clothes; a lot of wild, controlled desire that brimmed just under the surface. Lina was someone who knew exactly how to get what she wanted – she had the nous, the connections and the bravado. Could she compete? Kara wondered. Was it worth taking the chance?

She shook her head and tried to act careless. 'It's over with us,' Kara said. 'You can't make it any worse than I have already.'

'Maybe not. But I imagine the boy might need some comfort. Someone to give him the break he deserves. He's got potential. Nice pout, nice ass. I could take him places.'

Kara would have laughed at anyone suggesting Tam could be made into some kind of flunky, but the look on Lina's face made her hesitate. That dark deep longing had hardened into utter determination.

'How are his pussy-eating skills?'

'Cheap shot, Lina.'

'You're right. I forgot how you felt. And what about him? Is he hurting all over for you? Or has he already got his cock inside someone else?'

Kara pressed her lips together. Pictures flickered in her head – horrible, vivid pictures. She pushed them away and focused on her breathing. She wouldn't rise to it. Wouldn't think about it.

'I could help him get over it,' Lina continued. 'Take his mind off it. I do know some good ways to distract a man.' When she smiled, she showed the sharp points of her incisors. 'And I know Judy's foibles. I'd have him eating out of my hand in a week. Sex and success,' she said, toying with the pendant round her neck as though she was lost in thought. 'A lot of shiny promises. The perfect way to fix a broken heart. Only the more you promise someone, the harder it tends to shatter, of course. The next time.'

Kara stepped backwards as Lina approached her. The woman was hovering on the edge of somewhere scary.

'I could break him and make sure he never recovered,' Lina said finally. 'Give me his number.'

Kara felt sick. Lina could get Tam's number from Mike, of course, probably had it written down already somewhere. The bitch was just chasing thrills, trying to make Kara feel worse than she already did.

It worked.

'You've got nothing to worry about, Kara,' Lina said. 'So long as you turn Mike off you. I'll leave Tam alone and you'll have the best gig of your life. Instant stardom. That's a promise.'

Kara trusted Lina about as much as a rabid dog, but she didn't have a choice.

Quietly, flatly, she recited Tam's number. Lina punched it into her phone and, while she did so, Kara looked at herself in the mirror. She recognised the haunted, restless look that Lina had worn earlier when she talked about Mike. It was the look, she realised, of a woman who'd lost something very important and didn't know how to get it back.

She followed Lina back to the table to find a small crowd had joined Mike. Kara vaguely recognised some of their faces. They had a burnished, slightly unreal look that fascinated

Kara. One woman was a one-time pop star turned folk singer, another man Kara knew from the photo next to his newspaper column. She settled in her chair and tried hard to smile, knew that she should be making the effort. Rubbing shoulders with these kind of people was what made it all tick, what would get her noticed and keep the buzz going. She should do something outrageous – speak to the columnist who kept trying to catch her eye, flirt with the hangers-on, talk about her sex life, something.

But Kara found herself looking at Mike instead, the fine laughter lines that curled round his mouth and the way his eyes crinkled when he smiled. His hand reached for hers under the table and rested there, feeling her fingers one by one, massaging them with a steady insistent pressure.

Don't let him fall in love with you, Lina's voice echoed in her head. *Break the spell.*

So that was what she had to do. Play Mike's game, while she played Lina's at the same time. Hope that she could make Mike fall out of love with her, without spoiling her chances as a singer.

And all along, she had to keep her mind as far away from Tam and heartbreak and failure as she possibly could.

That night, when Mike took her back to his place and pulled her down next to him on the couch, she kept a part of herself distant. When he lifted her arms over her head and held her wrists pinned to the armrest, she closed her eyes and let her thoughts drift. He leaned down to kiss her and she opened her mouth and let him.

All the time, while he fondled and caressed her and turned her one way and another, she listened for signs. Clues or signals that would show her how to break the spell. The trick was, she thought, to make him believe it was his idea.

When he held her thighs apart and licked a very slow trail from her asshole to her clit, stopping just a hair's breadth from her nerve centre, she gasped. Her pussy swarmed with the need to be touched and she waited for the promised flick of his tongue with her breath held. But there was nothing – only empty air.

'Good,' he said, lifting his head up as she squirmed from side to side. 'You're back. I thought I'd lost you for a while there.' He looked down at her thoughtfully, keeping her hips pinned in place and her pussy exposed. 'What is it?' he asked. 'Not missing Tam, are you?'

Kara shook her head and kept her mouth firmly shut. In her head, she cursed Lina for making everything so complicated. Kara had always avoided exactly these kinds of messed-up situation – always chased the sweet straightforward fucks that didn't involved getting tangled in emotion. And now she was stuck right in the middle of the stickiest, messiest, most tangled fucking web she could imagine.

'Hold on.' Mike nodded at the armrest, and Kara gripped it tightly.

'Don't let go or I'll stop altogether,' he warned.

It was how he liked her – splayed and unable to pleasure herself. And, Kara realised, he didn't even need to tie her up. If he made the right promises he could control her precisely, dictate exactly what she should or shouldn't do. Just like everything else in Mike's world – if she wanted to win the game, she had to play by the rules.

Even when those rules left her hanging in midair with nothing.

'Make me come,' she said, through gritted teeth.

Her pride was always the first thing to slip away. But tonight she needed more than an orgasm from Mike. She needed to find out what drove him and, as she remembered Lina's threats, she struggled to keep a hold of herself.

Her body wanted otherwise. Her hips bucked down but the cushions under her were deep and maddeningly soft, so that she only sank into the spongy fabric. Her legs kicked at the back of the seat. Rolling her head from side to side, she swore under her breath.

'Please,' she said.

'Not tonight, Kara. You won't win just by playing desperate.' Idly, Mike drew one fingertip lightly over the top of her pubis, dancing across her pussy lips and dragging a line straight to her asshole. 'I think I want to teach you something new.'

His finger tickled at the entrance to her arse, circling and fluttering in a way that made her muscles clench up tight.

'You'll get your pleasure here,' he said, pushing just the very tip of his finger inside her tightly bunched hole. Kara's spine arched and she bit her lip. 'You'll love it.'

Dipping his head down to her lap again, Mike burrowed lower. The tip of his tongue flickered over her anus, strange and new. With his forefinger rubbing and nudging gently inside her, Kara gasped. He moved inside her, slow and firm.

'How does that feel?' he asked, lifting his head to watch her.

'Weird,' she said. 'Backwards.'

'But you like it.'

'Yes.'

He sank his finger in to the knuckle, taking her by surprise so that she didn't have a chance to tense up. She was stoppered by him, filled at the base. The dark intensity of the sensation made her hold herself very still.

Mike curled over her to suck one nipple into his mouth, still working at her arsehole. Each tiny measured stroke made her feel dense around his finger. Between the pleasant ache of her nipple in his mouth and the slow finger-fucking, her body wanted to fold over and scrub up against him. Her pussy and her mouth were wildly empty and she swore as he kept her pinned there, tormented with feeling and the lack of it.

This is just what he wants, Kara thought. To keep me pinned here, begging. And this time I can't give him what he wants.

All at once, she went limp. Though it took a vast effort, she stilled herself and breathed deeply. If he wanted to torment her, she could take it. Plugged at one end and sucked at the other, she could lie there calmly and let him try to drag more protests out of her.

He felt it immediately. 'Kara?' Her nipple slid from his mouth as he spoke and the cool air shrunk around her wet skin so that it puckered tightly. Mike hung over her. 'You don't like it.'

'Oh, I do. It feels nice,' Kara said, her voice very calm.

'Nice?'

'Mm.' Kara shrugged. Inside she was burning up, hanging in midair while she waited for more – but she held back. Was this a way of tormenting Mike? Maybe she could even the balance. She curled her hands into fists and squeezed them hard. Knowing he was still watching her, she forced a half-smile to float over her face, sweet and blank.

Mike pulled his hand away, letting her arsehole relax with a mixture of relief and tingling disappointment. With a flicker of excitement and curiosity, Kara wondered what he'd do next, how he'd try to win her back.

She didn't have to wait long. He grabbed her hips and turned her over; pulling her so roughly it was almost a mauling. When he'd hauled her onto her hands and knees he laid a warning hand on her ass. Kara understood perfectly – be still, he was saying. Wait.

The springs of the couch bounced as he got up and walked away.

She knew it wasn't over yet. Far from it. While she rested her forehead against the armrest, Kara allowed herself a real smile. Was he really that easy to rile? She waited, crouched on all fours, as docile as a horse waiting to be saddled. No wriggling, no squirming, no noise and no heavy breathing, she told herself. It wasn't going to be easy.

The slap that stung her buttocks took her by surprise and she had to hold her breath to stop herself from crying out. He spanked her slowly, drawing out a longer pause between each strike and giving her space to flinch or speak.

Kara was glad she had her back to him, because it was all she could do to screw her face up and stop from reacting. Gritting her teeth, she braced herself and steadied her resolve. She wouldn't gasp or moan and she wouldn't ask him to stop.

When he finished, the cheeks of her arse were hot and sore, buzzing all over and pleasantly tender.

'I'm going to fuck your arse,' Mike said.

Kara bit her lip. She held onto his promise as though it were a physical touch, tucked it away inside.

'Did you hear me?'

'Sure,' Kara said, shrugging.

She heard small noises behind her. For a moment she wondered what Mike was doing and then she jumped from the cold wet shock as he dabbed lube on her. He twisted his finger inside, going deeper this time so that the tight feeling in her ass spread up to the base of her spine and throbbed sweetly.

Mike may have been losing patience, but he kept his movements slow. The head of his cock replaced his finger and he held it there, nudging at the mouth of her ass, pushing just a little at a time.

Kara wanted to rock back onto him, to feel him open her in this new place, but she forced herself to hold still. His hairy thighs were tight and warm against the back of her legs. He cradled her hips firmly in his hands. Would he still do it? Did he need to have her playing the part before he fucked her?

It wasn't easy to think straight while his cock slid over the crack of her buttocks, but Kara persevered. To break the spell, she had to spoil his game. Mike liked to be the one in control, liked to feel he held all the power. All she had to do was diffuse the tension. Flip the balance. She gritted her teeth hard.

With one long movement, she sank back and pushed herself onto him, letting the tightness of her asshole close around Mike's cock, taking as much as she could. At last, she allowed herself a long exhalation, a sigh that made her whole body melt. He was in her firmly, unbelievably big, his prick bearing down on her with a breathtaking force.

'Yes,' she hissed, drawing herself forwards and taking him again.

Mike made a noise in the back of his throat – a strangled grunt that Kara recognised as his last attempt to control himself. She impaled herself again, taking pleasure in the strangeness of the sensation and the sound of Mike struggling to hold his orgasm back. It was thick, overwhelming pleasure to have him plugged into her reluctant arsehole and Kara opened her mouth wide as she inched back and forth on his prick.

Every movement was so intense she knew he couldn't last long. His orgasm was hovering right beside them. When he came it sounded almost as though he was in pain, his body shaking as though he was sobbing, his cock quivering inside her. He clutched at her hips and dug in his fingernails, bent over her back and laid his cheek on her spine. Kara heard him whispering curses into her skin, swearing bitterly as his orgasm finally robbed him of every last drop of power. She smiled.

'Make me come,' she said, grabbing his hand and placing it between her legs. Though he was shrinking inside her and his legs shook with post-orgasm weakness, Mike rallied. He frigged her with skilful finesse, his fingertips drumming against her clit and rubbing her towards climax.

'Good,' Kara said, her voice thick with pleasure. She placed her hand over his. 'Keep going.'

It was then, as she pressed his hand over her pussy and ground against it, that Kara felt the power start to fall away from Mike.

Crouched over her and sweating from his own exertions, his body sliding and sticking to her, she realised the balance had tipped. The orgasm was glowing at her centre, spreading across her body and overtaking her mind. But just before it hit, she held Mike's busy fingers still and opened her mouth to laugh, knowing that she'd finally found a way to break free.

At the studio the next day, Mike was subdued and fractious. Kara ignored the session guys he'd brought in – they may as well have programmed a drum machine and used a tape loop for all the attention she paid them.

'Diva,' she heard the guitarist mutter when they stopped for a coffee break and she turned to blast him with a hundred-watt smile.

'Fuck you,' she said sweetly, and slipped her headphones back on. She sang with her eyes closed, giving the songs a new edge – a flash of steel under the velvet slide of her voice. After she'd recorded the vocals for 'Turn on Me' in one take, flawlessly, she looked up at the control booth and nodded.

Mike sat with his hands steepled in front of him, his eyes dark and troubled. He broke eye contact when Kara looked at him and shifted uncomfortably in his seat. She blew him a kiss. Maybe she could play the game and win, she thought. If she was strong enough to make her own rules.

17

Lina flew in and out of the studio all afternoon, leaving papers with Mike and throwing critical, curious looks at Kara. It didn't matter. While Kara was singing and feeling this strange, bitter and bright new hardness to her heart, she was unshakeable. Nothing could faze her – not Lina's cautionary glares or the strawberry-red love bite on Judy's neck.

She'd lost Tam already, and it really didn't make much difference who he was fucking. So long as Lina didn't make good on her threat and get her claws into him. If he was with Judy, he was safe, Kara thought. What really mattered, right then, was the music. So she clamped her headphones tight to her head and sang as hard as she could.

The only thing that threw her off her stride came late in the session. The blond lank-haired keyboardist with the faded, check shirt and the 'diva' opinion was unable to pick up Jon's tightly scored melodies, playing them over and over but losing the tune every time.

'Shit,' he said as he fumbled the notes yet again.

'I thought you said you were hiring professionals?' Kara directed her question at Mike.

'Oh, give me a break,' the guy said, throwing his hands in the air and turning to Kara. 'I didn't write this shit and I haven't seen it before this morning.'

'That's not my problem.'

Mike's voice cut in on the headphones. 'Can we skip the squabble, please? Let's take that again, from the top.'

'Are you sure?' Kara asked, resting her hand on her hip. 'You don't want to come in here and take over? I know how you love to be in control, Mike. Why not sack this guy too and come and show us what you've got?'

He didn't answer.

'I'm sorry,' Kara continued, her voice growing louder as she felt more reckless. 'I forgot you don't play any more. Can't cut it. Don't have the balls –' She broke off as Mike rose from his seat and left the control room, slamming the door behind him. Around her, the musicians coughed and shuffled their feet.

For the first time that day, Kara felt anxiety swarm over her, prickling at her scalp and making her heart race. Had she pushed it too far? Mike wasn't the kind of person to put up with musicians insulting him in public. She wanted to stop him from falling in love with her, sure, but she didn't want him to cancel everything, junk the deal and trash her career. He might be out there right now shredding her contract. She tapped her foot nervously, felt the swimming feeling in her stomach.

When he opened the door and came into the live room, it was all she could do not to start stammering an apology. He had rolled up the sleeves of his shirt and he walked fast, cutting across the room like the slice of a knife.

'Get out,' he said mildly to the blond keyboardist. 'I'll pay you the full day's wages. But you can leave now.'

By the time the guy had sworn, scowled, shaken his head and left, Mike had slid onto the stool and rested his hands on the keyboard. He tipped his chin at Kara. 'Let's go,' he said.

Under his hands, the melody started to spill from the piano. Mike barely glanced at the score and instead kept his eyes fixed on Kara. It was as though he'd already learned the song by heart.

She had to admit he played expertly. All Jon's ragged, looping melodies turned into something different in Mike's hands; they became smoother, subtler ... sexier.

Kara found herself singing in a husky drawl, as though Mike was dragging new elements out of her voice with his playing. Eyes closed, she swayed in time with the background rhythm, letting Mike's counterpoint twist her deeper into the songs.

When he broke off halfway through and left her hanging in the sudden silence, Kara was bewildered. She looked round to see Mike sitting with his arms folded.

'I don't think it's the piano that's the problem,' he said. 'It's you.'

'Me?'

'You're singing flat. And a little too ... abrasive.'

Kara swallowed. 'No way,' she said. 'This is my voice, this is how I sing.'

'Hm.' Mike looked her over. 'Maybe your posture. Stand straight.'

Kara shook her head. She felt awkward all of a sudden, like she didn't know where to put her arms. The hired guitarist and drummer looked her up and down as though the criticism had stuck to her skin. When Mike stood and approached, she felt herself shrink away.

He placed his hand on her stomach, slid it down under the waistband of her skirt and rested it on the dip between her belly and her pubis. Aware that there was a room full of strangers watching, Kara tried to pull away, but Mike had his other hand on the small of her back and he held her in place.

'Take it easy,' he said softly, working his fingers down further until they were brushing the fringe of her pubic hair. 'Trust me. Now. Breathe into my hand.'

Kara glared at him. If she made a big deal she'd look ridiculous. And he'd had his hand down her skirt plenty of times before. Why should she get shy now? Keeping her eyes on his, she breathed deeply and felt his hand tighten against the swell of her body.

'Good. Keep going.' His hand slid upwards and rested on her chest, in between her breasts. His touch made her heart skitter about behind her ribs and Kara was keenly aware that everybody in the room was watching closely. She tried to slow her inhalations, but the more she struggled, the faster she breathed.

'Your bra,' Mike said. 'Take it off.'

You could have heard a pin drop. The drummer's eyes had widened like saucers and a lewd grin spread across the guitarist's face.

Kara tried to laugh.

'It's constricting you,' Mike said, reaching up to pluck at her bra strap. 'Take it off.' He nodded at the door, indicating the bathroom across the hall. 'Give your voice a chance to breathe.'

He was trying to make a point, Kara thought. Trying to embarrass her. She glared at him through her fringe, silently willing him to back down, but Mike merely raised an eyebrow.

'Don't get precious, Kara. Your body is an instrument. If you want to succeed, you'll have to treat it as such.' He was talking loud enough that everyone could hear, but now he leaned in close and murmured in Kara's ear. 'I thought you liked showing off. Now go to the bathroom like I've told you, and when you come back I want to see your titties jiggling about nice and loose under that top, OK?' He gave Kara a light pat on the bottom and his professional smile.

It was like waving a red rag at a bull. Kara's uncertainty dissolved, pushed aside by a reckless fury she could taste in her mouth.

Without a word, she grabbed her shirt and wrenched it up over her head. She dropped it on the floor and checked Mike's reaction. To her delight, his face had darkened with a mix of surprise and anger.

Behind them the musicians sputtered with laughter. But when Kara reached behind her back to unhook her bra, they fell utterly silent. She focused on the drummer as she loosened the fastening, watched his tongue flicker over his lips and his eyes dart back and forth.

'You can watch,' she said calmly. 'I'm not shy.'

She pulled her flimsy cotton bra off and draped it over a mike stand. Her brazenness and the sudden cold made her shiver, and she felt her breasts tingle, her nipples tightening as she bent down to pick up her shirt. As she slipped the shirt back on the tips of her nipples grazed against the light fabric, sticking out in proud points judging from where the musicians' eyes were fixed.

'So?' she said, putting her hands on her hips. 'You want to go again?'

'No,' Mike said, his gaze murky and furious. 'Not yet. Undo your skirt.' He jerked his chin at her.

'You think it'd help if I sang naked?' Kara demanded, but she popped the button of her skirt and pulled the zip halfway down. 'That enough?'

'What do you think, boys?' Mike asked, throwing the question over his shoulder at the musicians behind him. 'Will that help?'

The guitarist crossed his arms, flexing his curvy biceps as he considered Kara's déshabillé. 'Oh yeah,' he said. 'Looks good. But she can go ahead and take more off if it's going to help. You know, with the singing.'

'Fuck you,' Kara said sweetly. 'Mike, let's pick up the song again.'

Mike nodded. 'OK. But while you're singing –' he came in close and smacked her ass, grabbed a handful of flesh '– tense up here. Nice and tight.'

Kara's muscles contracted automatically. Memories of Mike as her teacher and Mike as her lover glanced off one another, the feel of him twisting his finger inside her and opening her up gave her another shiver. Mike kept massaging her bottom, watching how it made her chest rise and fall.

He leaned in to whisper to her so close his breath tickled her ear. 'That's good. Just think of me,' he said, 'fucking you there. Can you do that?'

Kara nodded.

Mike pulled back and talked loudly. 'Lovely. Loose in the chest, tight in the ass. If you can't keep it up, we'll do some more exercises and I'll get the boys to join in this time.'

Kara kept her eyes fixed straight ahead. Don't let him see you're embarrassed, she told herself, but the shame was clear on her face, and she was wet between her legs. Would Mike strip her and throw her to the wolves, let those gormless hired guys perv over her? Would he enjoy that?

Of course he would. Just another way to exert his control. He liked her in thrall to him, unsettled and horny. The trouble was, Kara thought as she gripped the mike and leaned into it, that she liked it too. He made her feel like a slutty fool, and she couldn't get enough.

The strange thing was that Mike's instructions worked. Whether it was because of his impromptu singing lesson or the fact that she was half aroused and agitated, Kara sang like she was on fire. They played without a break for the next two hours, laying down one track after the other. Everything rolled with unstoppable force until Lina came in.

Shut away in the wood-lined box of the studio, Kara had forgotten the rest of the world existed. There was nothing but sweaty tension, Mike and the other musicians, and the songs bouncing off the walls with energy so fierce it vibrated in her hair.

When Lina appeared, it was as though she had broken into their secret den without a password. For some reason, a rush of guilt swarmed over Kara, as though she'd been caught in the middle of doing something she shouldn't.

'Sounds good,' Lina said, leaning back against the wall and settling in to watch. 'Don't let me stop you, please.'

Kara wiped her face on the back of her sleeve. Tension flickered in the room, the presence of Lina disrupting the hothouse atmosphere as if a cold draught had blown in the door.

'What is that?' Lina was frowning at the bra hanging inelegantly draped over the mike stand.

Kara shrugged. 'Mike's idea,' she said, raising her eyebrows.

Lina nodded, very slowly. 'So you're all letting your hair down,' she said. 'And how's it playing out?'

'Very smooth,' said Mike. 'We've got something special happening.'

'I'm glad to hear it. Hope the pressure's not getting to you, Kara. I know it's not easy keeping up with Mike's demands.'

'Everything's lush. All going according to plan,' Kara said.

'Kara's been very good,' Mike added. 'She's got spirit.'

'I can see that,' Lina said, her eyes dropping to Kara's clothes, the obvious braless breasts under her shirt and the pulled-open skirt.

Kara straightened her spine, stuck her chin out and let Lina get a good look.

'Well, you're not shy,' Lina said. 'Can't wait to give everyone a show, can you?'

'My body is an instrument,' Kara said, not even bothering to keep the mocking tone out of her voice. 'I know how to play it.'

She was pinned between Mike and Lina, she realised, trapped by secrets and unspoken longing. The atmosphere was so sticky she could hardly breathe, desire and hate and jealousy ran circles round the room. And nobody was willing to let go.

'Nearly finished, aren't you?' Lina said. 'I can tell you've been working hard. But you want to be careful you don't burn yourself out. You'll need to be on fighting form soon.'

'For the gig at Polar?' Kara said. 'Can't wait.'

'Everybody will be there,' Lina said, slipping her hands into her pockets. 'Everybody. I'll make sure of it.'

There was a warning in her words. Kara heard it quite clearly, and had the sudden image of Lina priming a gun.

'I got hold of your old band mates.' Lina shrugged. 'Not sure if they'll make it. Tam seemed a bit ... preoccupied to be honest.'

There it was. The sound of the safety catch slipping off.

'Maybe he's upset you gave him the elbow. But he's hot property, that boy.' Lina smiled. 'Even if you did drop him, someone else'll pick him up –' she clicked her fingers '– just like *that*. I told him, but he still looked a bit pissed off to be honest.'

'Looked? You saw him?' Kara answered sharply, before she could stop herself.

Lina gave her a wide smile. 'He came by earlier. Must have been looking for Judy. Don't worry – I told him you guys were busy.' Lina studied the ceiling as though lost in thought. She shook her head and laughed, letting her hair shake free. 'He didn't seem to mind all that much. Damn. I'm keeping you guys back. Go on.' She gestured to the microphones. 'I can't wait to hear this special thing you've got going on.'

Kara hugged herself. The muscles in her neck were coiled so tight they cracked when she lifted her shoulders and her ears were ringing. She looked at the mike in front of her and the blank faces of her new backing musicians. There was a sharp ashy taste in her mouth and, as her eyes fell on Mike sitting coolly at the keyboard, she felt something snap.

'I have to go,' she said bluntly, reaching for the coat she'd hung on a chair and then shoving her arms into the sleeves, already walking. She was halfway to the door when Mike called after her.

'Kara.' His voice was hard and full of warning, and her spine went rigid at the sound.

'I'll be here tomorrow,' she said, 'don't worry.' She threw the last words over her shoulder and slammed the door behind her.

Outside the night was icy black, the pavements slippery with early-spring rain that was already beginning to freeze. Kara walked without thinking, inhaling the cold air in short quick breaths. She pushed past a knot of drunk students spilling across her path and hurried along the tunnel of trees that led to the messy heart of the West End. The roots of the old trees had burst through the tarmac and churned up the pavement, and she stumbled just as a car with dimmed head-lights crawled past.

Picking up her pace, she felt anxiety sparking in her fingertips as the car pulled alongside. The window scrolled down and the engine purred softly.

'Fuck off,' Kara said curtly, flicking her middle finger at the invisible driver.

He revved the engine and took off, leaving her behind in the dark with a metallic screech. She walked faster, heading for the orange glow of Gibson Street and the steep terraces beyond.

Her mobile was in her pocket and she gripped it tightly. It

was tempting, but this wasn't the kind of conversation she could have over the phone. She needed to see him face to face. Even if Judy was naked in his bed, even if it meant he ended up hating her. Christ, she thought, what if he isn't in? But then she gritted her teeth. Of course he was in. She knew Tam. If he had a new girlfriend, he'd be holed up in his bedroom fucking her senseless.

Kara reached his street and glanced up at his window – the light was on. Not sure if she was relieved or rattled, she made for the door and buzzed. This time, when he answered, she didn't run away.

'It's me,' she said, 'let me in.'

She jogged up the stairs, pulling on the handrail and reaching the second floor out of breath, her heart thumping in her ears. Tam stood in his doorway wearing just a pair of faded jeans with the zip half done up. He looked like he'd just got out of bed – hair all mussed and a confused look on his face.

Why did you have to be half naked? Kara thought. That skin was satin, dewy, bitable. She shook herself and met his eyes.

'Kara?'

'I have to speak to you.'

'It's kind of late.' Tam said quietly, but she was pushing past him already, swerving to avoid the half-open door of the bedroom and heading to the kitchen. Even dizzy and full of nerves, Kara knew she might be interrupting, and the last thing she wanted was a showdown with Judy. The kitchen should be safe.

She flicked the light switch on and walked to the sink, where she picked over the dirty crockery and found a glass that looked relatively clean.

'Did you just stop by for a drink of water, then?'

Tam was rubbing the sleep out of his scrunched up eyes. Kara stole a glance at him as she held the glass under the tap, wondering how he managed to look sweet and filthy at the same time. When his eyes cracked open and he looked at her, the heat of his brown eyes scorched her.

'I know everything went all ... wrong, with us,' Kara said. Now she was here, the desperate angst that had driven her out of the studio and along the night streets seemed to have suddenly evaporated. She was flailing around for words, for a way to broach the subject that wouldn't make her sound like a jealous bitch. Playing for time, she took a long sip of water and smacked her lips.

Tam had crossed his arms over his satin, dewy, bitable chest and now he gave her a cool look, raising one eyebrow as if to ask 'What have you got that's better than bed?'

'You saw ... You talked to Lina today,' Kara said.

The smile that curled across Tam's mouth almost broke her heart. 'Sure,' he said, kicking at the floor with his bare foot. 'We went for a drink. She's a pretty cool woman.'

'Oh, spare me,' Kara muttered before she could stop herself. She sighed and set her glass on the kitchen table with a firm knock. 'She's poison, Tam.'

'Ahhhh,' Tam said, nodding very slowly. 'I see.'

'No, Tam, you don't.' Kara shoved her hands in her hair and closed her eyes. She sighed again. It wasn't easy to concentrate with Tam standing there dripping bare-naked testosterone all over the linoleum. He wore his jeans slung low and every time her eyes dropped below his face they were instinctively drawn to follow the trail of hair that trickled over his belly and down to the wider tangle ...

'Do you have anything to drink?' Kara asked sharply. 'That works better than water?'

'I just finished the last beer,' Tam said, walking over to her and smiling right into her face. He dragged the tip of his tongue over his lips with a movement that made Kara's own mouth go dry. 'Want to taste?'

18

'I'm serious, Tam,' Kara said, putting her hands flat on his chest. She pushed him back with the equal and opposite force of what she really wanted to do, which was grab him and hold on to him hard.

'Please, listen to me,' she said. Meanwhile, she tried not to think about how warm and smooth he felt under her hands.

'You don't want me to see Lina. But you don't want to see me either. Can't have it both ways, Kara.'

Tam spun away from her and paced across the kitchen, stretching up to knit his fingers together behind his head. He rolled his neck as if to work out the kinks. 'Oh God,' he said, 'why do I fall for this crap. Every time.'

'I'm sorry,' Kara said. 'Tam, I'm sorry. I didn't want to –'

'You didn't want to what? Push me away? Or you didn't want to come round and screw up my life again?'

Tam walked up to the cupboard where a dartboard hung on the back of the door. He tugged a dart out of the cork and twisted it in his hands, smoothing the feathers back along the shaft. He's nervous, Kara thought. Seeing him this uncertain – cocky, irrepressible Tam – made her legs feel shaky. She leaned on the table and waited for him to talk.

'Lina's got a lot of ideas,' he said, testing the point of the dart against his thumb. 'She can hook me up with the right people.'

'She could,' Kara agreed. 'But she won't.' Lina's words rang in her head: *I could help him with that broken heart. And then shatter it all over again.*

Kara stared down at the table between her hands, looked at the knots in the wood and the scratches where knives had scored the surface. She'd rather break her own heart, she realised, than let Tam get hurt. So how did she end up in his kitchen acting the angel of doom, trying to crush all his hopes for the future?

'She's setting you up,' Kara said quietly.

'Right. And why would she bother?'

'To get to me.'

Tam smiled, but his mouth was bitter. 'Of course. It has to be about you, Kara.' He lifted the dart and feinted it at the board. 'Nobody else is allowed to take a shot at the limelight, nobody else is allowed to get any kicks. You couldn't give a fuck about anything but making sure you get everything you want. Admit it. You're just here because you're a selfish ...' He didn't finish the sentence. Instead, he hurled the dart at the board, let it clatter against the wire and fall to the ground.

He might as well have thrown the dart right at her. Kara shrank inside, felt bile rise in her throat and blood flood in her cheeks.

'No,' she said, 'no, you're wrong.'

He was standing half turned away from her, every muscle in his body tensed and hard, his hand opening and closing as if he was working at a cramp. She walked to him and reached out, tried to take his arm and soothe the restless flex of his fingers in hers. He went rigid when she touched him. Turned his face to the wall. His hand was a dead weight, his arm stiff and cold.

She wanted to shake him. Wanted him to fight. It would be easier to shout and scream than to feel him slip away like this. But Tam stayed solid and immovable, and when he spoke his voice was horribly calm. 'We said goodbye, earlier,' he said, 'and I wished you luck.' He shook his head a little. 'I want you to do well, I want you to go on and take everyone by storm.'

'Tam.' Kara tugged at his arm, leaned into him and laid her cheek on his chest. She could feel his heartbeat against her face, hear the deep tick of the blood pulsing through his veins.

'I still wish the best for you,' he said, his voice wooden. 'But I want you to do one thing for me.'

'Tam. Please trust me.'

He laid a hand on her hair, stroking softly from her head to the tip of a tress. When he reached the end, he pinched the strands in his fingers and tugged gently. Kara closed her eyes as he wound a handful of her hair in his fist. Pull, she thought, pull hard. Pull my head back and just kiss me.

'I want you to leave now and not come back.'

She didn't cry, but her eyes were suddenly wet, smudging against his skin and turning it slippery under her cheek.

'It's because of Mike,' she whispered, her voice hoarse.

Tam pushed her away, so that she had to scrabble for a chair behind her to steady herself.

'I really don't want to hear it,' he said. 'That's enough.'

'Lina's in love with Mike,' Kara went on, her voice rising until she hated the sound of it. Hated the light of the kitchen, the night outside, the record that was half finished and waiting for her with all the promises of her life riding on it, hated everything that surrounded her and that she'd ever imagined she might love.

'What the fuck,' Tam said, taking a step towards her, his face so intent that she was almost afraid. 'What the fuck would you know about love?'

Kara's hand flew to her mouth. She shook her head as if she could erase Tam's words just by refusing to listen. She would have to scream or cry or throw something, anything that would make her breathe again. Nothing was working. She was free-falling, drifting out into the night where it was so cold she couldn't feel anything at all.

And then he was holding her. His arms were circling her and hugging her tight to him, pressing her face into the warm cleft of his chest where the wetness of her tears was still shining.

The kiss was as bitter as the one they'd shared earlier, but this time it wasn't as tender. He crushed her mouth under his and it felt like he was going to devour her. She didn't even get a chance to kiss him back, just opened her mouth and let his tongue crowd between her lips. Tam surged forwards so that all Kara could do was bend in his arms and let him maul her.

The rude stiffness of his cock stuck out under his jeans and stuck into her belly, promising her more than he ever could have with words.

He was all over her, working at her body with firm hands, grabbing her flesh and squeezing it as though to test how strong it was. How much she could take. Her ass stung as he pinched a handful of it and swarmed with feeling as he rubbed the sore spot, tugging her hips up to slide her backwards onto the table.

He grabbed hold of her legs and pulled them wide apart so that she was balanced precariously on the edge of the table, shoved his hips roughly against hers so that she felt the ache in the tendons inside her thighs.

And she reached for him, responded to his strong touch with a force to match, dug her nails into his shoulders and pulled him down to kiss her more.

More. It was all that was running through her head, and for the first time in days, it was just the one word that mattered. *More*.

The chair toppled and hit the ground with a loud crack, but Tam didn't even flinch. He just kept kissing her, filling her mouth with his tongue and bruising her lips, licking and sucking as he mauled her clothes and tugged them aside. When he plunged his fingers into the hot slick of her pussy and drove them up to the knuckle, she cried out. Burrowing her face into the crook of his neck, she rocked back and forth onto his fingers, letting him corkscrew into her and begging for more.

She tugged at his jeans, trying to pull them down without unbuttoning them. They snagged and got stuck on his hard-on, so she yanked the buttons undone and reached inside to feel the scalding heat of his erection in her hand. His hips pumped against her and his foreskin slid under her fingers, his prick obscenely dark and hard, swelling to the thickness of a hammer handle. A kiss of moisture at the tip of his cock wet her palm and made her feel like crying all over again.

Taking him inside her was like the first time she'd fucked. It hurt a little and the feeling was so new, so strange and surprising that her mind went blank. She could feel only him in her, that wide, expanding fullness that surged and over-whelmed her, rendering her tongue useless and her body nothing but a magnet, something that only existed when it was moving or touching, being touched. He drove into her with such force and fury that her ass was lifted off the table.

She needed it again, instantly. The push and pull.

'Oh God,' she said, 'back, go again, m-more.'

Tam gave a rough laugh, his breath ragged. 'You're not making any sense,' he said, gripping her chin in his hand and pulling her mouth to his. 'So shut up.' His breath was hot in her mouth as he leaned in to kiss her again.

With his tongue churning in her mouth and his cock sliding in her pussy, Kara finally lost all sense of herself. There was only blackness, a burning blackness that twisted and surged within her.

As he slammed her against the polished wood of the table, bringing his body tight and close to hers, the water glass tipped over and fell. The shock of the cold splash on her flank made Kara inhale sharply, curl her hands into Tam's hips and dig her nails in. His body was all bone and hard muscle, so compact and tightly coiled. Underneath her, the puddle of spilled water sucked and splashed. The table was all slippery and Tam had to anchor her down to get deep inside her. Kara tipped her hips upwards, like a begging bowl.

She wanted to ask him to fuck her harder, but instead she smiled, bit her lip and narrowed her eyes. He knew what she wanted. Always did.

The smile fell from her face when they ground into one another. It was hard to breathe, being so close and so tightly joined. Every time Tam withdrew, it gave Kara that feeling of being at the top of a swing, the way the weight in her belly would rise and she'd be held in suspension, waiting for the next rush. She'd twitch her hips, pulling herself forwards to meet him, almost unable to stand the moment of emptiness without him inside her.

Tam gave a full stroke, stabbed her deep with his cock and held himself right up against her. His heart hammered in his chest hard enough for Kara to feel it against her own. She couldn't let him go this time, hooked her legs around his narrow hips and locked him in place, crossing her ankles behind him.

Like that, they swayed back and forth, feeling the subtle tremors of him inside her and their ribs swelling and emptying. Kara let herself soften as they embraced each other, the movement no longer violent but pulsing inside them like a bass note that you can hardly hear but feel in the soles of your feet.

'Oh God, I've missed you,' she whispered, the words spilling from her mouth as though someone else was talking.

'I told you to be quiet,' Tam murmured, thrusting his fingers into her hair and pushing her face into his shoulder.

There, tucked into the crook of his throat, she licked his skin and tasted the salt. 'You're the only one . . .' she said, whispering it into his skin, so quietly he might not have heard it over the hum of the kitchen strip lights and the faint traffic noise outside. But he squeezed her hard, and she felt him start to move again inside her, gathering speed that she knew would soon be out of his control.

Their movements grew larger as they tipped over the edge, not meaning anything any more and not slowing or relenting. Kara thought she could hear them, a pounding noise like the thudding of a tom-tom drum.

'The only one I trust,' she said, as Tam's rhythm increased and all the muscles in his body tensed to breaking point.

Three final thrusts, and he cried out, a ragged yell as coarse and blunt as an animal's.

Kara felt her own climax uncurl, explode out in fractals, spin its way from her sex to the tips of her fingers. Underneath them the table shook and the glass rolled in a drunken parabola to the edge of the table where it tipped and fell, crashing to the floor and bursting into hundreds of shards.

For a long minute, they held onto each other and didn't speak. Kara was shaky and her head swam, the fluorescent tube light overhead suddenly so bright it dazzled her. She felt like a newborn thing, tender and stiff, and clung to Tam wishing she could stay there for ever.

When Tam pulled away at last, his skin was stuck to her and the buttons of his jeans had left red indentations on her thigh.

'Marked,' she said, as she pointed to the little circles impressed on her skin.

'You're not the only one,' Tam said, pulling his trousers up and leaning down to touch his foot.

'Oh God,' Kara said. A chip of glass had cut his ankle, leaving a thin red line of blood across the gold of his skin.

'It's OK. It'll give me something to remember you by.' He licked his thumb and rubbed at the scratch.

'Better than a notch on your bedpost, I suppose.'

'Yeah,' Tam said, stretching up and catching her by the waist. He kissed her stomach, his stubble rasping at her. 'Especially 'cause I don't have any bedposts.'

'Right,' Kara said, squirming away from his ticklish kisses. 'Just that damn bare mattress.'

'I know.' Tam lifted his head to look up at her. His eyes were as clear as Kara had ever seen them. 'I don't have much. But what I do have is yours, Kara. If you want it.'

His lips were lush and full and still a little swollen from their rough kisses. His eyes were deep dark pools that she could drown in. He was on his knees in front of her, holding her tight, and letting her know how he felt. Tam wasn't the most eloquent of men, but Kara knew what he was offering.

Too much.

She squirmed, disentangling herself from his grasp. 'Come on, let me out,' she said when Tam held his arms fast either side of her. She pushed at his arms. 'There's water spilt everywhere. I'm sitting in a puddle.'

'Uncomfortable?' He had her pinned to where she sat on the table and he wasn't moving.

'Yes, Tam. It's cold.'

'It certainly is.'

She didn't meet his eyes. She knew what was there. But at last he moved away and let her struggle to her feet. He watched as she got up and tugged at her clothes.

'You can be so sweet. When you want something.'

Kara clutched her head. 'Please, Tam. Don't freak out. It's just –'

'You can't handle it.' Tam walked across the kitchen to the fridge.

'Watch your feet,' Kara murmured, looking at the broken glass on the floor.

Tam ignored her, pulled a beer out of the fridge.

'I thought you were out of beer?' Kara said.

'I lied,' Tam said, without missing a beat. 'I know how it goes.' He jammed the bottle on the side of the counter to pop the cap off. 'Now you've had your shag you'll be restless.' He took a swig. 'Scratch one itch and you switch to another.'

Kara shook her head. 'It's not like that –' she started.

'No?' Tam cut in. 'You're not that greedy? Not so selfish you'd crash your way to the top of the heap without giving a fuck whose heart you broke or who you left behind?'

His words were harsh, but he was calm. Almost as though he'd been expecting her to cut loose and run, Kara thought.

'Admit it, you'd screw over your best friend if it meant you got a taste of the limelight,' Tam continued, flicking the bottle cap towards the sink. Kara frowned. Something wasn't quite right about his speech. While Tam had a lot to criticise her for, he couldn't bleat about her trashing a friendship that had never really existed.

'Tam, we were never great friends,' she said. 'We fuck, we make music, we have a laugh. But you're not what I would call my best buddy.'

'I don't mean me,' Tam said.

'Then what are you talking about?'

His face looked almost sad, she thought. As though he knew his answer was going to hurt her more than he wanted it to. He looked down, slowly peeling the label off his beer bottle and speaking in a low voice. He sighed. 'Have you spoken to Ruby lately?'

It had been three days since she was home. In a way, the flat she shared with Ruby didn't even feel like it deserved the name any more. Not when there was a chance World War Three might break out as soon as she showed her face.

Kara stood outside looking up at her bedroom window. It was dark, but a light was burning in the living room and she could hear Ruby's music even from three storeys down. Leonard Cohen, wailing for mercy.

Not a good sign.

Tam was right. There were things she had to fix, even if it meant swallowing her pride. She climbed the stairs to the front door and slid her key into the lock, turning it with a resentful jerk. It didn't catch. She rattled it in the lock, but nothing happened. She swore to herself. Had Ruby changed the locks? Already?

She ran down the steps and walked backwards into the middle of the street, leaning back to watch for movement behind the blinds. As she lifted her chin up towards the sky a few prickles fell on her face, speckling her cheeks and eyelashes with cold moisture. The rain was starting. It was spitting now, but in the Glasgow winter a downpour was likely any minute.

If Ruby didn't let her in, where would she sleep? God knows what Mike would say if she turned up soaking wet at his flat. She'd run out on him in the studio, and he wasn't likely to welcome her. Tam had offered her his single bare mattress and she'd run from him as well. This is the last-chance saloon, Kara said to herself. With her hand shoved deep in her pocket, she crossed her fingers.

'Ruby, I hope you're in a good mood.'

19

'You can pack your stuff and get the fuck out.'

Ruby glared at Kara. There were sooty rings around her eyes and black smears on her cheeks and she was clutching a handful of crumpled tissues. Behind her, on the living-room stereo, Leonard chanted 'There are no diamonds in the mine' at top volume.

'Ruby, can you give me a minute –'

'To what? Apologise to me for dropping me from the band? Or for having my boyfriend's face in your crotch? Did you think we could have a laugh over it, or did you want to compare notes?' Ruby had to raise her voice over the music.

She turned round and kicked the stereo, sending the needle skidding over the record and making a horrible tearing noise. Leonard stopped singing and the two girls stood in a silence that warped nastily.

'You need to listen to me,' Kara said at last. 'Everything is all fucked up, but it's not what you think it is.'

'Oh no. Everything's just peachy.'

'How long have we known each other, Rube? That must count for something.'

'Apparently not.'

'OK.' Kara walked across the room to the cupboard in the corner. It was stuffed to overflowing with assorted junk – broken drumsticks, old tapes, paint tins. Kara stretched up to the top shelf and felt around for a moment. She grabbed a large dark bottle and pulled it down, turning it so that Ruby could read the label.

'Remember this?'

A flicker of recognition showed in Ruby's eyes. She sighed. 'How ironic. The special fizz.'

Kara nodded, brushing dust off the label. 'For when we hit number one, remember?'

'It was a joke anyway. We might as well pour it down the sink.'

Kara went to the kitchen and returned with a couple of empty teacups. She pulled up a rickety chair and held the bottle between her knees, twisting the wire cage off the neck. Ruby watched without speaking, her face grim and pale.

Kara pushed the cork carefully with her thumbs, coaxing it out of the bottle. The pop sounded ridiculous in the silent room – a celebration that had died before it began. She poured a cupful and held it out.

'Come on. Sit down.'

Ruby stood with her hand on her hip, tapping out a silent tattoo with her fingers.

'Please?' Kara asked, hoping she didn't sound completely pathetic.

Ruby reached out slowly and took the cup. 'You want to propose a toast?' she said. 'Or shall I just throw this in your face?'

Kara held her cup cradled in her hands as though it was warm tea instead of cold fizz. She took a sip and watched Ruby. 'We've known each other so long, Rube. The last thing I ever wanted to do was hurt you. It was just a –' The wine tasted sharp and cold in her mouth. She swallowed and started again. 'Me and Jon –' At the sound of his name, the pain that darkened Ruby's eyes made Kara wince.

'Don't,' Ruby said, 'you dare mention his name.' She whirled round and flung her cup across the room, where it hit the wall with a dull clunk and cracked in half. A pale splash streaked over the wall and dripped onto the floor. Ruby looked at the wall as though she wanted to pull it down with her bare hands. 'Jon is gone. History. Over.'

Her shoulders sagged then and Kara saw her crumple as though she were about to collapse.

'Ruby.' Kara jumped up and ran to her, putting her arms round her and holding on tight while she cried. Ruby didn't make any sound, but she shook hard and Kara was shocked at how small and fragile she felt.

'This is crazy,' Kara whispered into her hair. 'Nothing happened, Rubes.' She felt the other girl shudder. 'I swear to you.'

'Don't lie to me,' Ruby said, her voice low and bitter.

Kara sighed. She took hold of Ruby's wrists and pulled her back to look her friend straight in the face. 'I thought about it. OK, for one moment the very wrong thoughts ran through my head.'

'I saw the photos.'

'You saw pictures that Lina had set up. She did it on purpose, Rube.' Ruby struggled to free herself, but Kara held her fast. 'Tell me what you saw,' she demanded.

'Fuck you. Take your hands off me.'

'Not until you tell me what you saw in those pictures.'

Ruby was breathing hard. Her lips were drained of colour and her cheeks flushed a mottled red. She looked like she had a fever. 'I saw Jon with his face in your lap.'

Kara nodded. 'Yeah. They posed us like that.'

'His mouth was on you.' Ruby's voice was tight, as though she was being strangled. 'And you were holding his hair.'

Kara closed her eyes and swallowed.

'You were enjoying it,' Ruby continued. 'I could see it in your face.'

'Just a kiss,' Kara whispered. 'One stupid kiss.'

She dropped Ruby's hands and walked to the window. Outside the rain was falling steadily, wetting the streets and making them shine. The city was beautiful in the rain, Kara thought. Shame nobody ventured out to see it.

'So hate me,' she said eventually. 'OK. That's understandable. But don't punish Jon. He doesn't deserve that.'

'After he gave my best friend's pussy "one stupid kiss"?' Ruby spat the question out.

'He loves you.'

Behind her, Ruby was silent.

'Don't throw away what you've got,' Kara said quietly. 'Call him.'

As soon as she spoke she thought of Tam. She'd left him standing in his kitchen, eyes as black as tar and an atmosphere in the room that made her ache all over. What if she had stayed? What if she'd let him say the words that had been hovering on his lips?

'Oh God. Is it worth it?' she asked out loud, almost to herself.

Behind her, Ruby laughed softly. 'I miss him so much it makes me feel sick,' she said. 'I can't sleep, I can't concentrate on anything and the only person who could make it better is the one that hurt me in the first place.'

'I'll take that as a "maybe",' Kara said with a faint smile.

By 1 a.m., they'd finished the champagne. Ruby had pulled out her old indie records and they sat listening to Belle and Sebastian while they watched the rain.

'Looks like we're staying up all night then,' Ruby said, hugging the blanket that she had wrapped round her shoulders.

'Yeah, just a few hours till morning.'

'I don't think I want to see it.'

'Brand new day,' Kara said, pulling a face. 'We'll fix everything.' She waved her empty teacup at Ruby. 'And live happy ever after.'

Ruby raised an eyebrow. 'Right. Your big gig.'

'Yes. The mother of all concerts. Launch party.' She leaned back and closed her eyes. 'And the papers and the important people and the money.' She waved her hand vaguely.

'You're not making any sense.'

'Funny.'

'What is?'

'That's what Tam said. And then he kissed me. Hmm.' Kara frowned. Her hand moved slowly to her mouth and she pinched her lips between her fingers.

'OK,' Ruby said, 'I have a proposal.'

'What is it?' Kara was feeling drowsy, lulled into an exhausted reverie by the music and the wine and the familiar surroundings of her flat.

'I'll call Jon,' Ruby said, 'if you sort it out with Tam.'

Kara opened one eye and peered at Ruby. 'There's nothing to sort out,' she said sharply.

'Apart from the fact you're in love with each other and won't admit it?'

'What?'

Ruby shook her head. 'Oh, don't try to deny it.'

'It's good sex that's all.'

Ruby smiled. 'Sure. And you have good sex with plenty of people.'

'Yes.' Kara shrugged.

'And Tam's nothing special.'

'I don't –' Kara stopped. For a moment her mouth hung open but no words came out. She shook her head. 'We fight. All the time.'

Ruby played with the fringe of the blanket, pulling the threads straight against her knee. 'You're scared.'

'What would I be scared of?'

'That you might love him so much. That it might end up hurting.' Ruby looked closely at Kara. 'Like it is for me now.'

'Oh God! I know you're upset. So fix it! All you have to do is pick up the phone. He'll be here in ten minutes, Ruby.'

'Don't change the subject.'

Kara stood up and walked stiffly to the phone, pulled it up to Ruby and handed it over. 'Call him.'

Ruby stared at the receiver for a long moment, as if she was scared it was a dog that might bite her.

'Call him,' Kara repeated.

Ruby scowled and snatched the phone out of Kara's hands. She punched in a number and closed her eyes while she waited for him to answer. Kara noticed she was holding the receiver so tightly her knuckles were white.

Jon was there within an hour. When he knocked, Kara opened the front door with a limp smile. She knew Ruby was watching them both closely. Anything she said might be interpreted the wrong way.

'It's late,' she said, clumsily, 'I'm going to, uh, go to bed.'

Ruby barely glanced at her as she withdrew into her room, just off the living room, and closed the door.

She leaned against the door and looked at her bed, unmade and unslept in for days. After all the hours in the studio, the scenes in Mike's house and Tam's kitchen, her room looked very small and very empty. Somebody in the next room walked across the room and Kara listened to the footsteps and the floorboards creaking. She heard Jon's voice, low and broken, his words hard to make out.

Shaking herself, she walked to her bed and started to

undress. As she dropped her clothes on the floor, stepping out of her skirt and pulling at the buttons on her shirt, she heard Ruby, her voice rising louder and breaking off. Kara bit her lip.

She slid under the covers, shivering as the cold sheets touched her body. They were arguing now, Jon and Ruby's voices alternating through the door. Kara closed her eyes and pulled the pillow over her head, hoping the storm would pass soon.

It didn't work. Their raised voices reached her even through the pillow. What made it worse was when she heard her own name among the angry stream of words. Kara groaned. She'd have to be in the studio in a few hours. Another day of high-octane games with Mike and Lina, another day of singing her hardest and running on empty. It was like balancing on tight ropes, only the ropes kept swinging and twisting underfoot.

Don't look down, Kara told herself.

She gritted her teeth. She needed one thing to hold on to if she was going to get through the next day and the concert afterwards. The concert. She had to perform, tomorrow, in the biggest deal of her life. A thousand people. Her thoughts flailed about, mixing in with the sounds of Jon and Ruby ripping each other to pieces in the next room. She had no time. What if she fucked everything up?

Her feet slipped on the wire and she felt the great seething gap of empty air underneath her. Willing herself to concentrate, Kara recited song lyrics into her pillow:

> *'In the morning we're going to scream*
> *blue murder . . .'*

Tam. The song led her straight to him. The lines of his body, the way he curved over his guitar so intently. Just as he'd held on to her earlier that evening. All his attention focused on her, his eyes wide and dark.

When she remembered Tam's words the buzzing noise in her head grew so loud she couldn't think any more. In the next room Ruby shouted and furniture scraped across the floor. If they loved each other so much, why were they trying to rip it all to shreds? Jon and Ruby were *golden*. The two of them were always entwined, holding hands, practically joined at the hip. Onstage, they threw little glances at each other, secret smiles that nobody else understood. They played off each other. Made each other stronger. It wasn't right that they would break up. It didn't make any sense.

Could something that solid and certain really be torn apart so easily? One momentary slip, a meaningless mistake. And more Kara's fault than Jon's. She tried to burrow deeper into the bed.

Add it to the list, she thought. Just one more fuck-up in a week of bad judgements. She'd been so badly wrong. She'd let so many people down. And it was quite possible she'd crushed Tam's heart because she couldn't handle her own fears.

Outside there was a crash – an explosion that sounded like glass shattering against the wall. Instinctively, Kara jerked upright, her frayed nerves pushed to breaking point. As she listened to Ruby cry, sobs jerking out of her like a stuck record, something snapped. Kara got up, wrapped herself in the sheet and walked to the door.

Jon and Ruby turned at the sound of the door opening. Tear-stained and angry and hurting, they both looked wrecked. Just like I feel, Kara thought.

'This is insane,' she said. 'What are you doing?'

'Stay out of it,' Jon said, his usually soft voice harsh and bitter. 'You're not going to help.'

'Because it was my fault in the first place,' Kara said. She turned to Ruby. 'Your boyfriend is a beautiful man. He's sweet and quirky and talented. Yes, I did want him for a moment. I wanted to fuck him.' She pulled the sheet tighter around herself, gripping it hard. Ruby's expression was so cool it was unreadable. She took a deep breath. 'You're not the only one who wants him and you never will be. Didn't you ever notice the girls hanging round after gigs?' Kara gave a grim smile. 'I don't suppose you did. Because the two of you were so wrapped up in each other. For God's sake, so much in *love*.'

Ruby let out a long breath. 'It's not that simple, Kara.' She looked straight at her old friend. 'If you'd ever let yourself fall for someone you might understand that.'

Kara shivered. The room was cold and the first glimmer of dawn was already seeping through the blinds. Standing there wrapped in her sheet, exhausted and strung out with the wreckage of her friendships around her, she almost laughed.

'Maybe I have fallen for someone,' she murmured.

'It means more than just having good sex,' Ruby added spitefully.

'Yes.' Kara nodded. 'It means more.' She looked at the starburst stain on the wall from Ruby's earlier breakage and the smashed bottle lying on the floor in pieces. Her gaze caught on the ancient record player sitting nearby. It had taken a direct hit and the needle arm hung at an awkward angle. 'Shit, Ruby. We were going to play our first record on that,' she said.

'And then throw it out the window,' Ruby agreed. 'Like proper rock stars.'

'That's never going to happen,' Jon said. 'Probably won't even release it on vinyl anyway.'

Both girls turned to look at him.

Ruby frowned. 'Were you always this weird,' she murmured, 'or did I just not notice because the sex was good?'

Jon's eyes shifted uneasily, as though he wanted to smile but thought he might be walking into a trap.

'What do you think, Kara?' Ruby continued, keeping her eyes on Jon. 'Is he worth it?'

'I can't answer that,' Kara said.

'But you had a taste,' Ruby said quietly. 'Wasn't it to your liking?'

'I told you,' Kara said. 'Jon's a beautiful man.'

'You wanted to fuck him.'

'I . . . Ruby, don't be like this.'

'Be like what? You're right, I'm not the only one who'll ever want him.' Ruby walked towards Jon. His eyes were pleading with her and, as she reached out to touch his face, he swallowed hard. 'I just want to know that I'm the only one he'll ever want.'

'You know that –' Jon started to cry out, but Ruby moved her hand over his mouth and silenced him.

'I don't want to hear it,' Ruby said. She lowered her hand, dragging it over his chin so that his mouth pulled open. 'I want to see it.'

'What are you doing?' Jon asked, his voice nearly a whisper.

Ruby was tugging at his buttons, undoing his shirt slowly. She pulled it aside and bared his stomach. Kara tried to look away, but she was mesmerised. Not only by Jon's naked flesh, the white shock of his hairless chest and the rapid rise and fall of his ribs as he breathed, but by Ruby's deliberation. She was wrestling with the fly of his jeans now, tugging at it despite the look of panic and confusion that flashed across Jon's face.

'Ruby, stop,' he said, reaching up to grip her wrists. Kara turned her face away.

'I want to see you,' Ruby said.

In the half-light of dawn, the room was grainy and the tension made everything seem dreamlike. Kara heard the soft clicks as Ruby unbuckled Jon's belt and pulled his zipper down. Her movements were slow, but she didn't pause, and Jon seemed shocked into silence.

'Kara, come over here,' Ruby said. Her voice was calm, but there was an edge to it. Kara knew she couldn't argue.

She moved closer to the couple, closer to forbidden territory. With his clothes half undone, Kara felt that she was seeing Jon at his most vulnerable, the delicate fuzz of his pubic hair and the pale root of his cock just showing.

Ruby shoved her hand into the open maw of his trousers, gripping his cock in her fist. 'Kiss him,' she said to Kara, without breaking her gaze with Jon.

'Ruby this is crazy,' Kara said.

'I don't care,' Ruby said. 'It's what I need.'

Kara held back, wondering when the dreamlike atmosphere would turn into a nightmare.

'Do it,' said Ruby.

Jon didn't turn his head until the last moment, but when he did Kara saw the desperation in his eyes. His mouth was soft and yielded to hers, letting her bite on his lower lip and push the tip of her tongue between his lips. His body swayed and Kara could hear Ruby's breath speeding up. She kept kissing Jon, feeling the strangeness of it. It was almost like incest, she thought, not like kissing a lover.

Kara felt a tug. Ruby was pulling at the sheet she had wrapped around her middle. Silently, Kara dropped her arms and let the cloth be unwound. Ruby let it fall to the floor and pushed Kara closer. She was naked, inches from Jon, with her mouth fastened to his and his girlfriend's hand on her ass, kneading her flesh.

It was strange how she could feel so many things at once, Kara thought. Fear, arousal and guilt all mixed up in a cocktail shaker and poured down her throat.

20

'How does it feel?' Ruby asked, watching Kara's face closely. 'Do you like that?'

But when Kara broke away from Jon to answer her, she got a sharp slap on her bare ass. 'Don't stop,' Ruby said. 'I want to see this.'

Kara's head dropped, her gaze focused on the floor. The situation felt very wrong, yet there was such a charge surrounding their tight triangle that she couldn't pull away. With Jon half-undressed and Kara completely naked, Ruby was the one in control. Such a small girl, swamped in a baggy striped jumper that was fraying at the cuffs, with her hair wild and her face pale under her freckles. But the force of her will, her anger and burning intensity meant she took on the role of director just as surely as Mike. If not as calmly.

Ruby pushed at Kara, nudging her closer to Jon. Now there was only a sliver of air between the tips of her naked breasts and his chest. In the cold of the room her skin puckered with goosebumps and she was keenly aware of the heat of Ruby's hand resting on the small of her back.

At last she stumbled forwards, pressing up against Jon, feeling his shirt crushed between them and the smooth hot strip of skin where their naked bodies touched. Ruby's other hand was between them, curled round her boyfriend's cock, and her knuckles bumped against Kara's pubis as she manipulated Jon.

The dull pressure of Ruby's fist on the root of Kara's clit was a pleasant shock and part of Kara wanted to press harder against her friend's hand. Something held her back though, knowing that this was Ruby's game and she had to play by Ruby's rules.

'Down,' Ruby said, as if reading Kara's mind. 'Kneel.'

Kara slid to the floor silently, with Ruby's hand on her shoulder guiding her. When her face was pushed into Jon's crotch and she inhaled the sweet sharp smell of him, Kara closed her eyes. Ruby's fist was against her face now, feeding her the tip of Jon's cock. Automatically, she opened her mouth. The soft head of his cock rolled on her tongue, already stiffening so that she had to stretch her jaw to take it all in.

'Suck him,' Ruby murmured, working the length of Jon's shaft deeper into her mouth. Kara didn't need any encouragement. She sucked obediently, letting Jon swell and harden until he filled her whole mouth.

Her hands hung uselessly at her sides. She didn't even need to be tied to know that she could only touch what Ruby told her to. This was a kind of penance, with the floorboards hard under her knees and the cold air chilling her.

Above her, Ruby and Jon were lost in a deep kiss. Jon's knees were shaking and he made small meaningless noises in the back of his throat. Kara felt him twitch in her mouth and tasted a salty drop of pre-come.

'Stop,' Ruby said, pulling away and breathing hard. She looked at Jon, face screwed in a grimace as he tried to hold himself back.

'God, you look so pretty when you're going to come,' she said. 'But I'm not ready yet.' She looked down at Kara, still kneeling on the floor. 'I want to see you finish what you started. In the pictures,' she continued, 'you kissed her pussy. I want you to do it again.'

Kara met Jon's eyes. Guilt flared in his expression, his big doe eyes wide and uncertain. Was this a second betrayal? Even with Ruby's blessing the act felt dangerous.

'Ruby, you don't have to do this,' Kara said, even as she felt the pulse start between her legs.

Ruby tossed her hair back from her face. Her eyes locked on Kara's and she nodded. 'I don't have to. But it's what I want,' she said. Her voice was so soft and calm that Kara believed her.

Ruby yanked her head towards a rickety wooden chair by the stereo. 'Sit on there. And spread your legs.'

Kara walked to the chair and lowered her ass onto the cold seat. She positioned herself as Ruby had instructed. Sitting with her legs open and her hands on her knees, she felt more exposed than ever. The pose was completely obscene. The brush of her pubic hair didn't conceal the deep-pink bud of her clit and the wet gleam between her legs advertised quite clearly how turned on she was. No matter the rights and wrongs of the situation, she was aroused. She squirmed on the chair, the glimmer of shame only heightening the tension.

'Isn't this making it worse for you?' she whispered to Ruby.

To her surprise, the other girl smiled. 'What hurt was the secret,' Ruby said, leading Jon over to her. 'This time when he licks you, I'll be right here watching.'

Jon crouched in front of Kara and bent his head to her lap, following Ruby's instructions perfectly. Kara tried to keep herself still as she felt his warm breath on her. It was a replay of the photo shoot, she realised, only this time there was a backbeat of uneasy emotion. Should she feel less guilty because Ruby was directing the scene? When Jon's tongue flickered over her clitoris, Kara suddenly reached out for Ruby's hand.

'Hold still,' Ruby whispered. Jon was lapping at her now, his tongue blunt and clumsy. He could have been a dog drinking milk. The lips of Kara's pussy were slippery wet, and the soft licking made her melt as though she were dissolving from the centre outwards. There was nothing to hold on to, nothing hard to rub up against.

Kara clenched the muscles of her inner thighs, straining for something more intense, but Jon kept sucking her relentlessly, turning her whole body to jelly. She wanted his tongue to penetrate her, or his fingers, anything that she could tighten around.

'Don't let her come,' Ruby said. 'Just lick her softly.'

Instantly, Jon slowed his movements and lessened the pressure, so that he was dabbing gently at Kara's pussy with the tip of his tongue.

'Please,' Kara gasped, the little tickling touches infuriating her. She gritted her teeth and tried to push herself against the edge of the chair to feel something more solid than Jon's butterfly kisses.

'Stop it,' Ruby said, mildly, reaching down to pinch Kara's nipple. She squeezed hard, sending a burst of fabulous pain through Kara's body. From the smile that curled on her lips, Kara knew Ruby enjoyed the act. Somehow the intensity of the sensation soothed Kara's need and she sank back onto the chair to let Jon continue teasing her with his mouth. He darted his tongue in tiny circles around the mouth of her pussy, flicking at her lips and nudging the base of her clit.

Kara felt like she was falling, as though the tightrope was lurching underneath her and unravelling at both ends. She'd known when she and Jon got mixed up in that twisted photo shoot that what she was doing was wrong. Her desire had been the problem, that reckless shimmer of temptation that seemed to trip her up so often.

When Mike tied her up or held her down, he fixed her desire. Sharpened it to a point. The rules were clear and all she had to do was play along.

But now her best friend's boyfriend had his head buried between her legs, and everything was getting tangled and strange. The rules didn't make any sense any more. Kara's knees were shaking and the soles of her feet burned as Jon's head nodded between her legs and his tongue stroked her up and down. She thought she might slip and she wanted to shift in the seat, but any movement might make him stop.

'Please, Ruby,' Kara said. She knew everything was up to the other girl.

Kara's fingers were still twisted in Ruby's. The other girl shook her hand free and stuck it down her skirt. So she was turned on, Kara thought, before the next stroke of Jon's tongue sent her spinning. She clung to the seat of the chair, her hips lifting off it to meet Jon's maddeningly soft mouth.

'Please,' she called again, without really knowing what she was asking for. 'It's too much.'

In response, Ruby pulled her hand out of her skirt and thrust her fingers into Kara's mouth. The roughness of the gesture and the shock of it was what Kara needed, only in the wrong place. Still, she sucked on her friend's fingers, grateful for the sensation of having something hard crammed into her. They left a slight metallic taste on her tongue, foreign and dirty.

When Ruby pulled them away Kara gasped with the sudden emptiness. But she knew better than to complain.

'She says it's too much, Jon. You can stop now.' Ruby gave a dismissive toss of her hair as she spoke, as though she was shaking Kara off. For the moment, she seemed to have finished playing with her toys.

Her face set, Ruby slid down on the floor next to Jon and pulled him to her, kissing him with a violence that made Kara's heart pulse with envy. She sat on her chair, sticky and unsatisfied, watching Ruby and Jon tongue each other. The stiff pole of Jon's cock stuck out of his trousers and Kara knew that Ruby was going to take him right there in front of her.

If that was her revenge, it was perfect. Claim her boyfriend with Kara watching on helplessly, unable to protest or join in. Kara felt the pulse stringing her along, the want and the lack booming inside her. She opened and closed her hands, but didn't dare move to touch herself the way she wanted to.

Ruby and Jon were devouring each other, falling back onto the floor and pulling clothes out of the way. Kara envied them so badly it hurt. She was transfixed, every muscle in her body wound up and tense. Ruby straddled her man and drove down on his cock, crying out through gritted teeth. She shook her wild dark curls over her shoulder and rode him, her hips bucking hard against his.

On her chair, Kara rocked her hips from side to side, moving in sync with the couple on the floor. It was fascinating and bizarre at the same time.

'Oh God, Ruby,' Jon said, reaching up to touch her.

She grabbed his hands as they flailed in midair and pinned them back over his head. 'You want to come?' she whispered.

'Yes.'

Ruby smiled. Slowly, her movements stilled, until she was motionless over Jon's body. She held her face inches from his. 'No,' she said, her voice all velvet and treacherous. 'Not yet.'

Jon groaned. Ruby hushed him and stroked his face. She let her fingertips rest on his lips, very gently. Something in the touch was so intimate that it embarrassed Kara. It was as though by witnessing this one small gesture she was trespassing on territory even more private than the sex.

Jon kicked and tried to lift his hips. He turned his head to bury his face in Ruby's palm, whispering something into it that Kara couldn't hear. Ruby stayed where she was, unmoving, her thighs locked over Jon's hips.

'Come here,' she said.

Kara knew she was talking to her and she responded instantly, slipping onto the floor and crawling over to them. She felt like a beggar at a feast, waiting to see what Ruby would offer her – something to suck or something to put inside her. It really didn't matter. She hovered next to their entwined bodies, ready to do whatever she was told.

But Ruby had a different plan.

'Watch us,' she hissed, drawing herself up straight. She leaned back, arching her spine like a dancer so that Kara had a clear view. Her eyes were drawn to the point where their bodies joined, the cleft of Ruby's sex with Jon's cock buried inside it. When Ruby started moving again, Jon's shaft slid out of her, his skin dark and glistening with moisture.

'This is what you don't get,' Ruby said, breathing heavily. 'This is what you'll never have.'

She locked eyes with Kara as she swayed over Jon, rising up and sinking down again, over and over. Although Jon was pleading with her, she didn't increase her movements, just kept rocking at a steady pace. Her eyes were glittering, with arousal, but also with the thrill of victory.

'You get to be the star. You get to win the race.' She panted as she spoke. 'You get to win all the games, Kara. But you don't get Jon.'

'No,' Kara said, 'I wasn't playing games with you.'

But Ruby wasn't listening any more. Her body had curled over Jon's, her hands splayed on his chest while she ground her hips into his. Kara spread her hands on her knees and watched as Ruby rode Jon into the floor. She was locked out of their tryst, outside of the circle. Neither of them were even looking at her any more, just moving against each other, their movements perfectly in sync.

Kara could tell they were going to come from the way Jon's

fists were curling and Ruby's screwed-shut eyes. It wasn't a performance any more – their bodies were lost in each other. Ruby slammed down, fucking Jon with short swift thrusts.

Kara held her breath, listening to the broken cries and the short panting breaths. She watched as Ruby curled over and spilled across Jon, raining kisses all over his face and cupping his head in her hands. Words tumbled out of her mouth, softly whispered, something Kara couldn't quite hear. There was a catch in her voice, as though she was crying.

Jon repeated her words back to her and the two of them collapsed, sagged against each other. Ruby buried her head in the crook of her boyfriend's neck and breathed hard.

Sitting next to them, Kara heard the heartbeat in her ears match the pulse in her womb. It was the same restless rhythm that pushed her forwards every day – the one that she heard just before she went on stage or when she was about to have sex.

Jon stroked the small of Ruby's back, a rhythmic soothing touch that Kara suddenly longed for more than anything. She hugged herself tightly and listened to the birds singing outside.

Her phone woke her – the jangling ring tone screeching into her dreams and jerking her awake in seconds. She was in her own bed, wrapped in the sheet and lying flat on her stomach. Bright sunshine sliced through the curtains and the sky outside was a hard flat blue. Kara swore and scrabbled through her clothes for the phone. Mike's name showed on the screen, and when she caught sight of the clock displayed under his number, Kara winced.

He didn't even bother to say hello.

'Where the hell are you?'

Kara started to stammer an explanation, all the memories

of the long strange night flooding her brain and making her stomach twist. But she was still foggy and half asleep, and the words wouldn't come out right. She was sure she could hear Mike grinding his teeth on the other end.

'I don't want to hear it. I'll pick you up in twenty minutes. Be ready.'

Kara counted in her head. Three hours until the sound check. Four until the doors opened and the audience started filling the black cave of the Polar. Five hours until she had to be up there, with a new set of backing musicians and new songs, making her big impression on all the people who mattered.

She stumbled out of bed and stubbed her toe on the way to the bathroom. Lucky that adrenaline dulls the pain, she thought to herself as she jumped in the shower and blasted herself awake with scalding hot water. She thought about doing some vocal warm-ups in the steamy room, but decided she couldn't risk waking Jon and Ruby.

The night had been intense, weird and sexy – a strange way of making peace. But Kara still felt as if the ground underfoot was treacherous, that there were still pitfalls and tripwires between her and Ruby.

For some reason, after all the charged sex and emotional confrontations, the image that stuck in her head was of Jon and Ruby holding each other so tight they looked like they'd been carved from a single piece of stone.

Kara dressed in her lucky red Converse and favourite vest top – grey with neon flowers spilling across the chest and a deep-slashed neck. She pulled on a pair of jeans and shoved her make-up bag into a backpack, along with her song sheets. As a final thought, she packed the silver guitar pick Tam had given her for her twenty-first birthday. She tried not to think too hard about what Tam might be doing or thinking.

There was no time to call him or worry about Lina's threats.

In a few hours Kara would be on stage. This was what she'd been working towards for the past five years – nothing else could get in the way.

By the time she heard Mike's horn outside, Kara had drunk two cans of Coke and put on her brightest, reddest red lipstick. She clattered downstairs to his car and slid into the seat, barely getting the door pulled shut before he was pulling away from the kerb.

'Morning,' Mike said brusquely. His normally calm face was scored with deep lines and his eyes were flashing deep violet. 'Good to see you.'

Kara ignored the sarcasm in his voice. She looked out of the window at the fruit shops and cafés that were passing as they sped down Great Western Road. Mike ran two red lights and took the corners way too fast – swearing bitterly when the car got snarled up in the Saturday traffic.

Kara watched a couple walking over Kelvin Bridge, the man with his arm slung over the woman's shoulders, their heads turned in to snatch a kiss.

'Is Lina at the venue?' Kara asked, trying to keep her voice even.

'She'll be around,' Mike said, keeping his eyes on the road. 'Why?'

'No reason,' Kara said.

'Wherever the action is, you'll find Lina,' Mike muttered.

Kara threw him a curious glance. Was there more to his mood than stress and the fact she'd run out of the studio the night before? 'You fell out?' she asked, before she could stop herself.

Mike crunched the gears as he pulled up at a junction and braked hard. 'What else is new,' he said, almost to himself. Then he twisted in his seat to look at Kara. 'We've been up most of the night trying to set up this gig.' His gaze tripped over Kara as if hunting for clues. 'While you've been up to God knows what.'

'I had stuff to sort out,' Kara answered, pulling at her fringe.

'What stuff? With whom?'

The question, or the fierceness of Mike's tone, startled her.

The light had changed to green, but Mike sat motionless with his hand on the gear stick, waiting for her to talk. Behind them a taxi sounded its horn.

Kara opened her mouth to give him a choice reply, but bit her lip when she saw his face. Something told her this was something she really, really didn't want to get into.

21

Polar was a very different place during the day. The whole place reeked of pine disinfectant layered over the lingering smell of stale beer, and the black walls were scuffed and shabby. Without the lighting and the crowds, and with the pulsing background music silent, the place echoed like an empty gym hall. Stagehands and engineers shouted to each other across the stage, wires lay coiled on the floor and bursts of feedback crackled at random through the speakers.

Kara followed Mike through the warren of corridors behind the stage, glancing through half-open doors and trying to keep her bearings. Backstage spaces always disoriented her – windowless, functional labyrinths with the feel of an engine room. There was always the sense that everything was humming with purpose, counting the hours until show time. Mike knocked on a white door and tried the handle. It didn't budge.

'Shit,' he muttered, wheeling round and letting Kara see the tic of irritation that jerked in his cheek. 'The instruments are in there. Lina has the key.'

Kara took a deep breath and exhaled through her mouth. She could tell the tension was getting to Mike. Before a gig, she and Tam would be wound up and brimming with nerves, ready to spark a fight or a fuck at any moment. She found sex usually helped take the edge off. But they had hours to go yet – and Mike looked like he was suffering from something worse than stage fright.

'Is everything OK?' she asked, unsettled that Mike wasn't as cool and in control as he always seemed to be.

He bit his lip. 'It's been a long time,' he said.

'Since you played on stage?'

Mike sighed. He rattled the door handle again, as if it might magically unlock itself. 'Go and find Lina,' he said, abruptly. 'Get the key and bring it back here.'

He kept his back to Kara as he spoke and she hovered for a moment waiting for more information.

'Go on!' Mike said, and Kara spun on her heel and jogged back the way they'd come, retracing her steps until she emerged in the auditorium. She caught sight of the hired guitarist sitting on the edge of the stage.

'Seen Lina?' she called, not willing to say more to him than she absolutely had to. Every time he saw her, Eric's face took on a contemptuous leer.

Now he sat back and spread his legs wide, giving Kara a greasy smile. 'Who wants to know?'

Kara nearly spat on the floor. 'Just tell me where she is,' she said, putting her hands on her hips.

'Surely Mike doesn't want to see her,' he continued. 'Ever again, I'd have thought.'

'What are you talking about?'

Eric frowned. 'Of course, you disappeared last night. That did not go down well. Want to hear what happened next?' He beckoned to her, patted the stage next to him. 'Come and sit down, I'll tell you everything.'

Kara swallowed. She edged closer to the stage, keeping Eric at arm's length. 'So spill.'

'What, you don't want to cuddle up next to me?' Eric raised his eyebrows.

'Eric. Tell me what happened,' Kara said through her teeth.

'OK,' Eric sighed. 'Let's just say – "hell hath no fury". After you left, Mike freaked out. He shouts at Lina –'

'And Lina shouts back, no doubt,' Kara filled in, impatient to hear the rest. 'Then what?'

Eric screwed up his face and winced. 'It wasn't pretty. Lina tells Mike he's going to mess it all up like he did the last time.'

'What, the concert?'

'Yeah. Hasn't played for six years. But she also said ...' Eric stopped talking and pulled at a thread on his jeans.

Come on, Kara urged him silently. She slid a little closer and put her hand on his knee, forced herself to smile at him. 'Said what?'

Eric looked at her. His eyes were as wide as a startled animal's. Underneath that sleazy exterior, Kara realised, he was just an insecure kid. She squeezed his thigh hard.

He cleared his throat and kept talking. 'She said you were using him. That you didn't need him. And that you had probably gone to, uh ... to get together with Tam.'

'What did Mike say?'

'He just went really quiet. And then he left. Lina went after him,' Eric said. He shrugged. 'They drove off in his car. Left us standing about like spare parts. So we packed up our gear and called it a night.'

Kara realised she was gnawing at her bottom lip. Had Mike listened to Lina's outburst? Would he care? Maybe she was using him. It seemed everybody had marked her down as a selfish bitch lately. She slid off the stage and wandered towards the ticket desk, turning things over in her mind.

Lina was crouched over the desk, phone clamped to her ear, laughing with that smoke-and-gravel voice she had in the mornings. Kara waited at a discreet distance, trying to make out what the conversation was about. Whoever she was talking to, Lina was turning on the charm.

'Well, just make sure you do,' she said, playing with a lock of her hair. 'OK. See you then.' She looked up and caught sight of Kara, hovering behind a pillar. Her expression slipped for a moment, and then she nodded. 'Bye, Tam,' she said sweetly, and folded the phone slowly shut. 'Kara. What is it?'

'That was Tam? How is he?' Kara asked. The blood buzzed in her ears and she had a crazy impulse to wrench the phone out of Lina's hand.

Lina stared at her for a moment and raised an eyebrow. 'What do you want, Kara?'

Of course, the way Lina played her games included never giving a straight answer. Keep cool, Kara told herself, although her heart was squeezing. 'We need the key for the dressing room,' she said.

Lina plunged a hand into her pocket and pulled out a keyring. She held it out, dangling it on the end of her fingertips. Kara reached for it, but Lina swung it aside, leaving her hands to close on empty air.

'You failed,' Lina said.

Kara noticed the other woman's lips were rimmed with colour but pale in the centre, as though she'd chewed off the berry-coloured lipstick that was usually so perfectly applied.

'Failed at what?' Kara asked. She wondered if Lina and Mike had been up all night like she had. If they'd been together.

'Better pay special attention to your lover today,' Lina said, her voice as brittle as spun sugar. 'He missed you last night.'

'Mike?' Kara asked, noticing how the name made Lina flinch.

'Of course, Mike,' she said. There were dark shadows under her eyes, grey and heavy. 'It seems you didn't break the spell. Despite our deal.'

'I left last night, you saw me. I didn't spend the night with him,' Kara said.

'I know,' Lina said bluntly. 'But I did.' She looked up at Kara and her eyes were as hard and grey as granite. 'It should have been just like old times. But no matter how tightly he closed his eyes and tried to pretend, it didn't work.' She looked down blankly at the papers strewn over the desk in front of her. 'Even when he was in me. I knew he was thinking of you.'

Kara swallowed. She couldn't quite picture self-assured, commanding Mike missing her. She could imagine the other stuff. He and Lina playing out their power games. Fucking like they were fighting. She couldn't imagine him pining for anyone.

'Hard to believe, isn't it?' Lina continued. 'I suppose you'd never have guessed it. Too wrapped up in your own dramas.'

Kara remembered what Tam had said to her the night before. Lina echoed his words almost exactly. Was she really that oblivious?

'I know him better than you. I can tell when he's faking it,' Lina said. She took a deep breath and leaned forwards over the desk, covering her eyes with her hand. 'Better get moving. You're on stage in –' She flicked her wrist and looked at her watch '– just over five hours. Make the most of it,' she said, dropping the keys on the table with a loud clatter.

'Is Tam coming tonight?' Kara asked, leaning forwards to snatch the keys.

'Yes.'

'Lina. Please.' Kara never thought she'd find herself asking Lina for anything. Her voice shook a little. 'Please leave him out of this.'

Lina turned away from her and started leafing through a list of numbers she had printed out on the desk. 'I'm busy, Kara. Got to make sure everybody turns up tonight.' She lifted her gaze and the intensity of it made Kara take a step backwards. 'Got to make sure it's a big success,' she said. 'Don't I?'

When she got back to the dressing room, Mike was slumped on the floor with his head in his hands. Kara slowed as she approached him.

'I got the key,' she said. Mike didn't move. 'Is everything OK?' Kara asked, almost scared to hear his answer.

Mike laughed. In the narrow corridor the sound bounced back flat and hollow. He looked up at her. He was smiling, but there was no light in his eyes. 'I don't know why I'm worried,' he murmured. 'Nobody would even notice if I sat there and knocked out Stravinsky's "Piano Rag".' He stood up and leaned towards Kara, caught hold of the hem of her top and tugged it down to expose the cleft of her breasts. 'That's all they want to see.'

Kara frowned and pulled away. 'They're coming to listen to the music. What else have we been busting our arses for?'

He laughed again, shaking his head so his hair flopped forwards. 'Don't be ridiculous. We're selling them you, Kara. Not music.' Mike sighed and pulled himself up to stand above her. 'All we need to do is provide a little background noise.' He reached round to cup her buttocks with his hand and squeezed. 'Face it, Kara. You're a product with sex written all over it. Nobody gives a damn whether you can sing or not.'

Kara tried to pull away. She reached round Mike and slid the key into the lock, all the time keenly aware of him watching her. Her shoulders were pulled up high and she was gulping air. She flung the door open and made for the bathroom, with Mike following right on her heels. He grabbed her shoulder and pulled her up short.

'Oh come on. You win the jackpot, Kara! After tonight you'll have the world at your feet. All the glory. Silver and gold. What more could you want?'

She spun round to face him. 'It's not enough,' she said, searching his face for some glimmer of understanding.

'Everything you've ever wanted is not enough?' Mike said, raising an eyebrow. 'Now that is breathtaking ambition.'

He licked his lips. Kara noticed the gleam in his eye and knew what was coming next.

'I know what you need,' he said, running his thumbs up and down her bare arms. 'To scratch that itch.'

His hand danced over her shoulder and traced a line across her throat, curling round her neck. He buried his fingers in her hair and held on tight, pulling her head back slowly.

'It's hard when your dreams come true, isn't it?' he murmured.

Kara knew she didn't have to answer the question. Mike was playing with her again. But this time something had changed. When his free hand flicked at the neck of her top, she noticed his fingers were unsteady, as though he'd been drinking.

'All the things you had to do to get where you are. They come back to haunt you, don't they?'

Kara closed her eyes. She thought of Ruby and Jon, of the fierce anger in her friend's eyes the night before. She thought of Tam kneeling on the floor in front of her, unable to ask her straight out what she knew he wanted to.

'You have to learn to ignore the jealousy, Kara.'

Mike let go her hair, took her top in both hands and tugged it. The slashed neck tore with a faint rasp as Mike ripped it to her waist. Kara stumbled backwards, but Mike had her tethered by the ragged handfuls of fabric. When she swore at him, he let go and the two tails fell back on either side of her exposed chest.

'You have to make sacrifices,' Mike said, giving her a half-smile. Kara held herself stone still. Mike reached out to trace the lace edge of her bra as though he were drawing patterns on the skin underneath.

'And what have you ever sacrificed?' she asked, keeping her eyes fixed on his. 'Apart from your conscience, that is?'

He nodded. 'Touché.'

Idly, he stroked the curve of her breast, sweeping his fingers over her nipple and scraping the cloth gently with his blunt nails. Kara itched under his touch, but still she kept herself motionless.

'I've sacrificed more than you know,' Mike said, his voice very soft. He bent his head to her breast and sucked at her through her bra, so that the damp fabric clung to her nipple and chafed against it, stiffening in the heat of his mouth.

Kara knew that someone might walk in at any moment. She also knew the risk would only fuel Mike's desire. A picture of Eric bursting through the door to find Mike suckling on her tit flashed into Kara's head and she twisted away. Her nipple was wet and stiff from his sucking and her legs were already going weak. God, he knew how to manipulate her.

'I can't do this,' she said, pulling her top across her chest and holding the torn fabric close to her skin.

'Crap. I bet you're already soaking,' Mike said, starting towards the button of her jeans. Kara took a step backwards and shook her head.

'I mean, the show. The record. The fuckable star with a forgettable soundtrack.' She waved her hand vaguely to describe what she meant. 'Everything. It all feels wrong.'

Mike looked at her shrewdly. 'Pre-performance jitters,' he said, rolling his eyes. 'Now don't be ridiculous.'

'I'm serious.'

'So am I,' he said, pacing across the room to a small fridge and pulling it open. 'It's far too late to get cold feet, Kara. I've given you what you wanted. Everything I promised.'

'I ... I've changed my mind,' Kara said. Her voice sounded like a whisper in a wind tunnel, so small and frail it could be blown away.

'No dice.' Mike shook his head. 'You'll be up there tonight. You will shake your arse to the requisite beat, you will flash your tits and you will knock the audience dead.'

'I can't.'

Mike pulled a bottle of Stolly out of the fridge and searched for glasses in the cupboard. He tore the lid open and poured a tumblerful of clear oily vodka.

'If you're not up to singing we'll just dub a recording over the musicians,' he continued. 'You can mime.'

'No!'

He took a long swig of his drink before he answered. 'Like I said, Kara. It's far too late to back out now. You know the deal. Do you want me to make some clichéd remark about how the show must go on?'

He approached and pulled her hands away from her top, forcing them to her sides. 'Just do exactly as I say and everything will be fine,' he said. He plucked at the top button of her jeans. 'Take those off,' he added, nodding at her while he took another sip. His fingers made wet smudges on the side of the glass.

Half of Kara wanted to knock it out of his hand and scream him out of the room. There was a storm thrashing inside her, a gathering, tumbling sensation that she'd never felt before. Yes, there were nerves before a show. But that was light, jangly electric excitement. This was different. Dark and sour.

She was on the tightrope again, scrabbling at thin air. Underneath her a thousand people swarmed, eyes glittering in the darkness. And instead of the rush of anticipation, Kara was aware of a rising seasickness, the sensation that the crowd only wanted to rip her apart and consume her.

Mike waited for her to carry out his instructions. He faced her with the cool certainty that she would do as she was bid, watched her with that mild curiosity that made her hair stand on end.

'Why do you want me?' Kara asked.

Mike frowned at her like he didn't understand. 'The usual reasons. It's not that complicated, Kara.' He thrust a hand into his pocket and cocked an eyebrow at her like she was mad for even asking the question.

A week ago, Kara would have let him get away with that answer. She would have felt unsettled and aroused by his casual rebuttal, and then she would have done as he'd asked and stripped for him. The force of his certainty and the focus of his desire had been blinding.

But today, she needed more than clever replies. She waited.

'I always wanted you,' Mike said bluntly.

Kara shook her head. 'No. No, you enjoyed that I lusted after you. I think you liked the power it gave you. But there was no way you would have made a move back then.'

'You were my student.'

'That had nothing to do with it.'

Mike turned and paced, taking a couple of gulps of his drink. Kara watched the way he moved, agitated but still self-possessed. He was fraying at the edges, Kara thought, but he still had that mesmerising quality.

'You only want me now because of this,' she said, waving her hand at the dressing room. 'Because of where I'm going.'

Mike sighed impatiently. 'For God's sake. Yes, your ambition, talent, it's sexy. Does it really matter?' He threw himself into an armchair and watched Kara over the rim of his glass. 'I don't see what the problem is.'

Silently, Kara pulled open the buttons of her jeans. Mike lay his head back and watched. She slid out of her trouser legs and peeled off her knickers, dropping the clothes in a pile on the floor.

'Good,' Mike said, quietly. 'That's a good girl. Now come over here and kneel down.'

Kara ignored him. She pulled her ripped top over her head and reached behind her back to undo her bra. A shadow passed over Mike's face. He opened his mouth to speak, but Kara lifted a finger to her lips.

'Shh,' she said, tugging her bra off and dropping it on the pile. Naked, she stood in front of Mike and let him look at her.

'What is this?' he asked. 'You want me to give you marks out of ten?'

'This is me,' Kara said. 'No lights, no audience, no background music.'

Mike shifted in his seat and turned his head away. It was cold in the windowless room, and Kara shivered a little.

'Not a star, Mike. I'm just a singer in a band. That's what I choose to be.' She walked over to the chair and stood close enough for him to reach out and touch her. 'Is this what you want?' she asked. 'Is it enough for you?'

He held his glass in his lap and turned it, shaking the liquid so that it sloshed against the sides. 'You really do pick your moments, Kara,' he said. There was a note of sadness in his voice.

'I need to know,' she said.

'If I want you.'

'If you want me.' Kara nodded. 'Or if you're just trying to fix something that went wrong a long time ago.'

22

Mike didn't answer. He stayed silent for so long that Kara began to sweat. She shifted warily, somehow feeling more naked as time went on. Thoughts screamed silently in her head – what was she doing? Risking everything, ruining all her chances? Someone could burst through the door at any minute, and Kara knew she would be more ashamed at being caught like this, laying herself bare, than she would if they walked in on her and Mike screwing.

At last, he dipped his forefinger into his glass and wet the tip. He lifted his finger and reached out to touch her chin, using it like a paintbrush to draw a line down her body. The cold trail burned from her throat to her lower belly, shining against her pale skin and the sweet pungent smell of the spirit prickled in her nose. He caught her wrist and held her steady, dotted a finger on the veins as if anointing her with perfume. Kara curled her fingers; this was different from the games they'd played before.

Mike's eyes didn't have the glowing intent that she was used to. If she didn't know him better she would have said he looked a little sad. He was stroking lines up her inner arm and down the side of her breast very deliberately. As though he was carrying out some ritual with a hidden, secret meaning. The alcohol left a sweet burn as it evaporated. He drew a line from her stomach to her pussy. When he dabbed at her clit with his finger, she flinched.

'Don't worry,' he murmured. 'It won't hurt.' He pinched her little bud between his fingers and looked up at her.

Kara felt the cold wet vodka on her skin and the intense heat that centred in her pussy. Mike didn't caress her or play with her, just trapped her tender hood lightly in his hand.

'Is it burning yet?' he asked, a dull curiosity in his eyes.

As he spoke, a tingle blossomed on her clit, the nerve endings suddenly alive and urgent with heat. Kara inhaled sharply. The warmth was spreading through her pussy and, for a moment, she panicked.

Mike caught the worry in her eyes and laughed. His fingers pressed, still, against her. 'It will pass,' he said. 'Once the spirit has evaporated. Highly volatile, alcohol.'

Kara felt the beat in her womb again, the hunger for sex that Mike knew so well how to evoke. All she had to do was rock forwards and rub herself against his fingers. If she bore down just an inch, she'd feel the relief that she'd been denied and the light burn on her clit would transform into scorching pleasure.

'You haven't answered me,' she said, her voice strangling in her throat.

'Remind me.' Mike said, 'What did you want to know?'

Kara was balanced so precariously. Her body was connected to Mike through one slight touch and her thoughts see-sawed back and forth between what she wanted and what she was scared of. It would only take one small movement to tip her into chaos.

'Do you want me?' she said, the question sounding ridiculous even as it escaped her mouth. She shook her head. 'No. This is crazy.' She clutched her hair in handfuls and swore.

Mike waited, holding her pinched between his fingers as lightly as if he were touching something breakable.

Kara took a deep breath and blew it out through her mouth, exhaling until her whole body softened. She opened her eyes and looked straight at Mike. 'You won't ever tell me, will you?' she said. 'You'll keep me hanging for ever.'

Mike licked his lips very slowly, making Kara imagine how it would feel if he were to lean forwards and do the same to her.

The burning that had played across her pussy had retreated inside her now, the heat fading into a low steady want. It was the same need that had been tormenting her for the past night and day.

Sex wouldn't fix it. Kara realised with a burst of sadness that Mike wouldn't fix it either. He might play with her for a month or a year, so long as she was a bright shiny new star, but eventually the glitter would wear off and he'd want some new kick.

'Not enough,' she said quietly, shaking her head. She took a step backward and left him with his hand held out. 'I'm sorry Mike.'

At that moment, the speaker above the sink crackled and burst into life. The sounds from the stage intruded noisily into the room: Eric tuning up, feedback warping in a high-pitched whine. Mike withdrew his hand like he'd been scalded, looking at her with cold disgust. She'd expected to be upset, but instead Kara's whole body sagged with regret and relief.

At last, everything that had tied her to Mike had come undone. There was nothing but a dull gleam in his eyes, full of bitterness and anger. Kara realised that even though it was a day too late, she'd eventually done what Lina asked. Three hours before she was due on stage with Mike, she'd broken the spell.

The sound check was over in a swift forty minutes. The session musicians ran through the songs with swift, businesslike ease and Mike seemed utterly focused on the keyboard. He didn't look up at Kara once and barely spoke a word as he played each melody, smoothly and impeccably.

Kara sang without thinking. She fixed her gaze on a point somewhere in the dazzling white blindness of the stage lights and repeated the lyrics as if she'd forgotten what they ever meant. She was perfectly in tune and didn't miss a beat.

When the sound engineer gave them a thumbs-up and flicked the speakers off, she stood on stage for a moment, looking into the fathomless black space of the auditorium. Even when empty, the place seemed to hold the ghost of an audience, the expectations and the hunger of a thousand invisible people.

Lina pulled her out of her reverie, clapping her hands loudly. 'Less than two hours, Kara, move it.' She waved Kara backstage and led her along the corridor.

Kara had stitched her top together with a couple of safety pins. She stood picking at a loose thread where the fabric was fraying and looked at Mike's empty glass, discarded on a table. Someone walked along the corridor, whistling loudly, and she turned with a sudden rush of irrational hope. The engineer winked at her through the open door and carried on past.

'Break a leg,' he said, and Kara tried to smile at him.

Around her, everyone was moving faster as the concert approached, but she seemed to be in the eye of the storm. She walked to the mirror and looked at herself critically. Everything rested on her now. On the body reflected in the blue-tinted glass.

Lina swept in without knocking, carrying the plastic-wrapped rubber dress over her arm. She hung it on a dress rail and smoothed the plastic down. Kara looked at it blankly.

'Time to change,' Lina said, pulling a packet of cigarettes out of her back pocket. 'You all set?'

Kara nodded.

'What's the matter, got cold feet?' Lina asked. There wasn't an ounce of sympathy in her voice. 'I don't blame you.' She turned the cigarette lighter over in her hands. 'Don't let Tam worry you,' she said. 'He's my concern now. My next project.'

'He's a good man,' Kara said quietly. 'What difference will it make to you? To break him?'

Lina shrugged. 'I have to take consolation where I can get it,' she said. 'And right now it looks like revenge is all I've got left.' She gave Kara a brittle smile. 'You'll learn,' Lina said. 'It's a treacherous business. You can't trust anyone.'

As Lina swung round to leave, Kara called to her. 'Lina.'

The other woman halted in the doorway but didn't turn round.

'Why are you here, if you hate me so much? You're the one turning this into a big event. The newspapers, the big fancy venue, all the publicity. Why even bother?'

Lina stood with one hand on the door frame. 'It's my job. I don't back out of things,' she said abruptly. Then her eyes narrowed with a sly look, and her next words were as sweet as syrup. 'Besides, launching you into the music business is just what you deserve.' Lina tapped the door frame lightly. She turned to smile at Kara. 'You're going to be a star' she said. 'Do you have any idea what that really means?'

'It means I get to sing in front of a thousand people.' Kara shrugged. 'I get to do what I love.'

Lina shook her head. 'No. It means you dance to whatever tune you're told to.' Her eyes glowed the colour of malachite. 'Congratulations, Kara. You just sold your soul. Remember to shake your money maker now.'

Lina's footsteps echoed softly along the corridor as she walked away.

Kara ran through the corridors to the fire exit and jammed the handle down to spring the wide red doors. Outside, the streets were busy with people and the rain had washed the pavements to a slick sheen. Music blasted out of open cars as she turned to see the queue of people waiting outside Polar – a long line of strangers moving one by one towards the ticket desk.

Kara scanned the line frantically, looking for familiar faces. A few people called to her, but she didn't recognise them and moved on. In the cold of the night her scrappy top with the gaping holes and the safety pins provided no warmth at all and she shivered as she walked past the chattering crowd. Whispers broke out as she walked down the street, but Kara didn't hear them. At last, she saw who she was looking for and rushed towards him.

'Tam!' He was looking at the ground while Judy held on to his arm and chatted to him. His eyes swam up in response to her call and narrowed when he saw her.

'What are you doing out here?' he said, rocking back on his heels. 'Shouldn't you be inside getting styled or something?'

Kara gripped his arm. 'There's no time,' she said. Hesitating, she nodded at Judy and tried a small smile. 'I just have to talk to Tam,' she said. 'For a moment.'

'Be my guest,' Judy said and released Tam with a little shrug.

Kara pulled him to the edge of the pavement, where they were buffeted by passing couples and close to the stream of traffic. 'Lina invited you,' she said.

'I'd have been here anyway.' Tam said. 'But yeah, VIP tickets and free drinks don't hurt.'

Kara wanted to shake him. Instead she squeezed his arm hard. 'Tam, do you trust me?'

A taxi rushed past and Tam pulled Kara away from the gutter. His jaw flexed as he looked steadily at her. 'I used to,' he said. 'Even when you were a raving bitch you were still safe, you know.'

'Do you trust me right now? Right here?'

Tam pressed his lips together as though he had a sour taste in his mouth. 'It's doubtful, Kara.'

Kara blinked hard. She was about to lose him for good. Behind them, the queue was surging forwards as the doors opened, and Judy called out. Tam shook Kara's hand from his sleeve and started to pull away.

'I don't want anything from you, Tam,' Kara said as he moved away. 'I just want to know that you'll be in there, somewhere. Looking out for me.'

Tam glanced over his shoulder as he joined the queue. 'Always,' he said, bluntly, taking Judy's arm and moving forwards.

Kara watched as he disappeared into the tide of people pouring slowly into the doorway.

Suddenly, she felt very cold and naked out there in the street among the traffic and the shouting crowds. She turned to slip through the open fire exit and back to her dressing room.

Mike was waiting for her when she got there. He wore a white shirt and his dirty-blond hair was combed back so that his cheekbones and the sculpted lines of his face stood out. Standing in the centre of the room, he held himself tall and straight. Kara recognised the dark magnetism – the fascinating presence that had first made her fall for him.

'You're not dressed yet,' he said as she came in. He glanced at his watch and swore. 'The support's on already. You have half an hour.'

'Where's Lina?' Kara asked, brushing Mike's instructions aside with a wave of her hand.

'She'll be out front taking care of the VIPs,' Mike said. He frowned. 'Leave it to her. None of that is your concern – all you need to do is pour yourself into that dress and be ready to perform.'

Kara nodded. 'Yeah. Only I need Lina to give me a hand.'

'For God's sake, I can do up your zip for you.' Mike shoved a hand in his pocket and cocked his head on one side. 'I'm sure I can manage to keep my hands off you. If you're feeling coy.'

'It's not that. It's just that it takes a special technique, you know, with the thing being so delicate.'

'I can be delicate,' Mike said, his voice loaded with meaning.

It almost made Kara hesitate, remembering just how well he could temper his touch. How he knew just when to give pleasure and when to withhold it, how to work her up into mindless delirium. He was skilled. And she was tempted.

She thought of him drawing ice-cold lines over her skin and the dark bitter look in his eyes, and shook herself. She set her mouth in a stubborn line and repeated her demand. 'I need Lina.'

'You can't get away with pulling the diva act just yet, Kara.'

She didn't answer, just crossed her arms and stared him down. On the corner speakers, the sound of applause came through as the support act finished up.

Mike swore, but he went to his jacket and pulled out a walkie-talkie. Holding down the button, he spoke clearly into it. 'Lina.'

Static roared as he let go of the talk button, and then Lina's voice came through, strained and keyed up.

'Busy as hell, Mike. What do you want?'

'We need you back here.'

'What, now?'

'Now.'

Mike released the button and turned down the volume. He gave Kara a look that could have melted granite. 'Happy?'

'Yes.' She smiled. 'Thank you.'

It took Lina all of three minutes to burst in the door, bringing the faint roar of the crowd in behind her. She was in full flight – lipsticked and booted and wearing a slight frown that only made her look more formidable.

'I just left a hack from a national newspaper alone with a double whisky,' she said. 'Make this quick.'

Mike gestured at Kara, who stood by the dress rail in her jeans and dishevelled top.

Lina's frown deepened and her eyes flashed with alarm. 'What's going on? You're not ready?'

Kara nodded to the rail and walked over to close the door behind Lina. She stood with her back against it, the door handle digging into her back, watching the two leading lights of Blue Star Records try to avoid looking at each other.

'This is a farce,' Lina growled, stalking across the room. 'So fucking unprofessional.' Her voice was growing louder with every word. Kara heard the fear in it and the anger that her plans were going awry.

'And it's only going to get worse,' Kara said quietly.

As one, Mike and Lina swung round to look at her.

'What?' It was Mike who spoke.

Kara gave him a smile. 'You're so good at all this,' she said. One last time, she looked around the dressing room – the bouquets of good-luck flowers, the light bulbs studded round the mirrors. 'Both of you. A couple of star-makers.'

Lina drew her hand onto her hip and looked at Kara critically. The walkie-talkie in her hand bleated and hissed, but she ignored it. 'Well, it's nice that you noticed,' she hissed, 'but you can save your Oscar speech for *after* the show.'

Kara bit her lip and pulled a face. 'Afraid not,' she said. She looked down at her feet, at the battered red baseball boots and the faded jeans she was still wearing. 'The thing is, there isn't going to be a show.' She looked up at them through her fringe and couldn't help the smile that quirked the corners of her mouth.

Mike barked – a short loud laugh that had nothing to do with humour. Before he could say a word, Kara had pulled the door open and slipped outside. Just as she was going to slam it shut behind her, though, she hesitated. Leaning back through the narrow crack into the room, she nodded at Mike and Lina's shocked expressions.

'You two have so much in common. You should really work it out, you know.'

With that she pulled away and tugged the door closed. From her back pocket she pulled out the bunch of keys that Lina had given her earlier and screwed the key into the lock just as Mike reached the door on the other side.

She walked down the corridor as the handle rattled. Mike started pounding on the door and she quickened her steps.

Eric was sitting in the wings with his guitar slung across his knees, and Kara laid her hand on his shoulder.

'Eric.'

'Woah, thank God for that, I thought you were –'

'You brought your acoustic guitar with you, right?'

'I – yes, but I'll be using the electric one for most of the –'

'No, you won't.' Kara gave him her bravest smile. 'Can you go fetch the acoustic for me?'

Eric shot a wary glance at the stage and the restless audience beyond it. The auditorium was packed with people and the murmur and noise of the crowd swarmed in Kara's ears. While Eric ran off to fetch his guitar, Kara closed her eyes and rubbed her face. There were whistles and shouts from the crowd, the noise growing steadily louder as the minutes ticked by.

Kara thrust her hand into her back pocket, pushed the dressing-room key aside and felt deeper. For a moment she couldn't find it and her heart thumped with panic. Then her fingers closed over the slim cold metal of the plectrum. She ran her thumb along the edge and turned it over in her hands. It was a thin sliver of metal, but it was solid and it felt good in her hands.

'I wish I knew where you were,' she muttered, squinting into the black mass of the crowd.

Eric skidded to a halt beside her, holding the guitar by its neck. Kara took it without a word and breathed out deeply through her mouth. She waited for the leaping, jangling sensation in her stomach to quiet a little, and then she turned towards the stage.

'Kara?' Eric said. 'What's going on?'

She smiled at him and gave him a little wave as she walked on into the blinding white glare of the spotlights.

23

There was a surge of noise from the crowd as Kara walked onstage. Beyond the edge where the blackened boards dropped into darkness, all she could see was a vaguely shifting mass of people. The crowd surged closer. Kara held her spine straight as she reached the mike at centre stage, tried not to let her nerves show. With both hands, she clung on to the stand and felt it sway slightly.

This was it. This was the nightmare she'd been having for the past week – the formless dark and herself high above it, about to slip and fall. Across the crowd, the first low roar of noise died back as everyone waited for the rest of the band to follow Kara. She was painfully aware of how she must look – one small figure in a static spotlight, wearing her ratty jeans and the safety-pinned top, looking out nervously across the auditorium.

The harsh light pinned her in place – without his cue, the engineer wouldn't dim it – and Kara was blinded by the hot glare. She missed the feel of the band behind her, the knowledge that they would start the song with layered sound. Then she'd have a drumbeat to follow and a guitar to sing with, and Jon's keyboard would pull it all together.

Not tonight. She glanced to the wings, where Eric stood watching, his face drained of blood. How long until someone opened the dressing-room door? Kara steeled herself. She faced the audience.

'The New Rakes will not be playing tonight,' she said, and

heard her voice boom in the stage monitors. A murmur rose from the audience, a wave of disappointment and anger. There were shouts from the back of the venue, but she ignored them.

'I'm sorry,' she said, raising her voice over the angry noise of the crowd.

'The New Rakes –' she had to swallow to stop her voice catching '– will not be playing again.' Kara bowed her head and tried to stop her voice from shaking. 'It's my fault,' she continued, not caring if her voice was lost in the chatter of a thousand people. Just so long as one person heard her. She spoke with her eyes screwed shut and her lips tight to the mesh of the microphone, focusing on one thought and one thought alone. 'You were right. All along. I just never saw it until it was too late.'

Hushing noises came from the floor and, for a moment, Kara thought they were hissing at her. When she realised that people were falling silent, she felt another wave of fear wash over her in a cold surge. There was little movement in the crowd now, just a growing silence as everyone focused on the stage. Rubberneckers, Kara thought. Watching the train wreck. She shrugged.

'So this has all gone really wrong.' She plucked at her jeans. 'I know I'm not going to blow anybody away.'

Kara heard the thud of a door. She looked round wildly, expecting to see Mike coming for her from the wings. But it was the exit at the back of the hall, the door swinging back and forth as a small trickle of punters started to leave. They'd come to hear The New Rakes or see Kara giving her usual floor show. They weren't hanging around for some broken-hearted apologies. Light from the hall outside spilled into the auditorium as the stream of people leaving pushed the doors open.

Kara bit her lip. All her dreams were collapsing around her.

So many nights leading up to this and she'd screwed it up about as badly as was humanly possible. She felt in her back pocket and pulled out the silver guitar pick.

'I have one song,' she said quietly. The people who remained were growing quieter, waiting to see what, if anything, would happen. They waited as Kara slung the guitar over her shoulder and plucked a few notes. It had been a long time since she played guitar. She was grateful for something to hold on to, even if it was a hollow piece of wood. She cleared her throat and started strumming a chord, over and over.

'So. We were The New Rakes,' she said. 'Ruby on drums.'

She gestured behind her, imagined Ruby playing a roll. 'Jon on keyboard.'

Did she look ridiculous, introducing her imaginary band mates? She smiled to herself. No doubt.

'And on lead guitar, the man I should have said yes to.' Kara's voice grew stronger. She strummed harder, picking up the tempo. 'Tam, I can't believe how stupid I've been. This song's for you. Always.'

With just her voice and the guitar, the song sounded very different. But when she sang the opening lines of 'Turn on Me' there were still a few shouts of recognition from the audience. Kara smiled as she mouthed the lyrics. Some of their old fans were still out there, she thought. Then she closed her eyes and put everything she had into the song. It was her, just her on stage, and she was singing to one person in all that throng of people. Her voice rasped as she remembered everything: the nights she'd spent with Tam, the dark nights she'd spent without him. His smile and his dirty mouth. The way he held her nestled in after they'd fucked, or leaped up to fetch his guitar so he could play her the tune he'd been working on.

Kara wasn't aware of the crowd or the people waiting in the

wings to pull her off as soon as she stopped singing. She lost herself in the song and let the meaning of the words wash over her stronger than they ever had.

By the time she finished and opened her eyes, she was surprised to find there were tears caught in her lashes, threatening to spill.

Slowly, the applause reached her, growing and lasting as the half-full auditorium responded. The noise washed over her, drummed in her ears and wrapped her in sweet relief. It was almost enough to take the edge off the way her heart ached.

But then there was a flurry of movement at the side of the stage and Kara turned to see Mike stalking from the wings to the centre of the stage, the angles of his face so sharp they could cut butter. Her heart flipped as she saw Lina behind him, arms crossed and mouth grim.

'Kara!'

It was the voice that caught her attention – the lusty rough timbre that could only belong to one person. Tam was crowding in at the foot of the stage, waving to her. Around him, the crowd surged and broke apart as security guards in fluorescent jackets pushed through to reach him. He was holding out his hands and smiling at her, and his eyes were shining. She just had time to wonder how brown eyes could be so bright before she ran to him, hesitating for one second as the crowd thinned underneath her, and jumped.

She sank into a forest of strangers and Tam's hands slid around her waist. Bedlam exploded around them, but Tam's mouth locked on hers long enough for her to taste him and feel the rough reckless joy of his kiss. His arms held her fast and the length of his body was alive and hard against hers, fitting her perfectly from her mouth to her toes.

She heard voices calling to her through the confusion – some cheering, some hard with anger. A bouncer reached his strong arm across the crowd to grab her shoulder and, for a moment, she was torn in two directions as Tam pulled her deeper into the dark melee. Kara saw a jumble of images scatter in front of her – a boy with a pierced lip clapping in her face, girls whistling at her, bodies standing aside to clear a path for her and Tam. She thought she caught a glimpse of Ruby's corkscrew curls, a dark smile flashing behind the hair.

And then she and Tam were running, breaking away from the crowd and making for the square of light at the exit doors. They burst through them and into the yellowy corridor, clattering down the steps two at a time, heading for the street. She could smell the cold fresh air outside and hear the traffic roar and screech, and she could feel the heat of Tam's hand wrapped round her own.

'Tam,' she said, pulling up short. Two steps below her, he turned. 'There's no going back. You'll be making enemies. If you run with me now.'

Tam watched her for a moment, catching her breath. A slow smile spread across his face. 'Well, I s'pose that leaves the two of us going nowhere together.'

Tam leaned forwards and Kara bent down to kiss him. People pushed past them on the stairs, heading out into the street. They were jostled and bumped, but Kara barely noticed, only aware of the taste and feel of Tam's mouth – hot skin and a faint trace of beer, and the way he was kissing her like he hadn't ever before.

Tam broke away first, tugging at Kara's hand. 'Come on then,' he said, half dragging her down the stairs and out into the night.

Kara's mouth was still burning when they reached the street, and the sudden sense of the loud busy city rushing around them made her dizzy. They ran a block, dodging drunk football fans and a flower-seller necklaced with neon-light sticks, Kara struggling for breath and laughing at the same time, chasing Tam across the uneven pavements.

The thought of what she'd run from sent shivers of fresh adrenaline bursting through her veins, and urged her onwards towards the junction where the motorway cut through the city and the roar of traffic finally drowned out the music and noise of the streets. As soon as they rounded the corner, Tam pulled her into a doorway and wrapped his arms around her again, his chest heaving as he took in huge lungfuls of air.

'Think we lost them?' he said, looking down at her with his brown eyes.

Kara laughed. She was gasping for breath, but her mouth was already seeking Tam's and pressing against his.

A taxi sounded its horn and the driver whistled out the open window as he passed. Passers-by turned their heads to look at the lovers in the doorway. Tam didn't break their embrace, but pulled Kara deeper into the shadows and jammed himself up against her. He gripped her upper arms and squeezed hard, like he was trying to convince himself she was real. Kara felt it too, the disbelief that she was there with him, grinding into him and kissing him with an artless joy that made all her fears disappear.

She slid her hands under his T-shirt and felt his skin leap under her cold touch. His skin was smooth and hot and tight and she wanted to feel all of it all at once. Pushing him back against the door, she tugged at his jeans and pulled the buttons open so that she could slip a hand inside. His cock was huge and hard in her palm and she gripped it tightly, listening to the moan that escaped from his mouth and loving the sound of it. Still riding the adrenaline buzz, she was dizzy with want for him, and when Tam turned her round to undo her jeans she had to grit her teeth not to cry out loud.

Just a few feet away, the cars swept past, their headlights

raking the building and catching Tam's hair so that he was lit up briefly from behind. Kara stroked his face as he lifted her hips up and pinned her in the corner, dragged her fingers over his mouth. He snapped at her and caught her fingers in his mouth, sucking them hard as he shoved clothes aside to get them naked next to each other.

'Traffic,' Kara said, but her voice was failing her.

'Nothing's going to stop me fucking you,' Tam said, holding her tightly and pushing his cock between her legs.

It wasn't an easy angle, leaned up against the wall, and they sagged against each other, scrabbling for purchase on the sandstone wall. Laughter spilled out of Kara's mouth as she slid and scraped over the bricks. Tam raised an eyebrow and grabbed her leg, lifting it high so that her slit spread open. When his cock slipped and surged deep into her, Kara caught her breath.

He fucked her like nothing else mattered, with a certainty and urgency that made the rest of the night dissolve. She could think of nothing but how they were joined, how he took her and held her and drove into her. With every stroke he slammed her against the wall and brought her closer to the moment, closer to the stone at her back and the hot skin against hers and the blinding lights studding the thick navy blue of the city sky. With his cock plugged into her, Kara opened her mouth in a soundless scream, saying to herself over and over – yes, yes, yes.

To be there and have Tam inside her, have him holding her tight and fucking her roughly, was worth more than anything. She wrapped herself around him and held him so hard she could feel his heart thump against her chest.

His breath was ragged and Kara knew he wouldn't last long. His cock was so full and rigid inside her she could feel it pulse as he started to come. At the same time, she felt the buzz and the adrenaline in her veins warm up and sweeten, her whole body throb with the rushing joy of her own approaching orgasm.

She held on to him hard. He thrust into her, deep. Her mouth opened again and her hands clenched into fists as she felt them rock together, swimming in a swift and beautiful burst of ecstasy. He fell forwards and buried his face in her hair as he came, whispering her name hoarsely. It sounded like music, and the beat of her heart counted a steady rhythm as he cried against her neck.

For a moment they were still and silent, letting their pleasure ebb slowly. A lingering warmth spread through her limbs as Kara still held on to Tam, not yet ready to pull away.

Headlights swept over them and dazzled her. Kara came down slowly and found herself back on the street where they were half hidden, only a few feet from the pavement. They kissed again, smiling into each other's mouths. Clumsily, she unfolded herself and pulled her clothes straight, while Tam leaned against the wall and rolled his head to look at her.

'Does this mean you're looking for a new band then?' he said, reaching out to brush a tangle out of her hair.

Kara laughed. 'I suppose it does,' she said, before catching his hand and planting a kiss on the knuckles.

'You know, I might be in need of a singer.'

'Oh yeah?'

'Mmm.' He leaned in to kiss her again. They couldn't get enough of touching each other. As though all the words in the world could never equal the feel of each other's hands, mouths, bodies. As though they'd been dying of thirst and their kisses were clear, cold, sweet water. Kara pulled away at last. She smiled. No rush. They had all the time in the world.

'The thing is,' she said, tugging on his collar thoughtfully, 'I do most of my songwriting in bed.'

'Yeah? I think I can handle that.'

'And I've just blown the biggest chance I ever had of cutting a record.' Kara bit her lip.

Tam nodded. 'Yep. We'll have to work hard to get another deal.'

'Write a whole bunch of new songs.'

'In bed.'

'In bed. With each other.'

'You know –' Tam kissed her in between each word '– that sounds like a plan.'

He slung his arm round her shoulder and together they walked up onto the bridge, with the traffic and the motorway snaking away underneath and the lights of the city sparkling brightly in every direction, sending a steady hot glow of noise and light up into the atmosphere, nearly blotting out the stars. Nearly.

But not quite.

Visit the Black Lace website at
www.black-lace-books.com

FIND OUT THE LATEST INFORMATION AND TAKE ADVANTAGE OF OUR
FANTASTIC FREE BOOK OFFER! ALSO VISIT THE SITE FOR . . .

- All Black Lace titles currently available
  and how to order online

- Great new offers

- Writers' guidelines

- Author interviews

- An erotica newsletter

- Features

- Cool links

BLACK LACE – THE LEADING IMPRINT OF
WOMEN'S SEXY FICTION

TAKING YOUR EROTIC READING PLEASURE
TO NEW HORIZONS

LOOK OUT FOR THE ALL-NEW BLACK LACE BOOKS – AVAILABLE NOW!

All books priced £7.99 in the UK. Please note publication dates apply to the UK only. For other territories, please contact your retailer.

THE NINETY DAYS OF GENEVIEVE
Lucinda Carrington

ISBN 978 0 352 34201 0

A ninety-day sex contract wasn't exactly what Genevieve Loften had in mind when she began business negotiations with the arrogant and attractive James Sinclair. As a career move she wanted to go along with it; the pay-off was potentially huge.

However, she didn't imagine that he would make her the star performer in a series of increasingly kinky and exotic fantasies. Thrown into a world of sexual misadventure, Genevieve learns how to balance her high-pressure career with the twilight world of fetishism and debauchery.

LUST AT FIRST BITE
Anthology

ISBN 978 0 352 34506 6

In the realm of the paranormal there is nothing as sexy as a vampire – demonic lovers who exist to seduce and be seduced . . . forever. *In Lust at First Bite*, Black Lace creates a unique spin on the hypnotic allure of these charismatic creatures of the night. So turn down the lights, secure the latches, gather whatever protection is necessary and dip into a dark volume bursting with the appetites, the desires, and the loves of this legendary spectre.

To be published in December 2008

THE GIFT OF SHAME
Sarah Hope-Walker

ISBN 978 0 352 34202 7

Sad, sultry Helen flies between London, Paris and the Caribbean chasing whatever physical pleasures she can get to tear her mind from a deep, deep loss. Her glamorous lifestyle and charged sensual escapades belie a widow's grief. When she meets handsome, rich Jeffrey she is shocked and yet intrigued by his masterful, domineering behaviour. Soon, Helen is forced to confront the forbidden desires hiding within herself – and forced to undergo a startling metamorphosis from a meek and modest lady into a bristling, voracious wanton.

TO SEEK A MASTER
Monica Belle
ISBN 978 0 352 34507 3

Sexy daydreams are shy Laura's only escape from the dull routines of her life. But with the arrival of an email ordering her to dress provocatively, she wonders if her secret fantasies about her colleagues are about to become true. Unable to resist the new and more daring instructions that arrive by email, she begins to slip deeper into dangerous water with several men. But when her controller finally reveals himself, she's in for a shock and a far greater involvement in his illicit games.

ALSO LOOK OUT FOR

THE NEW BLACK LACE BOOK OF WOMEN'S SEXUAL FANTASIES
Edited and compiled by Mitzi Szereto

ISBN 978 0 352 34172 3

The second anthology of detailed sexual fantasies contributed by women from all over the world. The book is a result of a year's research by an expert on erotic writing and gives a fascinating insight into the rich diversity of the female sexual imagination.

Black Lace Booklist

Information is correct at time of printing. To avoid disappointment, check availability before ordering. Go to www.black-lace-books.com.
All books are priced £7.99 unless another price is given.

BLACK LACE BOOKS WITH A CONTEMPORARY SETTING

- ❑ THE ANGELS' SHARE Maya Hess — ISBN 978 0 352 34043 6
- ❑ ASKING FOR TROUBLE Kristina Lloyd — ISBN 978 0 352 33362 9
- ❑ BLACK LIPSTICK KISSES Monica Belle — ISBN 978 0 352 33885 3 — £6.99
- ❑ THE BLUE GUIDE Carrie Williams — ISBN 978 0 352 34132 7
- ❑ THE BOSS Monica Belle — ISBN 978 0 352 34088 7
- ❑ BOUND IN BLUE Monica Belle — ISBN 978 0 352 34012 2
- ❑ CAMPAIGN HEAT Gabrielle Marcola — ISBN 978 0 352 33941 6
- ❑ CAT SCRATCH FEVER Sophie Mouette — ISBN 978 0 352 34021 4
- ❑ CIRCUS EXCITE Nikki Magennis — ISBN 978 0 352 34033 7
- ❑ CLUB CRÈME Primula Bond — ISBN 978 0 352 33907 2 — £6.99
- ❑ CONFESSIONAL Judith Roycroft — ISBN 978 0 352 33421 3
- ❑ CONTINUUM Portia Da Costa — ISBN 978 0 352 33120 5
- ❑ DANGEROUS CONSEQUENCES Pamela Rochford — ISBN 978 0 352 33185 4
- ❑ DARK DESIGNS Madelynne Ellis — ISBN 978 0 352 34075 7
- ❑ THE DEVIL INSIDE Portia Da Costa — ISBN 978 0 352 32993 6
- ❑ EQUAL OPPORTUNITIES Mathilde Madden — ISBN 978 0 352 34070 2
- ❑ FIRE AND ICE Laura Hamilton — ISBN 978 0 352 33486 2
- ❑ GONE WILD Maria Eppie — ISBN 978 0 352 33670 5
- ❑ HOTBED Portia Da Costa — ISBN 978 0 352 33614 9
- ❑ IN PURSUIT OF ANNA Natasha Rostova — ISBN 978 0 352 34060 3
- ❑ IN THE FLESH Emma Holly — ISBN 978 0 352 34117 4
- ❑ LEARNING TO LOVE IT Alison Tyler — ISBN 978 0 352 33535 7
- ❑ MAD ABOUT THE BOY Mathilde Madden — ISBN 978 0 352 34001 6
- ❑ MAKE YOU A MAN Anna Clare — ISBN 978 0 352 34006 1
- ❑ MAN HUNT Cathleen Ross — ISBN 978 0 352 33583 8
- ❑ THE MASTER OF SHILDEN Lucinda Carrington — ISBN 978 0 352 33140 3
- ❑ MIXED DOUBLES Zoe le Verdier — ISBN 978 0 352 33312 4 — £6.99
- ❑ MIXED SIGNALS Anna Clare — ISBN 978 0 352 33889 1 — £6.99
- ❑ MS BEHAVIOUR Mini Lee — ISBN 978 0 352 33962 1

❑ PACKING HEAT Karina Moore   ISBN 978 0 352 33356 8   £6.99
❑ PAGAN HEAT Monica Belle   ISBN 978 0 352 33974 4
❑ PEEP SHOW Mathilde Madden   ISBN 978 0 352 33924 9
❑ THE POWER GAME Carrera Devonshire   ISBN 978 0 352 33990 4
❑ THE PRIVATE UNDOING OF A PUBLIC SERVANT   ISBN 978 0 352 34066 5
    Leonie Martel
❑ RUDE AWAKENING Pamela Kyle   ISBN 978 0 352 33036 9
❑ SAUCE FOR THE GOOSE Mary Rose Maxwell   ISBN 978 0 352 33492 3
❑ SPLIT Kristina Lloyd   ISBN 978 0 352 34154 9
❑ STELLA DOES HOLLYWOOD Stella Black   ISBN 978 0 352 33588 3
❑ THE STRANGER Portia Da Costa   ISBN 978 0 352 33211 0
❑ SUITE SEVENTEEN Portia Da Costa   ISBN 978 0 352 34109 9
❑ TONGUE IN CHEEK Tabitha Flyte   ISBN 978 0 352 33484 8
❑ THE TOP OF HER GAME Emma Holly   ISBN 978 0 352 34116 7
❑ UNNATURAL SELECTION Alaine Hood   ISBN 978 0 352 33963 8
❑ VELVET GLOVE Emma Holly   ISBN 978 0 352 34115 0
❑ VILLAGE OF SECRETS Mercedes Kelly   ISBN 978 0 352 33344 5
❑ WILD BY NATURE Monica Belle   ISBN 978 0 352 33915 7   £6.99
❑ WILD CARD Madeline Moore   ISBN 978 0 352 34038 2
❑ WING OF MADNESS Mae Nixon   ISBN 978 0 352 34099 3

BLACK LACE BOOKS WITH AN HISTORICAL SETTING

❑ THE BARBARIAN GEISHA Charlotte Royal   ISBN 978 0 352 33267 7
❑ BARBARIAN PRIZE Deanna Ashford   ISBN 978 0 352 34017 7
❑ THE CAPTIVATION Natasha Rostova   ISBN 978 0 352 33234 9
❑ DARKER THAN LOVE Kristina Lloyd   ISBN 978 0 352 33279 0
❑ WILD KINGDOM Deanna Ashford   ISBN 978 0 352 33549 4
❑ DIVINE TORMENT Janine Ashbless   ISBN 978 0 352 33719 1
❑ FRENCH MANNERS Olivia Christie   ISBN 978 0 352 33214 1
❑ LORD WRAXALL'S FANCY Anna Lieff Saxby   ISBN 978 0 352 33080 2
❑ NICOLE'S REVENGE Lisette Allen   ISBN 978 0 352 32984 4
❑ THE SENSES BEJEWELLED Cleo Cordell   ISBN 978 0 352 32904 2   £6.99
❑ THE SOCIETY OF SIN Sian Lacey Taylder   ISBN 978 0 352 34080 1
❑ TEMPLAR PRIZE Deanna Ashford   ISBN 978 0 352 34137 2
❑ UNDRESSING THE DEVIL Angel Strand   ISBN 978 0 352 33938 6

BLACK LACE BOOKS WITH A PARANORMAL THEME

☐ BRIGHT FIRE Maya Hess	ISBN 978 0 352 34104 4	
☐ BURNING BRIGHT Janine Ashbless	ISBN 978 0 352 34085 6	
☐ CRUEL ENCHANTMENT Janine Ashbless	ISBN 978 0 352 33483 1	
☐ FLOOD Anna Clare	ISBN 978 0 352 34094 8	
☐ GOTHIC BLUE Portia Da Costa	ISBN 978 0 352 33075 8	
☐ THE PRIDE Edie Bingham	ISBN 978 0 352 33997 3	
☐ THE SILVER COLLAR Mathilde Madden	ISBN 978 0 352 34141 9	
☐ THE TEN VISIONS Olivia Knight	ISBN 978 0 352 34119 8	

BLACK LACE ANTHOLOGIES

☐ BLACK LACE QUICKIES 1 Various	ISBN 978 0 352 34126 6	£2.99
☐ BLACK LACE QUICKIES 2 Various	ISBN 978 0 352 34127 3	£2.99
☐ BLACK LACE QUICKIES 3 Various	ISBN 978 0 352 34128 0	£2.99
☐ BLACK LACE QUICKIES 4 Various	ISBN 978 0 352 34129 7	£2.99
☐ BLACK LACE QUICKIES 5 Various	ISBN 978 0 352 34130 3	£2.99
☐ BLACK LACE QUICKIES 6 Various	ISBN 978 0 352 34133 4	£2.99
☐ BLACK LACE QUICKIES 7 Various	ISBN 978 0 352 34146 4	£2.99
☐ BLACK LACE QUICKIES 8 Various	ISBN 978 0 352 34147 1	£2.99
☐ BLACK LACE QUICKIES 9 Various	ISBN 978 0 352 34155 6	£2.99
☐ MORE WICKED WORDS Various	ISBN 978 0 352 33487 9	£6.99
☐ WICKED WORDS 3 Various	ISBN 978 0 352 33522 7	£6.99
☐ WICKED WORDS 4 Various	ISBN 978 0 352 33603 3	£6.99
☐ WICKED WORDS 5 Various	ISBN 978 0 352 33642 2	£6.99
☐ WICKED WORDS 6 Various	ISBN 978 0 352 33690 3	£6.99
☐ WICKED WORDS 7 Various	ISBN 978 0 352 33743 6	£6.99
☐ WICKED WORDS 8 Various	ISBN 978 0 352 33787 0	£6.99
☐ WICKED WORDS 9 Various	ISBN 978 0 352 33860 0	
☐ WICKED WORDS 10 Various	ISBN 978 0 352 33893 8	
☐ THE BEST OF BLACK LACE 2 Various	ISBN 978 0 352 33718 4	
☐ WICKED WORDS: SEX IN THE OFFICE Various	ISBN 978 0 352 33944 7	
☐ WICKED WORDS: SEX AT THE SPORTS CLUB Various	ISBN 978 0 352 33991 1	
☐ WICKED WORDS: SEX ON HOLIDAY Various	ISBN 978 0 352 33961 4	
☐ WICKED WORDS: SEX IN UNIFORM Various	ISBN 978 0 352 34002 3	
☐ WICKED WORDS: SEX IN THE KITCHEN Various	ISBN 978 0 352 34018 4	
☐ WICKED WORDS: SEX ON THE MOVE Various	ISBN 978 0 352 34034 4	
☐ WICKED WORDS: SEX AND MUSIC Various	ISBN 978 0 352 34061 0